A Peculiar Curiosity

Melanie Cossey

Fitzroy Books

Published by Fitzroy Books
An imprint of
Regal House Publishing, LLC
Raleigh, NC 27612
All rights reserved

https://fitzroybooks.com

Printed in the United States of America

ISBN -13 (paperback): 978-1-947548-06-0
ISBN -13 (hardcover): 978-1-947548-07-7
ISBN -13 (epub): 978-1-947548-00-8
Library of Congress Control Number: 2018945501

Interior, cover image and design by Lafayette & Greene
Cover image C. B. Royal
lafayetteandgreene.com
Cover images by Lynea/Shutterstock and Whitevector/Shutterstock

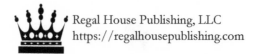
Regal House Publishing, LLC
https://regalhousepublishing.com

To my husband, who participates in my love of horror,
and my kids, who give me ideas

Chapter One

England, 1990

The rising anxiety was churning in my gut, constricting my chest, making it hard to breathe. In spite of the freezing weather, a bead of sweat formed on my brow. Gripping the wooden railing by the front door, I fought the urge to turn and flee to my car, but it was useless to run from this panic, as I well knew. I needed to face it head on, slow my breathing, and let the anxiety attack pass. Besides, I had already rung Mrs. Walker's doorbell—I was committed. *You are in control, Duncan,* I told myself.

With unsteady hand, I pulled a handkerchief from my pocket and dabbed at my brow. The opening line from Poe's "A Tell-Tale Heart" crept through my mind: "True!—nervous—very, very dreadfully nervous I had been and am…"

I took a deep breath and attempted to distract myself from the catastrophic events that had taken place earlier that morning.

Focus on the curiosities, Duncan, that's why you're here.

In our earlier phone conversation, Mrs. Walker hadn't elaborated much, except to say that the crates were at least one hundred years old and contained "horrid things" from the Victorian period. Doubtless a mixed bag of authentic oddities and sideshow gaffs—fake props used to bilk crowds of curiosity seekers out of their money.

But I had little else to do, now that classes had adjourned for the winter break. Perusing a collection of antiques and perhaps adding a few objects to my own collection of Victoriana would serve as a nice distraction from sitting at home and stewing about my bleak future in academia.

At last, I heard steps approach from inside.

The door opened to reveal an elderly woman in an insipid brown housedress with a cardigan sweater.

"Ruth Walker?"

"Yes. Dr. Clarke, is it? I'm so glad you're here. Oops, no, Missy!" With a glide of her pink-slippered foot, Mrs. Walker intercepted a tortoiseshell cat who seemed intent on dashing out the door. The feline spun and bounded down the hall. "She's a hunter, so I have to keep her inside or she destroys every bit of wildlife for miles around. I'm sorry, do come in." She stepped back into the narrow foyer, allowing me to enter.

Mrs. Walker took my coat and muffler while I bent to unzip my boots. "My, your cheeks are red. Oh dear, how long have you been standing in the cold, ringing that blessed bell? I just don't hear it as I should, and my son Robert must have his head in a box in the loft." She motioned for me to precede her into a small sitting room.

"Oh, no matter," I shrugged and forced a smile.

The dimly lit sitting room, wallpapered in a dated brown and orange floral design, was brimming with boxes, their contents spilling out to occupy every inch of useable space. In the corner, a Christmas tree glowed with blue and green lights; shiny metal ornaments glinted in merry contrast to the melancholia of the outmoded, disordered room. Mrs. Walker invited me to sit. I inched around the boxes, making for the only available seat—a tapestry wingback chair with a stained coverlet.

Sitting opposite me, Mrs. Walker apologized for the condition of the room. "We are in the process of clearing out the loft for the grandchildren. This is all my late husband's stuff. Most of it is for the bin, but there are these…things. I wanted to throw them away, but I don't think such things can just be tossed out. Robert thought they'd best go to the university as they might be of interest, you know, historically. They belonged to John's great grandfather, who, as the family story goes, was quite eccentric; did I mention that on the phone?"

"Eccentric? Mm, no, I don't believe so."

"Didn't I? Well, Edward was his name. He was a Victorian trader of curiosities who died after one of his excursions—supposedly from some tropical disease. I gather his widow didn't care to deal with his horrid acquisitions, so they were packed away and forgotten. The collection stayed in the family, however, having some importance as an heirloom. But what does one *do* with such things? Robert discovered it yesterday, tucked under the back rafters covered in cobwebs. John always said he would go through it, but he never managed… Oh, excuse me, I've not offered you a cup of tea."

I waved her off. "Thank you, no. Tell me about these curiosities, please."

"I couldn't bring myself to look through them all—I just had a peep. Once I saw those God-awful stuffed things and those…those *terrible things* in the jars, well, that was enough for me. It all had to go. Imagine, me living all this time in John's mother's house, blissfully unaware those disgusting creatures were up there." She shivered again and drew her sweater around herself. "Makes me feel right ill. There are two crates and a box altogether." She pointed at the crates, thick with dust.

"So, they contain preserved animals, then?"

"Heavens, no," Mrs. Walker whispered, grimacing. "The things in jars are, well, *human*. Or at least they were."

My heart skipped a beat.

"But as for the items in the second crate, you'll have to go through them and see what's important to you. Please dispose of whatever you don't want. I don't want any of it back. Ever."

"Yes, yes, of course," I replied.

Mrs. Walker rose and indicated the wooden box. "There, take it over to that desk and have a look." I stooped to retrieve the box and opened it on the desk, as she had suggested.

I lifted the lid and was hit by the acrid smell of aged things. Stifling a sneeze, I unwrapped a glass dome followed by a creature both gruesome and pitiable in its crumbling state—a two-headed white rat. One head protruded from the neck of the other, the single spine dividing into two at the shoulders. The rat stared back at me through two sets of murky glass eyes. It was an odd specimen. With my finger, I parted the hair around the rat's neck, but discovered no evidence of stitching. Nothing to indicate the head of a second rat had been sewn on to the first. Perhaps this was just the Cerberus I needed to ward off my recent mice infestation at home.

Next, I withdrew a stuffed tuxedo kitten with an enlarged, deformed skull and a Cyclopean eye in the middle of its forehead. These specimens were excellent examples of Victorian taxidermy and were quite well preserved. They made a rather frightful team. Pair these two with the poison and I was ready for some serious rodent genocide.

"Aren't they just terrible? You'll take them for the university, won't you?" Mrs. Walker gave a nervous half-laugh.

"They *are* terrible, but I do like them, and would be happy to take them off your hands."

"Thank goodness!" Mrs. Walker exclaimed in relief. "Let me get my son to help you carry them out to your car." She left the room for a moment and I could hear her calling for Robert.

"Thank you for your donations, Mrs. Walker," I told her when she returned.

"Well, thank you for relieving me of these relics; I hope they will be of some use to you and your department."

"That is my hope, too."

Robert Walker pushed past me with a soft, "Excuse me, sir." He leaned towards the portly side, his movements rigid, protected. I felt a pinch of pity for him.

"Dr. Clarke will take the crates and those dreadful creatures too, thank God. Please re-pack them for the doctor, would you, Robert?"

"Right-O." Robert grabbed the deformed kitten and proceeded to roughly wind it in newspaper before jamming it back in the box. I winced, worrying that much of the collection might be damaged should Robert be left in charge of packing.

"Here, I'll help with those." I took the box from him.

"Have a go, Doctor Clarke. I'll drag out the crates for you."

I carefully returned the items to the box and fastened the lid's metal clasps. "I'll put these in my car and return to help you with those crates. They look rather heavy," I said to Robert as I headed down the hallway, shadowed by Ruth Walker.

"I heard on the news that we're in for a storm. You don't have far to go, I hope?" she asked as she rummaged through the hall closet for my coat and muffler.

"Just down to Great Dunmow. I'll be fine. Oh, let me give you my number, just in case you come across anything else of interest." I pulled my wallet from my back trouser pocket and withdrew my business card—*Dr. Duncan Clarke, PhD, Lecturer, Social Anthropology, North Roads University.* I spied a pen on the writing desk in the hallway, scratched out the university number, scribbled my home number underneath, and handed it to Mrs. Walker.

"With much of the university deserted over the Christmas break, it's best to call me at home. I'm grateful for your donations. Again, thank you, Mrs. Walker."

The old woman reached past me to tug open the front door. Low leaden-blue clouds had gathered in the late afternoon sky, plunging the Linton neighborhood into a moody Renoir painting. Balancing the box of antique oddities in my arms, I trudged down the street to my car, salt crunching underfoot. Unlocking the boot, I laid the box inside. *The Oliver Typewriter* was stamped in black lettering along the side. The box was probably as old as the antiques within.

Returning to help Robert, who was staggering under the weight of a crate, I gripped the wooden handle, my lower back protesting in angry spasms. Glass clanked within as the crate shifted, and I leaned in to steady it.

"Easy there, she's a heavy one," Robert acknowledged.

"I've got it." Together we muscled the crate to my car, easing it in beside the typewriter box, before returning to the house for the second crate, which was, fortunately, not as heavy as the first.

"Do you have any idea what's in this one?" I asked Robert breathlessly as we lifted the crate into the car.

"Couldn't be bothered to look through it, to be honest. Sometimes it's best not to when getting rid of things or you'll just convince yourself to hang on to it. So, happy Christmas, Dr. Clarke."

Extending a hand, I shook Robert's dusty one and wished him a happy Christmas in return. With one glance at the darkening sky, I climbed behind the Volvo's steering wheel. Leaning over the passenger seat, I opened the glove box and pulled out a rag to clean my hands. The vial of chloroform that I had borrowed from the anthropology lab rolled out on to the floorboards. My gut lurched. That damned chloroform. Pocketing it had been a terrible idea—just another nail in the coffin of my academic career.

CHAPTER TWO

It began to rain, shyly at first, but as I turned south onto the back road toward Great Dunmow, frozen raindrops pelted my windshield and slid down the glass in thick grey clumps. I flipped on my wipers—a metronome that kept tempo with the torrent and tire orchestra. The road darkened, undulating beneath overgrown trees. My fingers tightened on the steering wheel as administrator Christopher Poirier's droll voice echoed through my mind…

"There have been complaints, you see." Poirier shuffled through his papers, reading random sentences aloud: "'…did not receive final marks in a timely fashion.'" More shuffling. "'…felt Dr. Clarke did not provide adequate assistance.' And: '…lectures seemed thin, basic, not reflective of the course syllabus.' Need I read more, Dr. Clarke?"

I felt my face growing hot.

"Then there's also a matter of an item taken from the lab," Christopher Poirier continued. "I think you know what I'm talking about, don't you, Dr. Clarke?" He glanced at the two other administers who mirrored his stern look before all gazes turned to rest on mine.

I prattled some reply, explaining that while I had had trouble focusing recently, it was all behind me now, and I was much better. And the business about the chloroform? Well, I had merely borrowed it to deal with a small rodent problem at home. It was nothing, really. I had intended to replace it…

"All the same, we feel you should take some time over the holiday to rest up." I was struck by the shift—by their trotted-out glances of guilt, lowered voices, and throat clearings of candor. "The thing of it is, we want you to deeply consider a leave of absence."

Recalling the incident caused the frustration to surge within me. I slammed down on the accelerator, the adrenaline rushing through my veins, then screeched to a halt at the first intersection in Saffron Walden. A family, burdened by shopping bags and thick winter wear, crossed in front of me.

A leave of absence? Clearly, they felt I wasn't doing my job, and judging from those bloody complaints, it seemed they had the proof. True, I hadn't been myself lately, but I was managing. But what really concerned me was Dave Allen's contribution: "Come see us again, the first Tuesday in January, before the term starts up. That way we can assess how things are going with you and what steps are necessary to ensure your best interests, and ours, are served. Oh, and you might consider talking to someone."

"Talking to someone? What do you mean?" I'd asked.

"A professional, Dr. Clarke."

Damn them. What if I didn't want to rest, didn't want to speak to anyone? Would they axe me, just like that? And what was I to do then? A professor in his mid-fifties—what other university would take me on under such circumstances?

By the time I reached Dunmow, turned onto Godfrey Way and pulled into my driveway, the frozen rain had draped the countryside in ice. I retrieved the chloroform, slipped it into my pocket, and emerged from the warm car into the chilly sleet.

Fishing for the blanket I kept in the back seat, I placed it over the typewriter box and carried it to the safety of my study, then returned with the blanket for the next crate. Despite the agonizing pain in my lower back, I heaved the crate from the boot, struggled with it over the threshold and set it down on the hallway floor. Last, I returned for the lighter crate and brought it, protected in the blanket, into the study, closing the door behind me with my foot.

After hoisting the typewriter box onto my desk, I lifted the lid.

I unwrapped the gruesome twosome and set them on my desk—damned ugly beasts—and placed the glass dome over the rat. Searching for the kitten's glass dome, I dug through handfuls of packing straw until I felt the hardened leather cover of a book. Moving the straw aside, I read the embossed letters, faded with the passage of time: *Travel Journal.*

Slipping on a pair of white cotton gloves from my desk drawer, I pulled the journal from the crate, as well as a second burgundy cloth journal that lay beneath. The back cover of the leather journal formed a flap over the front, terminating in a tongue that slipped into a belt, concealing and protecting the page ends. Sliding the tongue back from the loop, I opened the journal to the title page: *Travel Journal of Edward P. Walker. Volume II.* Bits of leather flaked off in my hand and the acrid scent of aged pages rose to my nostrils.

A cursive scrawl covered the opening pages, with crossed-out lines and crowded sentences rendering it almost illegible in places. Splattered black ink marks, now faded to grey, jetted across the pages, suggesting a frantic speed of pen between inkwell and paper. The pressure of the nib was so hard in places, it had carved holes through the page.

The burgundy journal sported a similar protective cover, and wear at the spine suggested frequent openings and closings. Within, the similar formation of characters indicated it was penned by the same hand, only the script here was neat, readable, and unblemished. This was a man who knew the necessity of blotting paper and had mastered penmanship with a nineteenth-century fountain pen.

As I flipped through the journal, an ivory page came loose, floated aloft, and landed on the floor. Retrieving the errant paper, my heart jumped, for staring out from the page were the anguished eyes of an emaciated boy who was roped to a chair, a gag stretching his mouth into a grimace. Written beneath the ink drawing, in crudely scrawled letters underlined by multiple slashes, was *Specimen,* followed by a second word that was largely illegible. Only the first letter was clear—a Z. The date, *August 1865,* was written at the bottom of the page.

The child in the drawing was riveting. His gaze seared into my own, his arms and legs—sapling thin—were tied to the chair with rope. Beneath the pull of his shirt, I could discern the visible lines of his ribs, and two bony kneecaps were evident under the strain of his trousers. A crosshatched pattern across the cheeks and forehead suggested the ebony complexion of a boy native to Africa or perhaps the West Indies. I felt as though a hammer had struck me square in the solar plexus. *What in God's name?* The drawing simultaneously sickened and fascinated me. My chest felt tight and a clammy heat laddered up my back and gathered in beads of sweat across my forehead. I dabbed a hanky across my brow.

Leaving the drawing on the desk, I splashed my face with icy water in the hallway bathroom, tucking the vial of chloroform from my trouser pocket behind the shaving cream in the medicine cabinet.

In the kitchen, I spooned left-over curry from a take-away container onto a plate and pondered the alarming drawing. What was a drawing of a bound and gagged child doing among the possessions of a nineteenth-century curiosity trader? Had Walker drawn this or was it an item he had come across in his travels?

Leaving the microwave to reheat my food, I returned to study the sketch under the desk lamp. The starved child looked positively tormented, his eyes pleading for release. My gaze flicked to the inscription *Specimen Z*—Z what? Turning the paper over and holding it up to the light, I still could not make out the smeared letters that followed the Z. Zambia, perhaps? And why *Specimen?* Specimen of what? Was the boy a victim of some kind of sinister experiment? I was eager to comb Walker's journals for an explanation.

I pulled from my desk drawer a framed snapshot of my ex-wife and me vacationing on the French Riviera—a ridiculous photo where we displayed inane, toothy smiles, pretending we could stand each other, while some tourist snapped the picture. Why did I keep the picture when it only reminded me of how we'd failed each other? I removed the glass and tossed the photo in the rubbish bin, then edged the sketch of the agonized boy into the frame.

After I finished my supper on one of the few remaining Portmerion plates that Diane had left behind, I thoroughly washed and dried my hands and returned to my study. After sliding on the cotton gloves, I compared the journals' dates cited at the beginning of each and selected the earlier one—the burgundy cloth journal with the neater handwriting. Adjusting my lamp, I settled back into my chair, vaguely aware that the sleet outside was beginning to subside. I opened the cover. There in meticulously crafted script, with the swooping flourishes seldom seen today, was the title page, the pertinent geography, and the date.

My breath came in a shallow rush as I read what was written there:

Travel Journal of
Edward P. Walker
Caribbean Islands
Volume 1: Friday, March 3, 1865

The Carolina is to depart from the oily grey Liverpool seaport for the crystalline waters of the Caribbean at ten o'clock on this foggy morning. Betsy, being full with child, was more disquieted by my departure than was customary for her, but even with the promise of her mother, nursemaid, and trusted physician to attend the birth, she bitterly protested my departure.

After spending a fortnight with her wistful tears soaking my pillow and her arms so tightly entwined about my neck as to make a restful sleep quite impossible, I am again anticipating the churning sea lulling me into a deep and satisfying slumber.

The Carolina is a majestic vessel and I have procured for myself a most impressive first-class cabin. My lavish room boasts a spacious parlor, a stately bedroom, and even a serviceable lavatory. Mahogany paneling lines the walls, extending from floor to ceiling. My washstand is replete with a soap smelling of citrus and lavender, and fresh towels with the ship line's monogram boldly embroidered across the bottom. I am seated in a velvet-upholstered chair and a plush Persian carpet lies beneath my feet. My cabin possesses a modest porthole—although regrettably, the view of the moment is of the dirty and dismal Liverpool harbor. Further, without Betsy here to protest the habit, I am delighting in a rich draw from my pipe as I pen this journal entry. I have consulted my pocket watch. Ten minutes remain until departure. I recall, with some amusement, the sympathetic looks of those who have asked about the woven fob affixed to the end of my watch.

"Is it the hair of your betrothed, or a sister, perhaps, who has left this world too soon?"

"Why, no," I replied. "This is the hair of Samuel Sylvester Dumay, perhaps you have heard of him? He was executed in 1846 after the bludgeoned bodies of seven women were discovered in a root cellar in his garden. Flies aren't the best secret keepers, as you might imagine."

The women tended to retreat with faces pale, one had even fainted dead away, but the men always returned to discreetly inquire how they, too, might acquire a similarly gruesome piece. This little timepiece served as marvelous advertisement of my trade, and a fine example of the curiosities I could procure, for the right price.

The ship's whistle now sounds. I have settled in to prepare myself for the ten-day journey at sea, and plan to avail myself of the great advantages the ship's amenities offer.

I hope to make some unique and advantageous discoveries on my trip to the West Indies, and am particularly keen to acquire a jadeite axe blade of the kind recently discovered in Antigua. An axe blade such as this would doubtless fetch a small fortune in the curiosity trade. I have labored tirelessly, over the course of many a year, to obtain oddities for gentlemen desiring to understand our nature, our origins, and the very fiber upon which we are built. My unequivocal joy shall lie in acquiring an exclusive treasure—one that may fetch an incalculable price.

છ

The pages that followed recorded the delight Edward found in his journey—the shipboard extravagances of lavish meals and fine spirits. He told of his arrival in the swelter and heat of Jamaica, and how he procured accommodation in a hotel for English travelers. Walker wrote effusively of the emerald coastline, the turquoise waters, and the sweet scent of orchids that mingled with the tang of allspice. It was an appealing account of a Victorian gentleman's travels and included detailed records of the topography, social structure, culture, and practices of the native islanders. This journal was a great find for anthropologist and historian alike.

I read through three months of entries, documenting Edward Walker's travels through Jamaica and the surrounding islands. As the evening progressed, my eyelids grew heavy, but it wasn't until the book slipped in my grasp, jolting me awake, that I decided it best to quit for the night. I marked my page with a cloth bookmark and set the journal on my desk.

I proceeded about my nightly ritual of locking doors and shutting off lights, although my body felt heavy, my brain taxed. The other two crates could wait until tomorrow. Climbing at last into my bed, I lay my exhausted head on the pillow.

It was then that the incessant, horrid noise began again to bear down on me—the scrabbling, the goddamned scraping inside the walls. "Sod off!" I yelled, smacking the wall behind the bedstead with an open palm. The mice stopped for just a moment, then resumed, knowing I couldn't get to them, knowing they were safe to continue in their mousy ways, chewing, breeding, crapping inside my walls largely undisturbed. *Damn it!* I threw the covers back, stormed down the stairs, returned the journals to their box, and fastened the lid. *Go ahead, chew the bloody hell out of my house, but I'll be damned if you lay one tooth on these journals!*

CHAPTER THREE

The shrill demand of a telephone stirred me from sleep. I glanced at the clock—8:30 a.m.

"Daddy, did I wake you?" Clara's nightingale voice sang in my ear.

"I'll say you did," I grumbled, then feeling guilty, offered an apology. "I'm sorry, dear. I was up late last night doing…research."

"Research? Oh, Dad, you're supposed to be taking it easy so that you can recuperate."

"How the devil did you know that?"

"Mum told me, how do you think?" she said.

Diane. Sodding hell. The North Roads University rumor mill never stopped grinding and pulverizing.

"I thought we could take Winston down to Maldon, for a walk along the seawall. He's so restless cooped up in the house. It's Tommy's last day at nursery school and I've already started my holidays."

"A walk? After that storm? The streets must be sheer ice."

"Dad, have you looked outside yet? The sun is out, it's all melting away. Besides, retrievers are built for this weather."

"Maybe, but how about humans?"

Clara chuckled. "We'll do fine, I'm sure."

"But what about Thomas? What time does he finish school?"

"His class is on a field trip this morning to see the lights and then there's a Christmas party afterwards, so I've got till half-past three. That's more than enough time to—Say, stop trying to get out of it, will you? I'm not going to allow you to hole up in your study, doing whatever it is you do. You need to get out in the fresh air, get a bit of exercise. Come now, get up and I'll bring you some fresh muffins. See you in twenty minutes." She hung up before I could protest.

15

I rolled onto my side and stared out the bedroom window over the neighborhood rooftops to the distant fields beyond. As a child, I had combed meadows such as these, my trousers rolled up past my knees, the muck oozing between my toes, digging with a rusty spade I'd found in the garage. I'd dig for hours, sometimes the better part of a day and into the evening until the last light had drained from the sky. Only when darkness fell would I finally quit my digging, with nothing but my memory of the terrain to see me home safely. Mum would always catch me, no matter how many gin and tonics blurred her vision. She'd wrap her knobby knuckles around my biceps, scowling down at me, her hazel eyes a mixture of rage and pity.

"Dunny, it's not out there. It's gone. *Gone*. The Nazis took it and we'll never see it again. We'll never see *him* again. So just stop it. Stop looking!" Her black curls would bounce with fury as she trotted me down the hall, ricocheting me into my tiny room.

"Lights out, Dunny, lights out." Mum would click the heavy button on the wall and my room would plunge into blackness, relieved only by the slice of light from the hallway that cut through the crack of the doorjamb.

I'd lie there, counting how many times the ice clinked in her glass, and in my mind, I'd be digging, pulling gold watches out of the sodden earth, checking the back of each one for my father's inscription. My eyelids would grow heavy, lulled by ice clinks and Dad's words in my ear, the last before I fell asleep: "This will be yours when I die, Dunny, would you like that? Would you like that, eh?"

I sighed, rolled onto my back and stared up at the ceiling as the memory faded. I'd spent the last fifty years of my life digging but had come up empty-handed every time. I was tired of it and had long ago resigned myself to the fact that I was never going to find that gold watch.

My daughter and I spent a peaceful morning together, strolling along the seawall while the retriever stopped to greet every dog and human alike, tail swishing like a lazy fan behind him. Along the shoreline, derelict skiffs decayed in their muddy graves while yawls and fishing boats sliced across the River Blackwater, glinting as they passed. Gulls made slow circles overhead, their sharp cries accompanying the quiet lick of waves on the shore. As we sat at the pub for lunch—with one end of the dog's leash tied to our table leg and my slush-wet leather boots chilling my toes—thoughts of the journals and crates returned to me, distracting me from Clara's chatter.

Then, drawing me from my reverie, she asked, "So, what's all this about a leave of absence? I mean, are you truly ill, Dad, or just in need of a little vacation?"

"What makes you ask such a thing?" I replied irritably.

"You don't look well. Your eyes seem dull, and you've clearly lost weight. And when did you get that deep groove between your eyes? You're beginning to look like Grandpa.

"Thanks," I muttered, rubbing my forehead self-consciously.

"I'm just worried about you, Dad," Clara admitted, leaning forward in her chair. "What happened when you met with HR? What did they actually *say*?"

I took a swallow of my tea and avoided her eyes. How could I tell my daughter of my academic failures?

"Oh, it's nothing, really. They feel I need a break, that I've been taking on too many responsibilities lately. I'm just a little run down, is all. Nothing to worry about." I managed a weak smile, but my stomach clenched and twisted. I ran a hand through my hair.

Clara moved her empty glass aside and leaned across the table. "Really, Dad? A little overworked? Come on. My whole life you've been overworked. What's really going on?"

I glanced down at my hands, marred with viciously half-chewed hangnails, then across the length of the pub as the heat rose to my face. I forced myself to look Clara full in the face. "You're absolutely right," I admitted. "I worked overtime for years. I *slaved* for that university position, and now, when I'm a bit run down from the divorce, they're ready to—bah! I can't even say it." My hands formed into convulsive fists in my lap.

Clara placed her hand on my arm. "Dad, I'm sure everything will be all right. Honestly, I don't think you've really come to terms with the divorce. You still need time to process it. Maybe some time away would be good for you. You know, recharge your batteries, so you can resume lecturing later, in the spring maybe."

"Time away? How is time *away* going to solve anything?"

"How is it going to solve—? Dad, you're so wound up. Give yourself a break." Clara looked at me with pity and concern.

It was true. Clara had only ever known a father consumed by his career. I was Dunny, the boy who always had his head down in the dirt while life went on around him. For as long as I could remember, I had relentlessly pursued my work, staying up late to formulate theories and write lectures, seldom sparing a moment for a bedtime story or a goodnight kiss. Was it too late or might I have another chance with this daughter of mine?

Meeting Clara's expectant gaze, I exhaled, and, despite my despondency, found a wan smile for her.

"When do you meet with HR again?" she asked.

"Beginning of January, before the term starts up again." I glanced down at the bill that had just arrived, and said with a forced resolve, "I guess that's when they'll determine if I've recovered enough to continue lecturing or if it's enforced leave for me. But, hey, it's Christmas. I've got a few quiet projects around the house that need attention. I am sure that will be a nice distraction."

"Projects around the house, eh?" Her eyes narrowed.

"Quite. I also have a few books to read. All very meditative and relaxing, I promise." I smiled broadly, mentally congratulating myself for my smoke-and-mirror phrasing.

"What projects exactly?" Clara folded her arms under her ribs. "You've still got those mice, haven't you?"

"Well…"

"Ha! I told you catch and release would never work. They make their way back, over miles. They never forget where to find the good stuff. Please call the exterminators. You don't need to be dealing with that lot."

I shot Clara a stern look. "Young lady, have you ever known me to fob off a job on a professional when I could do it myself? Don't worry, I've got a plan B." Clara rolled her eyes as I hurried on. "Listen, darling. I plan to cook us a big dinner for Christmas and I've got—"

"Actually, Dad, I'm sorry, but we have plans for Christmas." There was that pitying look again.

"I see. And what are they?" My heart slid a little.

"We are going to Stan's parents' place on Christmas morning and then we'll be having dinner with Mum and, uh, David." Clara's eyes darted away from me.

"Oh, all right then. Can we get together on Christmas Eve?" I brushed past the pain at the mention of Diane's new boyfriend— acquired just six months after the divorce—trying to show that I was a good sport about it.

Clara brightened. "Yes, that will be lovely." Then her face folded in concern. "You'd best have the mice problem sorted by then. I swear I'll jolly well scream if I see one."

"Indeed. I'm addressing that today. We'd best get out of here so I can go home and take care of it."

I tried to take the bill, but Clara laid her hand on mine. "I've got this, Dad."

"Oh, well, thanks." I blushed. I wasn't sure why.

Once home, I retrieved a large empty Mason jar and lid from the cupboard. In the utility room, I stooped beside the washer to check my live trap, a homemade concoction fashioned out of a plastic water bottle. It was empty. I crossed into my study and checked the trap under the bookcase. Empty too. The bottle trap beneath my bed, however, was not. It rocked in my grasp as a live mouse danced inside, frantic to find a way out. I raced downstairs to the bathroom with my prize and, with cotton balls and chloroform in hand, returned to the kitchen. No more releasing the bloody beasts. It was time to kill.

Holding the bottle trap by the bottom, I tipped it upside down over the Mason jar and opened the trap, hoping the mouse would fall out into the jar. The fool thing clung to the ridged sides of the plastic, suspending itself over the opening. I shook the bottle and the mouse lost its grip, landing with a plunk inside the jar. Turning my head to the side so as not to breathe in the fumes, I drenched the cotton ball with chloroform, tossed it into the jar, and clamped on the lid. Although this was, apparently, a more humane method of killing the little beggars than poisoning or pinning them between spring traps until they suffocated, I didn't care to watch my victim struggle for its last breath. Turning away, I baited the now-empty trap with peanut butter and returned it to my bedroom.

My study, by this time, was swathed in shadow; the high narrow windows let in only dim panels of light. It would be difficult to examine the crated items in the subdued late-afternoon light, even with the aid of the small study lamps. The lamps, however, were perfect for reading.

Pulling on my cotton gloves, I settled into my chair, opened the cloth cover of Edward Walker's journal, and resumed reading where I had left off the night before. Walker had, by this point in the journal, traversed Jamaica, sailed down to Trinidad, cut up to Martinique, and journeyed on to the Dominican Republic, before finally settling in Haiti where he had rented a small house and hired a servant girl to cook and do his laundry. Unfortunately, he made little mention of his acquisitions, but instead described, in lush Victorian prose, island life as he found it.

Some of the journal pages displayed rudimentary sketches of the various villages he visited. Palm huts and modest island homes were depicted amid sweeping tropical plants or rose against ocean backdrops. The descriptions were compelling, the drawings even more so. My eyes sailed over the script, pausing only in a few places where letters were hard to discern. I felt as if I had been lulled into a sort of waking meditation, my mind dancing over Walker's words, imagining turquoise waters and tropical vegetation swaying in a salty island breeze. Entranced, I could readily visualize market places abundant with handcrafted goods, while dark-skinned locals bartered with British travelers. All at once, however, my trance ceased, and, unable to believe what I had read, I stopped, transfixed, my eyes glued to the page. Excitement leapt in my chest. I held my breath and read on.

Chapter Four

Thursday, July 13, 1865

At an hour most ungodly, I was roused from my slumber by a tapping at my window. I struggled at the task of lighting my lantern in the pitch black. Turning up the flame, I held the lantern aloft, illuminating two dark faces silently surveying me through the glass. Shrugging on my dressing gown, I hastened to the verandah where two Haitian boys awaited me—one, tall and lanky, and of an early pubescent age; the other, smaller and a year or two younger than the first. The taller boy asked in Creole, of which I had a functional command, if I were the man the Haitians called "The Collector." I affirmed that I was, at which point he claimed that he possessed knowledge of an object that would be of considerable interest to me and that I must follow him, with haste, to his village.

I was at once suspicious as to this boy's motives. Why was this foray imperative in the dead of night? Bands of Maroons combed these hills, protecting *Vodou* society from outside incursions. I could only imagine the fate that awaited me, should I encounter such characters, to say nothing of the dangers inherent in traveling through a dark, unfamiliar jungle. I rejected his request at once, demanding that he disclose the nature of the object before I consented to follow him. The boy refused and, with a look of desperation that I could not discount, persisted in his entreaty. But I stood my ground.

"Out with it, boy," I insisted.

The boy spoke not a word but withdrew from somewhere about his person a small dark object and handed it to me. I turned it over in my palm. In the subdued lantern light, I discerned the roughly carved shape of a large-bosomed woman. A wide smile decorated

22

her face, and her eyes were closed, as if the woman were possessed of some kind of rapture.

"*Manman* says I give you dis. Come," the boy insisted, tugging on my hand.

I turned the fetish doll over in my palm—it was indeed a curious item, one for which several of my London customers would pay a handsome price. Perhaps this boy might lead me to similar or even more valuable curiosities. The boy's urgency, coupled with my own burning curiosity, convinced me at last to comply. I slipped the carving into my pocket and nodded my assent.

"Mister, bring dat," the younger boy said, pointing to the speckled grey mare under the shelter at the edge of the property.

And so, under the dim glow of my lantern, I readied my horse with bridle, blanket, saddle, and rope, taking pains to prepare for whatever awaited me in the boys' village. When I was done, the taller boy took my lantern in one hand, while I led the apprehensive mare up the footpath that disappeared into the black jungle.

The dangers of my potentially foolhardy decision dragged at my soul, but I felt driven to procure items from the West Indies that were so rare and so valuable as would astonish all of my gentlemen clientele. I kept one hand on my hunting knife, resting snug in its sheath at my hip, and quickened my pace.

The boys led me north for several miles, as we forged our way through the pitch-dark jungle, dense with palms, ferns, and orchids, their flowers veiled in the hush of shadow. Drooping palm branches painted our limbs with dew as we pushed deeper into the jungle. After an hour, the foliage yielded to the treeless clearing of a native village. I could just make out the profiles of thatched roofs amidst the backdrop of trees.

The older boy halted and, pressing his finger to his lips, extinguished the lantern flame. He took the reins from me and proceeded to tie the mare to a tree. Then, anxiously clutching my shirtsleeve, he motioned me to silence as we crept through the sleeping village. My ears were attuned to every sound—the padding of our feet on the hard-packed soil, the lament of the wind that wailed like a forsaken spirit of the dead, and the restless stirrings of the goats in their pens as we stole by.

The boy halted in front of a hut at the far end of the village and dropped my sleeve. The glow from within the shelter illuminated the threshold, upon which was scattered what appeared to be cornmeal. A dark viscous liquid that looked alarmingly like fresh blood was smeared on the threshold. The boy's behest to enter seized me with trepidation and my hand gripped the handle of my knife, ready to withdraw it from its sheath should the situation so demand.

Gathering my courage, I stepped over the befouled threshold and entered the candlelit interior. Within the dank hut, candles flickered on a trestle table, encircling a pile of withered mangos, papaya and other exotic fruits. Huddled in a corner, a woman, sheltering a dark shape, wept softly. Once aware of my presence, she gestured for me to approach and when I did, she seized at my trouser leg, whispering, "*tanpri...tanpri!*" The woman, it seemed, sought my assistance.

There in the humid gloom I bent over the lifeless shape. A terrible stench emitted from it—the dreadful odor of human waste and malaise, and something else...something putrid. I realized with dismay that this dark shape was, in fact, a small child, wretchedly ill.

Retrieving the lantern from the younger Haitian boy, I relit it and passed its light over the huddled shape. I almost dropped the lantern, made unsteady by shock—the child's eyes, large and vapid in the darkness, were spiritless, devoid of all gentle aspects of a compassionate soul. This boy, around the age of eleven or twelve, beheld me with an unnerving vacancy, regarding me without perceiving me. I crouched, transfixed, before a small hand on my wrist guided me to pull the lantern back, and the child's face sank back into shadow.

"Please, no light. It hurts brother's eyes."

Setting the lantern at some little distance, I returned my attention to the beleaguered child. His skin felt loose, like a lizard's, and cadaverously cool despite the tropical heat. I felt for a pulse in the child's limp wrist but could not locate it. The dread rose in my chest. Passing a hand under the boy's nose, I relaxed when a wisp of breath stirred the hairs on the back of my fingers. I placed my ear to the boy's chest. His breathing was shallow and labored.

My whisper cut through the darkness: "What is wrong with your boy?"

The woman sobbed in answer, rubbing the child's limp body vigorously as though to rouse him.

"*Zonbi*," the young boy murmured behind me. The darkness gulped the word, swallowing it like a secret.

His companion silenced him with a cuff to the ear.

"Emmanuel!" the younger boy exclaimed, then recoiled, his hand cupping his ear, and I wondered if I could possibly have heard him correctly. *Zonbi? Preposterous*, I concluded. *Nothing but myth and humbug.*

Instead, I insisted, in English, "He is dehydrated. Do you understand?" The boys regarded me with slack expressions, uncomprehending. "*Es'ke ou konpran sa mwen di'w?*" I tried Creole, but the boys shook their heads in unison.

"He needs water." I pantomimed the action of sipping water from my palm.

"No water," Emmanuel replied. "He no drink. No eat."

I demanded they relate what terrible fate had befallen the child. *Zonbi?* Upon what desperate situation had I stumbled?

"I will tell you," Emmanuel muttered, then leaned forward and whispered a terrible tale into my ear. "Henri was a bad boy. He no work but fight and steal. Our *manman*, she did not know what to do. One day he do something so bad. He steal from *bokor*. The next day, all kinds of trouble. *Bokor* come, he do dis—" Emmanuel lifted the boy's shirt cuff to reveal an abrasion on his forearm that wept blood and pus. "Then, Henri get sick."

"When did this happen? How many days has he been sick?" My voice sounded alarmed to my own ears, although why should it be so? I had nothing invested here. Why should I concern myself with the fate of a vexatious boy? Yet somehow, I was concerned, and the boy's declaration of *zonbi* tapped at my brain like a dripping faucet.

"Not long," Emmanuel shrugged. Then, leaning in to my shoulder, he whispered again in my ear, "The *bokor* has Henri's soul."

A shiver coursed through me. In the dim light I studied Emmanuel's face for any sign of deceit but saw only sheer terror. The boy had been beguiled by his own folklore. I, however, would require more convincing.

"The *bokor* make him *zonbi*, so now he do nothing. He no eat, no sleep. Just stare and stare all day and all night. He don't even use the *apanti*." The boy, I knew, referred to the privy.

"A *zonbi*, you say? Impossible. How did the *bokor* do this?"

"White potion and black magic." The boy gripped my arm, his eyes wide in the lantern light, his body rigid with terror. "You collect him, too? Take him home. *Your* home."

The very idea appalled me. I was in the business of collecting curiosities—dead and desiccated things, not living human beings. "Your brother needs to see a physician," I protested.

Emmanuel shook his head, his jaw stiff. "When the sun wakes, they will bury Henri."

His persistence began to annoy me, and, shaking his arm from mine, I replied tightly, "He yet lives. God willing, he shall recover with the aid of a medical physician. He needs to be examined thoroughly, fed, given water, medicine—modern medicine."

"The *bokor* no let him," Emmanuel scoffed. "He want take Henri from grave, make him slave." Then, dropping to one knee, he pleaded, "Mister, help my brother. Please take him away, where *bokor* not find him."

"The journey is long, and I fear he wouldn't make it."

"Please, mister, try!" He regarded me with urgent eyes. "The *bokor* sleeps now. We take Henri out—"

"See here, I need time to think."

"No time. Must go now." Emmanuel's eyes glistened with desperation.

The boy's compassion for his wayward brother moved me deeply, and I softened to his plight. It was clear that in this dirty hut, with no access to medical care, held captive to the deluded notion of *bokor* magic, Henri would certainly die. From such things, I confess, I could not easily turn away.

CHAPTER FIVE

Intriguing. It was rare to find a firsthand account of a zombie encounter as only a smattering of zombie reports were scattered throughout the last century of history. Some stories originated with native Haitians while others were described by anthropologists, who had made Haitian zombie lore a focus of study. If I remembered my dates correctly, however, this account predated the earliest surviving narrative by about fifty years. The boy had used the Creole word *zonbi*, instead of the Haitian French word *zombi*.

I recalled Zora Neale Hurston's accounts from the 1930s. She had believed that zombies were created, not through a magical waking of the dead, but by poisoning the living with a mixture of natural toxins that were designed to hurl the victim into a death-like state. Walker's journal account seemed to support that theory. Apparently, I had stumbled upon what promised to be a detailed account of a prepubescent boy undergoing this folk magic ritual. This wasn't an ordinary travel journal.

I searched the shelves of my bookcase until I found my copy of *Passage of Darkness* by the Harvard ethnobotanist Wade Davis. Davis described how the Haitian *Vodou* sorcerer—the *bokor*—administered a sedative drug to the victim, a drug comprised in part of a potentially fatal neurotoxin called tetrodotoxin, harvested from the puffer fish. This, combined with other dissociative drugs like Datura, derived from the plant *concombre zombi*, or the zombie cucumber, created a powerful concoction that caused the victim to slip into a death-like catatonic state. The victim retained consciousness but was unable to move, speak or otherwise indicate life. All vital signs plummeted, resulting in the frequent misdiagnosis of death—providing the poisoning didn't kill the victim outright, which often it did.

Scanning through Wade's writings, I followed up every reference to the elusive *bokor*, anything that would shed light upon this mysterious journal of Edward Walker.

According to Haitian zombie folklore, the *bokor* came in the night, after the burial, and resurrected the victim from the grave. Davis maintained in his book that it was the performance of a magical rite by the *bokor*, and not poison alone, that created the zombie. By capturing the victim's *ti bon ange*—the element of the soul that contains character, personality, and willpower—the *bokor* gained power over him. Bereft of the *ti bon ange*, the victim would be reduced to a hapless puppet, vulnerable to the commands of the one who possessed his soul.

Walker's account of the boy, Henri, was an interesting one. Davis' research seemed to support the account in Walker's journal, at least in part. The boy's respiratory difficulties could be symptomatic of tetrodotoxin poisoning. The slow heart rate, too, would be consistent with Datura poisoning, as would Henri's enlarged eyes and dilated pupils. Nobody knew exactly which plant ingredients combined to make up the poison; Hurston and others had tried unsuccessfully to obtain the formula. In the absence of fact, supposition factored into the herbal equation as much as science.

Judging by Walker's description of Henri's state, the boy had been in the throes of the poisoning, approaching the final stages of the ritual and, perhaps, his life. Were that the case, removing the boy from the village might save him from the clutches of the *bokor*, but it was unlikely to save him from death.

Pondering Davis' words, my gaze was caught by the macabre drawing on my desk. It was Henri, of course, the *zonbi* boy from the journal. The inscription below now made sense: *Specimen Z—zonbi*. I was riveted by the boy's tormented eyes.

"What's your story?" I wondered aloud. Settling into my armchair,

I picked up the burgundy journal and began to scan the passage where I had last left off. In the warmth of the room, however, I felt my eyes grow heavy. I was so very tired, after all...

I was looking out my bedroom window into the night when Henri's tormented eyes, bright with an eerie glow, appeared on the other side of the glass. Then, the window dissolved and the boy was within the room with me, his hand grasping my shirt, holding me captive as he screeched, *"Es'ke ou konpran sa mwen di'w?"* Frantically, desperately, I struggled to free myself, but Henri held tightly, his sharp nails raking my skin. "Do you understand?" he shrieked again, in English.

"No. No, I don't understand," I wept, trying in vain to wrench myself from his grasp. His claws scratched at my flesh, the sound curiously hollow and insistent. *Scratch, scratch, scratch.*

In fright, I managed to clamber my way, clammy and shaking, back to reality. The scratching sounds, however, had grown perplexingly louder and more persistent as I returned to the waking world. *Scratch, scratch, scratch.* Tiny rodent feet scurried within the wall behind my chair.

It took some time for my thudding heart to resume its regular rhythm, caught as I was between the terror of the dream and the aggravation of reality. How much longer could I stand this constant assault to my nerves? Rubbing my forehead in an effort to assuage the headache that was building there, I decided a cup of tea would be just the thing to steady my nerves.

Staggering to the kitchen, I put the kettle on, rinsed out the teapot and closed the kitchen blinds against the dark sky. When I opened the fridge to retrieve the cream, I realized that it was well past teatime and my stomach was growling.

Reaching into the cupboard for a container of rice, I discovered a cluster of mouse droppings deposited on the lid. "Damn it!"

Yanking all the cans and containers from my cupboard, I cursed aloud as I wiped them clean. I shoved a frozen entrée into the microwave for dinner, then pivoted, catching sight of the mouse in the Mason jar, now quite dead. My stomach turned and I moved the jar to the pantry floor, covering the offending sight with a tea towel.

As I drank my tea and picked at my entrée, my thoughts returned to Walker's dilemma. Had he, in the end, removed Henri from the village? And could it be that this journal might confirm what were now only theories about Haitian zombie folklore? Walker's account could well challenge standard assumptions and give birth to some new insights—insights that would indeed make quite a splash in the academic community. Eager to get back to my reading, I left the washing up for later and hurried back to my study where the journal and cotton gloves awaited me.

CHAPTER SIX

"Very well, I shall take him," I agreed. "But merely to provide him respite for the night while I consider a long-term solution. It would be quite impractical to transport him to England and unlikely that he would survive the journey, but I shall see that he receives medical attention in Port-au-Prince."

"*Wi!* Thank you, mister. *Mesi.*" Emmanuel smiled up at me, the remnant of tears dripping from his cheeks.

My heart lurched at the sudden appearance of a dark shape in the doorway. The candle glow illuminated the angular shape of a tall Haitian man. I froze, my breath tight and shallow within my chest. Emmanuel placed a finger to his lips and pulled the man inside.

"Papa," he said. Then he pointed at me and uttered the Creole word for "Collector": "*Pèseptè.*"

The man grunted his acknowledgement and stooped over Henri, bringing a hand to the boy's forehead. Emmanuel addressed his father in hushed whispers, to all appearances apprising him of my willingness to remove Henri from the village. The father smiled with relief and drew his wife to him, burying a kiss in her spongy hair. She wept and reached for my hand, whispering, "*Mesi, mesi.*"

"Come. We must hurry," Emmanuel urged, his eyes flashing in the dim light.

The two boys gathered up Henri's meager belongings—a pair of trousers, a white shirt and some linen with which to diaper him—and drew it up into a knotted cloth bundle. The mother enfolded Henri in her arms, wetting his drawn cheeks with her tears. Gently removing the sick boy from her grasp, I declared that I would do my utmost to ensure her son's welfare. I bundled the oblivious boy into a blanket and rose unsteadily to my feet.

"Vincent, the light," Emanuel said, and the smaller boy retrieved the lantern. Emmanuel peered out of the doorway and surveyed the quiet huts of the village, presumably searching for the presence of the *bokor* before stepping out into the night. The blood pounded in my ears, and my ragged breathing sounded alarmingly clamorous in the heavy tropical air. Well I knew that sounds in the night traveled like ghosts to the ears of those who lay sleeping, dragging them from their dreams. Perhaps the *bokor* was even now stirring in his sleep? The cornmeal scattered under my feet and I half slid, uttering a loud gasp before righting myself. Together we froze, waiting for the jungle to swallow the sounds of my stumble, preparing ourselves for possible repercussions. Emmanuel seized the lantern and cut the flame. Henri's bones dug into my chest as I pulled him tightly to me.

With Vincent clenching my wrist, we crept through the inky curtain of night, down the path, past the huts, in one of which slept the man who had stolen the soul of the boy I carried in my arms. Perspiration drenched my shirt and gathered upon my brow. I prayed, "Lord in Thy mercy protect me." We passed a fenced structure—I could barely discern the rising thrust of dark poles against the lighter shade of sky. The hollow jangle of dried bones, suspended from fence posts, danced on the wind, melodic, haunting, and sinister— the graveyard. I felt a sudden dampness spread across my chest. Was it Henri's tears I felt soaking the fabric of my shirt?

We fell upon the mare at the rim of trees that surrounded the village. Emmanuel hurried to untie the ropes as Vincent clambered onto the mare's back, dropping the pack at my feet. I hoisted the comatose boy—a tangle of bony limbs and a weightless torso—up into the saddle in front of his brother, who clamped his arms around Henri and held him fast. I manipulated Henri's legs to arc around the horse, took the rope that hung from the saddle and looped it into a strap, which I wrapped around Henri's waist, securing it to the saddle horn. Folding the blanket around Henri's shoulders, I pulled the loose end up over his head. In one fluid motion, I seized the pack, took up the reins, and led the horse away from the village.

Emmanuel refrained from lighting the lantern until the dense jungle foliage enclosed us, and even then, he kept the light low. I scrutinized the ambient sounds, anticipating the *bokor's* step on the path behind us. Was he coming to reclaim what was his? Coming, perhaps, to cut off our heads? I heard nothing—nothing except the wind rustling the palm branches and the clatter of bones on the graveyard fence, raking my soul.

As I moved through the jungle, senses alert and nerves jangling, I assessed the situation. It was as strange as it was dire. Henri would have died had I not intervened, and he might yet still. I wondered what the sorcerer had done to the boy to put him in such a trance. Most likely, the *bokor* had merely drugged the boy, as evidenced by his unseeing stare and his weakened, ruined body.

Henri resembled those drug fiends I had seen huddled in doorways, retreating into the dark shadows of the London slums, their bodies withered beyond measure, eyes vapid, countenances empty and broken. If the poisons were purged from his system, perhaps he might recover from his drug-induced state. If so, at what rate and to what degree? Would the drug have irreversible effects? I had heard tales of Haitian folklore, tales of an aunt or cousin doomed to roam the earth as a *zonbi*, but I scarcely believed such preposterous superstition. My scientific mind rejected these anecdotes as nothing more than the wild imaginings of an arrested culture. The Haitian *Vodou zonbi* ritual remained shrouded in mystery, and seemed likely to be little more than an ancient trickery. However, I mused, what if I *were* to take him with me to London? Within the privacy of my study, I could observe the boy and document his condition, as I aided him to recovery. If, under my care, the boy recovered, my notes could conclusively disprove *Vodou* magic once and for all. And even if I was unable to restore the boy, the process of extended examination and study would provide a unique opportunity to explore the spiritualistic practices of the *Vodou* culture. As an esteemed member of the British Association for the Advancement of Science, I could apply to the committee for a grant to aid in my research and present my findings at the annual meeting in September of 1866.

A detailed study of this exotic poison and the symptomatic effects on the body would be most beneficial to advanced medicine. My studies could be instrumental in the development of a highly effective form of sedation, for example, one that could lead to improvements in surgical outcomes and heaven knows what else! This Haitian boy was my opportunity to tangibly contribute to the scientific community, and certainly there was more profit and prestige in that than in the acquisition and sale of mere curiosities.

Some thoughts, however, did give me pause. London was teeming with poor unfortunate children and although my heart was dismayed at their plight, I had never considered caring for one. God only knew what kind of trouble one would invite with such a course. Such derelict children might be beyond all attempts at refinement, causing untold emotional and physical distress. What possible tumult might Henri introduce into my life? But what opportunities might I relinquish if I left him behind?

Betsy, too, must be considered. My wife abhors my specimens, deems them dreadful; she would never consent to Henri's presence within our home, particularly since it was likely that she was now a mother with a babe of her own to coddle and protect. Should I choose to defy what I well know would be her wishes and bring Henri home, I would have to conceal him. There was much to be weighed: the deception of my Betsy and the consequences thereof, against my own scientific pursuits and advancements. If all went well, I would make an indelible name for myself; Henri would ensure that my name was forever linked to the greatest discovery in modern science and medicine, never mind the ensuing riches that were sure to follow. And by that time, Betsy would surely forgive me for harboring this boy without her knowledge.

Lastly, and above all, I consider myself a humanitarian—and by now, doubtless, a father—and as such could no longer dismiss the suffering of children. While I felt it my duty to save this boy from his certain fate, I remain conflicted. There was time, still, to leave Henri at the hospital in Port-au-Prince, which would absolve myself of this responsibility and ensure the boy liberty from the clutches of the *bokor*. But would a boy in his state, bearing the stamp of *zonbi*, receive the proper care among a nation of superstitious people? Perhaps they would refuse to treat Henri, insisting that I return him to his village? What then would I do with this child? I wrestled thus with my thoughts during the night journey back through the jungle.

Once at my lodgings, I returned the mare to her shelter, unstrapped the poor unaware Henri and lifted him from the horse, his flesh cool beneath my hands. His breath caught—seemed, in fact, to cease altogether—before resuming its labored rhythm as I laid him down in my bed. Henri's brothers crowded around the bed, holding the lantern aloft while I checked the boy's vital signs. Henri's fixed unseeing eyes gleamed in the lantern's glow, and I shuddered at the sight of them, averting my gaze to take his wrist and time his pulse. It remained faint—an alarming thirty-five beats per minute. Holding my finger to my lips, I pointed to the closed door of the adjoining room, indicating that my servant, Fredeline, slept not far from us. How soon until dawn, until the *bokor* discovered someone had secreted the boy away during the night?

I checked my timepiece; it was nearing three o'clock in the morning. I dared not leave before the streak of dawn. It would be too dangerous to have the mare pull the heavily laden cart back along the dark, and oft-times treacherous, road to Port-au-Prince.

Filling a glass with water, I handed it to Emmanuel and instructed him to force Henri to drink. I then turned my attention to the packing of my belongings. My load was lighter than initially hoped for, but the curiosities I had already accumulated would cover my accrued expenses; and, I reminded myself, my study of Henri would enable me to not only recoup my investment but multiply its profits manyfold.

I had one remaining task to complete. I retrieved a piece of paper from my desk drawer and penned a document that accorded the guardianship of Henri to myself, Edward Walker. I signed an *X* for his parents' signatures. Under the circumstances, I was sure that Henri's parents would approve the forgery.

Returning to Henri's side, I discovered that his brothers had been unable to make Henri drink, but spilled water upon his shirt and bedding as a result of their efforts.

I pinched the skin on the back of the boy's wrist. It was slow to return to place and I knew he was grievously dehydrated. "It's not enough. He's going to need more. Much more!"

The boys and I continued in our attempts to administer the water to Henri, but he would not take to it. A few ounces entered his body, only for him to eject it forthwith in a coughing sputter—a useless endeavor. The sore on Henri's wrist was a festering mess of blood and pus. I irrigated the wound with water and bandaged it tightly in cloth.

I instructed the brothers to return to their village. It would be best for them to return to their beds before anyone noticed their absence. Perhaps they could keep the *bokor* off my trail long enough to secure my escape. The boys bid their brother goodbye, each kissing his forehead as tears streamed down their cheeks. Emmanuel, as he turned to leave, whispered, "Remember the carving. Keep it near. For protection." Protection from *what?* I shudder to think.

I am alone now as I pen this entry, save for the incessantly chirping tree frogs outside my window and my hapless companion, Henri. As I have recounted the day's events herein, and have mulled, once more, over the facts, it has become evident to me that I must take the boy back to England. I must proceed forward in the name of science, to say nothing of my own best interests. Henceforth, I shall record my observances in scientific detail so that I may begin to compile a comprehensive report on my findings.

I will monitor the boy closely during the homeward voyage, and will endeavor to get him to take liquids, and perhaps some treacle to build up his iron count and abate the poisoning effect. May God be with this boy, for the immediate days to come will decide his fate.

My eyes are heavy, but I dare not fall asleep. I cannot imagine what might entail, should the *bokor* track me here, but I must, indeed, be prepared for the worst.

Friday, July 14, 1865

I bolted awake at first light to discover that I had drifted off to sleep in my chair, despite my best efforts to stay awake. The morning heat was already thick and oppressive, and the reality of my decision weighed heavy on my heart. I was now the guardian of a Haitian child, and a very ill one at that—a realization that unsettled me.

It had been a harrowing night caring for the boy, and I had quite exhausted myself playing nursemaid. When I finally sought out my chair—a momentary respite from my duties—I could not evade the ivory gleam of his moonstruck eyes, like the hazy glow of lamplights in a foggy London night. I had closed my heavy lids against their invasion and that, doubtless, was when I had slipped into slumber.

I rose from my chair, my body stiff, bearish, and so weary from lack of sleep that my eyes refused to focus upon their task of loading the carriage and hitching up the mare. With my defenses diminished, it would be easy for the *bokor* and his clan to ambush me—a notion that hastened my movements and lent speed to my weary limbs. At last, I took Henri outside, laid him in the wagon, and covered him with a blanket. I gave a final glance toward the jungle, my last nerve strung to buckling, but no one appeared at the forested fringe; no man or *bokor* had come for Henri, or for me—yet. I slapped the reins and the wagon lurched ahead, down the rutted path toward the coast.

The boy uttered not a sound during the entire journey to Port-au-Prince, and I knew not whether he had expired behind me. I dared not stop the wagon long enough to find out. Instead, I drove the mare headlong through the waking dawn, desperate to reach the coast.

Brightly feathered parakeets and martins alighted on branches as we passed, watching our lone procession with curious, cocked heads. I perceived no other vehicles on the road; we were alone under God's watch—that is to say if He existed, for what God would subject His child to such a hideous fate as this?

By mid-morning, we had reached the port, where innumerable vendors advertised their wares, their shouts and calls an insufferable cacophony that aggravated the headache that was beginning to build behind my eyes. I was obliged to repeatedly mop the rivulets of sweat that poured from my brow. My thirst was unbearable. I tethered the mare to a post outside the ticket office and, closing the blanket about Henri's face, I carried him inside.

Setting the bundle that was Henri on a bench, in a half slump against the wall, I took my place in the queue. When I reached the ticket window, the port authorities, scrutinizing my certificate of guardianship, interrogated me regarding my intentions for the boy—

convinced that I intended to abscond with him for the purpose of making him a slave. Surveying the child wrapped in his blanket, they questioned me as to the state of his health. Henri, I informed them, was suffering from dehydration and malnutrition due to neglect. His parents had entrusted Henri to my care in order that I should deliver the boy to his extended family in London.

Despite my eventual success at procuring passage, at this short notice I was only able to obtain a single bed for myself in a cabin shared with two others. My attempts to obtain a bed for Henri in this same cabin were met with stern refusals, and since I did not wish to risk losing passage altogether by drawing further attention to Henri's ill health, I had no choice but to buy him a ticket in steerage with the second-class passengers.

I would be obliged to leave the boy unattended for many hours in the lower-deck berth. What might befall him without an attendant to nurture him and monitor his breathing? Or attend to his linens should he soil them during my absence? Without proper attention and care, the boy would die. Despite my gnawing worry, I had no choice but to surrender his fate to Providence.

And so it was that I hoisted Henri up over one shoulder, seized his small parcel, and joined the line of bedraggled passengers making their way into steerage. My trunks, meanwhile, were labelled and stacked on the dock, together with the baggage of the other passengers.

A steward checking our tickets looked askance at the boy in my arms. I explained that I was his guardian and would be attending him throughout the voyage, despite our disparate accommodations. The man sized me up, nodded, and instructed me to retain my steerage ticket and present it each time I came and went.

As I carried Henri and the bag of belongings down the ladder into the hold below, a foul stench reached my nose—the pungent sour odor of perspiring bodies wedged into a humid, stale space. Passengers lay claim to available bunks by throwing their satchels and clothing atop the mattresses. Half-concealed behind the ship's pipes, I espied a lone cot and hastened to seize it for Henri's use.

With relief, I laid Henri down on the straw mattress and covered him with a blanket. I prayed that the deplorable conditions would not worsen the boy's illness.

I stayed with Henri for some moments, checked that his breathing remained regular and his pulse constant. During my administrations, however, I was troubled by the thought that it might be ill-conceived to draw too much attention to the boy. Passengers, upon discovering the afflicted boy, might conclude some sort of illness had broken out on board, inciting a panicked riot. This resultant debacle would be singularly laid at my door, and doubtless result in the strictest of punishment. I could not risk it. I would have to conceal him from prying eyes.

Returning to the upper deck, I set about finding some suitable food for Henri. The waiters were serving a light lunch in the dining hall and I requested a small cupful of treacle, a cruet of milk, and a spoon for my ward who, I explained, was feeling quite ill. They happily complied, and I returned to steerage with the cup. Unwrapping the blankets from Henri's face, I was dismayed to discover that the child's looks had worsened—his eyes were lifeless still, dreadful in their vacancy, but his complexion had since paled to an ashen grey. Pulling down his lower eyelids, I noted the pallid nature of his mucosa. I placed an ear to his thin chest. Henri's heartbeat was almost imperceptible.

I raised a spoonful of treacle to the child's mouth. As I had expected, he would not or could not open his mouth of his own volition and so, with a thumb to the corner, I pried his jaw open and wedged the spoon inside. When I withdrew the spoon, there remained a sticky well of treacle. Despite my efforts to feed the boy, I succeeded only in smearing it across Henri's lips and cheeks. Milk, likewise, dribbled out the corners of his slack mouth, and it seemed beyond the boy's ability to swallow any kind of sustenance. I needed some kind of implement to deliver the foodstuff directly to his stomach. I needed a syringe.

Leaving Henri to the shadows once more, I returned to the upper deck and sought out the infirmary. Peering inside and finding it empty, I combed through the drawers until I chanced upon what I needed. Dashing back to steerage, I knelt beside the boy and retrieved the milk cruet I'd stashed under his bed. Stirring some milk into the cup of black treacle, I placed the syringe into the liquid, drew back the plunger and emptied the contents down the back of my ward's throat. He sputtered and coughed but much of the liquid seemed to go down as the swallow reflex engaged. Once I was satisfied that enough milk had reached his stomach, I laid him back on the bunk and drew the blanket over him.

Returning to the dining room, I procured a plate of lunch for myself, before continuing on to my cabin, from where I am now penning this entry. As luck would have it, my cabin mates are not present, affording me the opportunity to rest without disturbance. I have emptied my pockets of my prized watch and the small carving given to me by Emmanuel, which now regards me from the bedstead with a complacent smile. The constant care of this sick child, combined with my lack of sleep the night before, has caused a great depletion of my vitality. I shall look in on Henri before long but now I must rest.

It was half past four o'clock in the afternoon when I awoke from my slumber. The time had slipped past me, and I discovered to my chagrin that I had left poor Henri unattended for four hours. As I struggled to gather my watch and the carving, and put on my shoes and jacket, my thoughts were directed entirely to Henri's welfare. Bounding from my cabin and sprinting down the stairs to the lower decks, I encountered the steward, who recognized me and admitted me at once. I hastened to Henri's place but, when I got there, breathless and perspiring, I beheld only an empty bed.

CHAPTER SEVEN

The slam of a delivery truck's steel door echoing from across the street woke me late in the morning. I had stayed up late the night before reading Walker's journal—his account of sneaking Henri out of the village and on to the ship was engrossing and his reasons for doing so, compelling. *Vodou* rituals, in Walker's time, were shrouded in mystery, with the first cases described at the close of the nineteenth century. Walker's journal certainly represented one of the first documented cases of a *Vodou* experience, let alone the acquisition of an actual individual who had undergone such ritual poisoning. While Walker held the mid-Victorian designation of a "Collector," he was undoubtedly an early precursor of my own anthropological profession. My discovery of his journal promised to be valuable, but precisely how valuable I had yet to determine.

There would be no reading of the journal today, however. It was the twenty-third of December, and I had to get groceries for Christmas Eve dinner and pick up some last-minute presents. It was a bright morning—a shame to waste it. I could probably afford an hour to go through the crates before the English weather descended again. I pulled the first crate into the middle of the study floor. The lid was secured with silver nail heads and required considerable effort with a claw hammer before the nails could be pried loose and the lid removed.

Packed straw lined the inside of the crate, between which metal jar lids glinted. Lifting one from the crate, I examined it closely; the glass jar's exterior was caked in a semi-transparent, grimy film and as I moved the jar, something jounced within the amber liquid. Rubbing the film from the glass with my pocket-handkerchief, my heart lurched in shock at what I saw within—a two-headed male infant. The eyelids on each submerged face were mere slits through which clouded eyes peered; a pair of tiny noses breathed in the century-old liquid. When I held the jar up to the window light, the fetus's fragile skin glowed golden, like a Chinese paper lantern. I set the jar down on my desk and turned away.

Bloody hell, I thought. *Where did he get this?* While I had seen many specimens as an anthropologist—and prior to that during my studies in biology—it was unnerving to be confronted with this long-forgotten specimen, entombed in dust, pulled out of someone's loft space.

I gazed at the grey sky, trying to slow my erratic heartbeat. The oak tree outside my window swayed in the cold wintry gusts and a squirrel rooted in the bird feeder.

Returning to my desk, I again examined the jar, and determined that the two-headed infant was a set of newborn, or perhaps stillborn, conjoined twins. Each twin possessed their own head and neck but shared not only a ribcage but a single set of arms and legs, which folded about the body like the delicate petals of an unopened flower. As I turned the jar, I noticed a label on which was scrawled *7 D.* This form of categorization suggested that someone—Edward Walker?—had recorded additional information on the specimen in an accompanying ledger or logbook.

The contents of the second jar were equally disturbing. Within the viscous liquid was an infant with a parasitic twin's tiny arm protruding from its mouth. With a grimace, I set it down on my desk. The third jar contained a perfectly formed baby with its brain on the outside of its skull; the fourth, a hermaphroditic fetus, possessing both male and female genitalia; the next, a full-term fetus with the genetic mutation of hypertrichosis—its face and legs entirely covered with a thick carpet of hair. The last jar was home to an infant with anencephaly, a condition where the neural tube fails to close early in pregnancy, resulting in the partial absence of a brain and spinal cord. The subject looked quite unlike a human child, with the lack of skull and brain giving it a distinctly frog-like appearance. Like the conjoined twins of the first jar, all these specimens seemed to have been full-term infants or pre-term stillbirths.

I pried open the second crate and removed the straw to reveal several boxes of different sizes. Within the first lay what appeared to be the mummified remains of a human hand, well preserved and carefully wrapped. The Victorians used to grind Egyptian mummies to powder and ingest it, a remedy thought to cure such conditions as ulcers, migraines, or epilepsy. This hand, prized for its value in medical cannibalism, would have fetched a good price in the Victorian period. I held the mummified hand to my nose and inhaled deeply. Wisps of ancient herbs, earthy and sweet, swirled up my nostrils, chased by the slight sting of ammonia. The odor was exactly as it should be: indubitably an authentic sample of mummified remains.

The next box contained the mummified remains of a bisected human fetus, which came apart at my touch—the tiny dried organs grey and wilted, like dried beans. The shrunken head of a South American woman occupied the third box, her cranium the size of a large orange and sporting a shock of chestnut-colored hair. Despite the numerous fakes concocted by Victorian collectors, these specimens appeared to be legitimate, and a man like Walker would have certainly possessed documentation that authenticated these antiquities.

Of the two remaining boxes, the first revealed a medical trepanning kit, containing tarnished instruments of torture, with silver pick-like tools, a clamp, and an auger with several interchangeable bits. The kit was used to drill holes in the skull to relieve pressure, release evil spirits, and generally treat any particular infection that had to do with the brain. Whether the trepanning kit had been used or not, I could not tell, but the next, clearly, had seen frequent use. The last box contained a bloodletting kit. The gold velvet lining holding the cups and lancet in place had long since worn away, suggesting the instruments had been frequently removed and returned.

I emptied the crates of the remaining straw but found neither a ledger nor a logbook and could find no reference in either journal to the contents of the crates. I wondered if Edward Walker's descendants had removed the ledger, or if it had long since been lost or discarded. Disappointed, I returned the journals to the box and closed it.

Searching through my coat pocket for the scrap of paper where I had jotted Mrs. Walker's phone number, I cradled the phone piece under one ear and dialed her number. My heart lifted when Ruth Walker answered.

"Why, yes, Dr. Clarke. What can I do for you?"

"Good day, Mrs. Walker. I hope I am not interrupting your afternoon?" I waited for her politely dismissive response before continuing. "I wondered if there might be another journal or a ledger that went with these crates?"

"Oh, well now, I don't know. I'll have to ask Robert. Why do you ask?"

"Well, the crates contain scientific specimens, each of which is meticulously labeled with corresponding numbers. It seems logical that a ledger existed in which the details of each specimen were recorded."

"Oh, I see. We did just have the junk dealer by yesterday to take the rest of the boxes. I hope it wasn't in one of those."

"Oh dear," I groaned under my breath. "I hope not."

"Well, leave it with me and I will ring you back later, after I've checked with Robert."

"Thank you, Mrs. Walker, I appreciate it." I hung up the phone.

Sod it! An antiquity without official documentation or the presence of a detailed record could be difficult, if not impossible, to authenticate. I hoped that lug Robert Walker hadn't tossed it out. In the meantime, I recorded detailed notes of the contents of the crates and described each of the oddities, with a column for their numbered designation.

I pulled a stack of Victorian-era reference books from my shelves that would provide insight into the nineteenth-century fascination with human mutations. Working through my lunch hour, engrossed in my research, it was one p.m. before I became conscious of the time. Fixing myself a quick snack, I rushed out of the house.

The streets were full of last-minute Christmas shoppers, who, like me, had put off paying exorbitant prices for food and gifts for as long as possible. I found a parking spot in an alley near High Street, under a string of Christmas lights. The small shops were brimming with people and I felt claustrophobic, but soldiered on, selecting an attractive muffler for Clara, a shaving kit with handmade soap for Stan, and a wooden train for little Tommy. These gifts were, admittedly, the first items I saw, but the pushing, shoving crowds were a source of escalating panic. I pulled out my wallet, then paused—worried about the expense if I was about to get sacked. But if I chintzed out on the presents, Clara would know just how dodgy things were. My gut roiled and clenched. I grimaced at the sales girl and passed her my credit card.

Next, I stopped at the hardware store, where I bought a bag of fifty spring-loaded mousetraps—more than enough to put Clara at ease. Then, at the food mart, I gathered up a collection of root vegetables, selected some fresh rosemary, and finally stopped at the butcher's counter for some rabbit meat. Rabbit stew was on the Christmas Eve menu.

There was a long queue at the till, and as I waited for my turn, I surreptitiously eyed the cashier—a pretty young thing with long dark hair that brushed against her white blouse, under which two tiny mounds barely passed for breasts.

My eyes moved to the impulse-buy items on the wire shelf. There I spotted little tins of licorice allsorts—Mum's favorites. And I recalled once as a boy, while Dad was at war, I had scrimped and saved every penny to buy Mum a package of licorice allsorts. I had wrapped it in brown paper, decorated it with carefully drawn holly, and set it under the indoor fern that had served as our Christmas tree. When I woke in the morning and stumbled into the lounge, Mum was savoring a piece of licorice, my wrapping paper torn and lying before her on the table.

"Happy Christmas, Dunny," she said with a smile. "Look what Joe gave me—my favorite sweet."

My older brother grinned, his eyes crinkling with malice. *Joe gave her?* I snatched up the wrapping and saw that the tag I had made—"Happy Christmas Mum, love Duncan"—was gone, and in its place another: "Love from Joe."

"Wasn't it precious of him to think of me?"

"Sir?" the cashier asked in a lilting voice. "Do you need a carrier bag?"

"Oh, right. Yes, please," I stammered.

Trudging out to the car, I tossed the grocery bag in the boot, climbed in the driver's seat, and shut the door. That old familiar feeling of being pushed aside, my efforts unrecognized by others, consumed me. I did not need the reminder that I hadn't measured up, that I frequently didn't measure up, and possibly could never measure up. Thoughts of losing Diane, compounded by the possibility of losing my job, began to cloud my mind. Sadness and self-pity gathered like a weight in my chest. I put the Volvo in reverse and backed out of the parking lot, blinking away the welling tears.

In my driveway, soft snowflakes dusted the pathway to my door. I unloaded my bags of groceries and presents in the kitchen, then checked the machine for messages—empty. Either Mrs. Walker had forgotten about me, or she had been unable to locate the ledger. Time, no doubt, would tell. After putting my coat and boots away, I checked my homemade mousetraps for more captives and strategically placed a few of the recently bought snap traps. The bottle trap in my study contained a large brown mouse, which I brought, squirming, to the kill jar and administered the chloroform treatment. Gathering the freshly dead mouse, and the one I had previously left to die, I deposited them in the rubbish bin outside the rear kitchen door, then put the kettle on to brew a cup of tea.

Returning to my study, I observed the curiosities lining my desk—the bizarre assemblage of jarred monstrosities, and biological mutants. The perfect company, I decided, with whom to continue my reading of Edward Walker's intriguing adventures. And so, settling back in my chair with the journal on my lap and the tea at my elbow, I opened the book with gloved hands and found my place.

Chapter Eight

My eyes cast about the crowded hold, frantically moving from one passenger to another in my search for the missing boy. Perspiration trickled down the back of my neck as I spun on my heel, scanning the crowd.

I considered asking nearby passengers if they had seen the child, but quickly dismissed the idea. I was loath to draw attention to myself—and to the fact that I had brought an ill boy on board and then promptly lost him.

Overwhelmed by my quandary, I pulled a handkerchief out of my breast pocket and dabbed my brow. It was then that I caught sight of a squat, plainly dressed gentleman motioning to me with a curl of his forefinger.

"Aye, 'e's 'ere, 'e is," the man addressed me, "and you've got no right to 'ave 'im back, leaving 'im as you did, in such a state!" A woman seated by his side, whose leather-tough skin bespoke many a day in the Caribbean sun, nodded at the man's rebuke and shot daggers at me through kelly green eyes. She cradled the swaddled Henri on her lap, rocking him back and forth in her arms.

"What ails 'im? Poor child. You should be reported—bringing 'im onboard to infect the lot of us. I ought to toss you in the sea," the man admonished me. The temerity of the wretch!

Quelling my anger, I assured the man that this boy was my ward and that while he was, admittedly, dehydrated, he was certainly not contagious. I advanced slightly. The woman drew Henri possessively to her bosom and glared at me. "'E's been sick," she said in an accusing tone. "We've 'ad to change his shirt. What 'ave you done to 'is arm?"

"The boy was poisoned by a fellow villager, the result of which is the wound that you see on his arm. I have rescued him and need to administer ongoing medical attention. So, give me the boy, if you please."

"If it weren't for the missus and me," the man muttered defiantly, "this lad would've choked on his own vomit. Where'd you 'ave to rush to that was so all-fired important anyway? By the look of you, I'd say you ain't in steerage."

"No sir, I've got passage upstairs." I bristled at the necessity of justifying my actions to this ragged pair, but I was in a tight spot, unable to call for the assistance of the steward and thereby draw official attention to Henri's worsening condition. "I was resting in my cabin, having reasoned that the boy could sleep off the poison after imbibing the milk and treacle. I see now that I have made a grievous error. If you'd be so good as to release the boy to my care, I'll not repeat this error in judgment."

"And why should we believe you now? You 'ave only us to thank that this boy lives and breathes."

"Yes, and thank you, I must, sir and madam. I owe you a debt of gratitude. How can I repay you?" I withdrew my wallet—everyone had their price.

"My 'ealing services are quite talked about, back 'ome," the woman piped up. "Nursed the whole village back from typhus, I did—never lost a bairn above the age of three. That's gotta be worth at least four shillings a day, sir."

"Four shillings!" I exclaimed.

"Two quid by time we reach England and you daren't need come down 'ere again. Yer boy will be firmly on this side of the livin' when you return."

"Highway robbery," I muttered. However, I had little choice: I simply could not attend to the boy's needs in addition to my own so long as we occupied separate living quarters. Necessity decreed that I hire someone to care for the boy, and this couple seemed as likely as any I would find below decks. I extracted a few shillings from my wallet and deposited them in the man's dirty palm.

"Oh, thank you, sir," he said, plopping them into his pocket. "For this fee I'll also keep the rats away." He laughed.

"See that you do, Mr——?"

"It's William, sir, just William, and this 'ere's my lady, Mary."

Mary grinned, content enough with our arrangement to bestow a smile upon me. I accompanied her as she returned Henri to the cot and folded the blanket about him.

The boy demonstrated no visible improvement.

"Use the syringe to feed him, won't you?" I told her. "And keep him in the dark; the light aggrieves his eyes."

"Worry not, sir, I know me 'ealing." Mary patted the little bundle as if it were her own.

"I will return on the morrow," I said and took my leave.

It was with considerable unease that I retired to my cabin. Was I a fool to entrust the care of my ward to those two interlopers? I console myself with the thought that they seem sufficiently vested in his welfare, now that they have placed a figure upon it.

Sunday, July 23, 1865

Throughout the voyage, I have faithfully attended to Henri's welfare with the ongoing procurement of milk and treacle; Mary reports, however, that he continues to have the greatest difficulty in keeping it down. His comatose state continues, apart from intervening reflexive coughing fits, purging himself of any sustenance which we manage to force into him. At each visit, I take his pulse and pinch his skin, measuring the rate at which it returns to lie smooth against the bone. There are, as far as I can discern, no improvements in his health.

On one occasion, I concealed food from the first-class dining table and offered it to Mary and William as a token of my appreciation. I was horrified at the manner in which they ripped and tore into their meal, like predators to carrion; it so deeply insulted my sensibilities that I forebore to ever convey food to them in such a fashion again.

Monday, July 24, 1865

During the final hour of our voyage, while the ship neared Liverpool, I made my way down to steerage to gain advantage over the pandemonium that promised to burst forth once the ship docked. The rancid odor of the cramped quarters, after so many days at sea, positively overwhelmed me, and I drew a handkerchief to my nose to blot out the offending smell. Bedraggled passengers packed their belongings, their clothing stiff with salt and grime from the ravages of the voyage. Henri's temporary caregivers were collecting their accoutrements while the boy lay quiescent in the corner, enshrouded in his Haitian blanket.

"Aye now, there you be and just in time," William declared as I approached. "I was just sayin' to the missus, I thought a gentleman like you might not be bothered with a sick child and you might stick us with 'im. I was just about to lay bets that we'd ne'er see you 'gain. But 'ere you be," and he thrust forward a grubby hand for me to shake. I avoided the gesture by reaching into my pocket, removing my wallet, and producing the promised quid.

"Thank you, sir. I believe that is the agreed upon amount for your services." I nodded dismissively, wishing nothing more than to rid myself of them both.

"Aye now, 'and it over," Mary demanded, grabbing William's shoulder and pushing past him to get to me. "'Twas *I* who cared for 'im. I want me due."

"You'll get your due in good time." William smacked her bottom, seized the notes, and, with smug satisfaction, pocketed them in his dirty trousers. Mary squealed in protest as the two moved blessedly away, heading for the queue that had formed at the bottom of the ladder.

I retrieved Henri's belongings from beneath the cot, gathered his blanket about him and lifted the boy from the mattress. Gratefully exiting steerage, I pushed my way down the gangplank to the dock and located my trunks.

Hailing a cab, I instructed the driver to take us to the Lime Street Railway Station. He steered the cab through the snarl of carriages that glutted the roadways around the dock. Arriving passengers, burdened with their suitcases, struggled to escape the path of the oncoming carriages. Through the window I could see the ocean liner that had carried us across the Atlantic, belching thick black smoke from three towering smokestacks, mingling with the ochre smog of the Liverpool suburb. Dirt and soot painted the clothes, hair, and every pore of skin. Oh, how vexatious these industrialized metropolises are, the crowds of people, the noxious air, the overwhelming stench! I was already weary of being back.

At Lime Street Station, I purchased two second-class tickets and hastened toward our departing train, the child Henri in my arms. During the journey, passengers struggling to maintain their balance against the movement of the car jostled and pressed in upon me and the constant standing put a terrible strain on my lower back. How I longed for the comforts of my usual first-class coach. Several nearby passengers, I noticed, held handkerchiefs to their noses while others had turned away. The woman who sat beside Henri abruptly got up, pushing past me with a grimace. I quickly took possession of the vacated seat. Was it the pervasive odor of tired travelers in a cramped space that had so offended, or Henri's inexplicable stench? I caught a few stares and whispers directed at the boy. Tucking the blanket around his face to conceal those ever-staring eyes, I turned back and silenced the gossips with a scowl.

Finally arriving at Euston Station, we caught a hansom cab to London Bridge Station, and then a train to Greenwich. At last, I was able to find a seat for both Henri and me, which has allowed time and opportunity to document herein the chain of events from my waking until this present moment. I have been monitoring his condition at intervals during our travel. Henri's pulse continues to flutter weakly, and he appears increasingly closer to death and not at all improved, as Mary had suggested. The journey, it seems, has tried him beyond measure. I do not know how, but he yet lives, and I continue to direct all thoughts and prayers to his ongoing survival. Now our train is pulling into the station; therefore, I must leave off writing.

&

Outside Greenwich Station, with luggage gathered about me, I hailed a hansom cab to take us the short distance home. I positioned the gravely ill boy beside me on the interior passenger seat while the driver loaded my trunks and accoutrements.

"Where to, sir?" the driver inquired over his shoulder.

"Berkins Road," I replied.

As the carriage threaded its way through the tumult of the station traffic and onto the street, I thought on Betsy, and the little one whom she must have birthed and nurtured in my absence. I fervently hoped for a son and imagined him with my features—a straight and aristocratic nose, blue eyes, and the strong cheekbones of his grandfather. I think I should love him less if he took after his mother, with feminine features and the irritable whining manner that Betsy was oftentimes inclined to adopt. I knew if my wife ever discovered Henri she would object so fiercely that I would have no choice but to turn the boy out. But I would not do so! I am singularly invested in the study and care of this child, which will doubtless prove an astonishing scientific advancement. I refuse to sacrifice this opportunity, so that another might reap the rewards, or worse, consign Henri to an institution that is little more than a torture chamber for society's cast-offs—for I am well aware of the fate that oft befalls the infected and the insane, corralled as they are in such dreadful places. Henri is mine to study and care for, and I will entrust him to none other.

Thoughts dashed through my mind of how I might secret Henri into my study without arousing Betsy's curiosity. Since my wife was not expecting my early arrival, there was a chance she might not be at home. It was a beautiful July day. Surely there was an afternoon tea or some such event begging her attendance? Perhaps she had brought the baby round to her mother's.

As I neared home, a viable plan solidified in my mind. I would request the cab driver stop some distance away and I would leave Henri behind in the cab while I verified Betsy's whereabouts. If she were at home, it would be imperative that I thwart any attempts on her part to discover my secret.

Therefore, I had devised a plausible ruse to satisfy Betsy's curiosity—namely, that I had a special surprise for her and a premature viewing would spoil it. Of course, if this particular ruse was required, I would be obliged to produce a real surprise in place of the deception. No matter. I had contacts that I could call upon— contacts that could be trusted to keep things concealed, if it came to that.

The servants, however, were another matter entirely. They, who see all and cannot be trusted to keep the secrets of the manor, even under threat of dismissal, would prove a particular challenge. After much deliberation, I determined that the best way for me to succeed at trickery was to shroud it in as much honesty as possible.

As we neared the house, I bade the cabbie pull over at the curb.

"Very good, sir." He vaulted from his perch and held open the carriage door. As I exited, he nodded toward the child who remained bundled within and inquired, "And your charge, sir? Shall I assist you?"

"No, no!" I barked. "I'll be back for him."

I hurried up the walk that led to my house and as I reached for the door handle, the knob turned, and Mr. Turner opened the door. My butler was most surprised to behold me. After our perfunctory greeting, I asked that which most concerned me—was my wife at home?

I proceeded to explain the need to keep one item among my belongings concealed from Mrs. Walker until such a time as I was ready to bestow it upon her. I confided that this item was of considerable size and that I must convey it to my study at once. Mr. Turner nodded his understanding and revealed that Betsy was in the nursery with my son. Oh, despite my troubles and fears, I felt tremendous pride and pleasure upon this pronouncement—that my child lived and breathed and was indeed the son upon which I had set my heart!

I impressed upon Mr. Turner that not only did I need his assistance to keep Betsy occupied while I smuggled her gift into my study, but also, she must not yet know of my arrival, and, indeed, his job depended upon the successful execution of both.

Hastening down the street to the carriage, leaving, no doubt, a bewildered Mr. Turner in my wake, I hoisted Henri to my chest. Nodding to the startled cabbie, I half ran with my blanketed burden down the street to my door. I heard the wheels of a hansom approach from behind, causing my heart to leap into my throat. Was the passenger a neighbor who might, at some future dinner party, inform Betsy that they had observed me carrying a peculiar package into the house on the afternoon of my return to London? A package exhibiting a decidedly human shape? I hazarded a glance inside as the cab passed by—a woman looked at me with steel grey eyes that blinked once and then looked away. I breathed a sigh of relief; she was unfamiliar to me.

I ascended the steps as deftly as I could manage, my vision partially obscured by Henri's shoulder. The door fell open when I reached for the handle; it was my good fortune that Mr. Turner had neglected to shut the door, allowing for a swift and seamless entry. I rushed my human package down the length of the hall, weaving around so much ill-placed feminine frippery, designed to clutter up a perfectly functional space with its superfluous extravagances. Henri's left foot, which was protruding at an unfortunate angle, grazed an Oriental vase and sent it pirouetting on its stand. I turned his body and used his buttocks to steady it before racing onwards.

Breathing heavily, I felt my way down the basement stairs in the dark, unable to set Henri down in order to ignite the gas lamp on the wall. Stumbling at the bottom, I only just managed to stay upright, my overriding concern to protect the boy at all costs. A few steps further and I was at last before my study door. The latch was stiff, and I had to rattle it several times before it gave way.

The weak light that fell through the high half-window left the room shadowed. Propping Henri in a chair, I lit a kerosene lamp and held it aloft, arcing a pale-yellow glow about the room. My specimens glinted in their jars as the light illuminated their rare and marvelous forms. All appeared as I had left it—shelves laden with rare books and manuscripts, my varied inventory of precious curiosities, the origins of which had spanned the globe, and, less glamorously, the invoices that littered my desk, which I had neglected to file before leaving the country.

Spying the patchwork quilt I kept in my study for drafty evenings,

I spread it out on the floor, laid Henri upon it, and covered him with his own blanket. Finally exhaling in relief that the task was done, I dimmed the lamp, exited, and locked the door.

Approaching the parlor, I heard a shrill exchange of voices from the upper-level landing where Mr. Turner and my wife were having a spirited conversation. Pressing against the wall, I concealed myself behind the hallway armoire. My butler was the stoic recipient of a scolding; it seemed he had disturbed my dear wife with his announcement of a polecat spotted burrowing in the woodpile. Mr. Turner proclaimed stiffly that it was his duty to protect her and the young master from the most vicious and vile of garden pests during my absence. Betsy answered heatedly that she had lived all these twenty years with the strictest knowledge of garden pests and that she was not a shrinking violet and rejected the implication thereof. I did my best to stifle a guffaw behind my white knuckle.

Betsy then disclosed that she was retiring to her sitting room to work on a needlepoint while the baby slumbered and, with a huff, instructed Mr. Turner to deal with the polecat in the woodpile in whatever manner he saw fit, and to quit bothering her with such unimportant details of domestic maintenance.

My heart quickened at her declaration. I determined to exit through the kitchen, so that I might again re-enter through the front door as a new arrival.

Fate was kind and no servant lurked in the kitchen. I continued through the scullery and peered out the window into the garden. The housekeeper was hanging the laundry, and it would be impossible to slink past her without detection. Betsy's voice echoed from the foyer, and I ducked down in a corner of the scullery and waited breathlessly for her to enter her sitting room—located, as it was, at the opposite end of the house. If she should shut the door to the sitting room, I would be able to sneak outside by way of the front entrance. If the sitting room door remained open, she was certain to catch sight of me in the hallway as I attempted to make my exit. I was quite trapped, and, in my fright, was unable to think of a plausible reason as to why I was prowling around the house rather than heartily announcing my arrival in the conventional manner.

"Mr. Turner, have Cook prepare my tea," I heard Betsy say.

Mr. Turner informed her that Cook was at market, but he would be delighted to prepare the tea in Cook's absence. Betsy murmured something in response.

Moments later, the butler entered the kitchen. From my position in the scullery, I attempted to catch his attention with a *psst*, softly at first and then a louder, more determined *psst*! At which, Mr. Turner's head snapped around in startled surprise.

"I got caught out," I told him. "You were tasked with keeping my wife upstairs. What am I to do now?"

Mr. Turner replied that although he had done his utmost to keep Mrs. Walker upstairs, she had a will of her own and there was nothing he could do. I impressed upon him that now he *must* prevent Betsy from seeing me; that he must keep her captive in her sitting room by engaging her in a long conversation about the numerous possibilities for victuals to accompany her tea, thereby giving me enough time to slip out the front door. I instructed Mr. Turner to close the sitting room door, to eliminate all danger of Mrs. Walker spying me. With an expression of shocked indignation, he refused, reciting the code of conduct between male servants and their female employers, which confounded me all the more. I bade him instead to stand between her line of vision and the doorway, and in haste and exasperation, sent him forth.

Hawk-eyed, I watched as Mr. Turner traversed the length of the hallway. When he reached the sitting room door, I readied myself to make my move.

"I know that you usually prefer scones with your tea, ma'am, but I am afraid we are all out."

I hurried down the hall, keeping close to the wall where it would be harder to see me from the sitting room. The distance seemed to stretch on forever.

From within the drawing room came Betsy's fiery retort: "Oh, for blessed sake! Didn't Cook have the foresight to prepare anything for my tea *before* she left for the market?" Fortunately, the volume of her reprimands concealed the creaking boards beneath my feet as I cut down the hallway to the door. She continued denouncing the servants in general, finishing up with, "I shall have to have Mr. Walker bring me back a Toucan to perch on your shoulder and repeat my words all the day long!"

I reached the foyer and slipped out the door, turning to close it behind me. As I did so, I heard a shriek—"Why, Mr. Walker's home!"—and my heart skipped, and my breath entirely left me.

And so it was that the nursemaid, Mrs. Newbury, announced my arrival. In an instant, Betsy appeared from the sitting room. My heart gladdened to see her. She was a vision to behold in her afternoon dress of yellow, which duly complemented her blonde locks and rosy cheeks.

"Edward!" she exclaimed. "What the devil? No warning, and with me in my house dress?" Betsy paused somewhere between joy and dismay. Finally, giving herself over to happiness, she pulled me into her embrace. I smiled with contentment at having arrived finally home and relief that my charade had been so narrowly but successfully accomplished.

"Come now, time for that later," I admonished her gently, and called for Mr. Turner to fetch my belongings from the carriage. Betsy apprised me that I was just in time for tea, but first she must take the opportunity to introduce me to my infant son.

"Ah, so I have a son, then," I smiled broadly, feigning surprise. "I must first settle my luggage, my dear, and then I am solely and wholly yours." Betsy granted her permission with a kiss to my cheek.

Chapter Nine

The ringing phone in the lounge drew my attention from the journal. I let it ring for a little longer so that I might finish the page.

"Dr. Clarke? It's Ruth Walker. I'm sorry to say, but after much searching, Robert couldn't find the ledger. But good news, there was one. He remembers removing it from the crate when he took out those stuffed creatures, but he's not sure where it went after that. He thinks the junk collector took it."

Shit! "Well, what can be done?"

"I can give you the address of his shop. Give him a ring, maybe he still has it."

"Right then, just a minute." Grabbing a pencil and a *National Geographic* magazine, I scribbled the name, number, and address of the shop, Hugh's Collectables, on the back cover. Thanking her, I hung up. Another trip up to Linton. I had no time for this, but if I didn't act now, the ledger could well be forever lost to me.

I dialed the number of the junk shop, but the line was engaged. It was just past four, and I would need to leave immediately to make it to the shop before it closed. Shoving on my boots and shrugging into my coat, I seized the keys and left for Linton.

While driving north through the darkening streets, it occurred to me how alive I felt. Excitement coursed through me, like a giddy schoolboy at the start of summer break. Here I was driving up to Linton in search of an antique ledger that had belonged to a long-dead dealer in grotesque anomalies. What *was* I doing? There were presents to wrap, a dinner to start, and a house full of mice to exterminate. An irrepressible grin crossed my face. I was rediscovering my passion—the desire to dig, the drive to find, the hunger to know. I pressed down on the accelerator and strengthened my grip on the steering wheel, my heart thudding under my ribs.

Hugh's Collectables sat at the end of a narrow row of buildings. A motley selection of chairs, a battered bike, and an overloaded clothes rack lined the sidewalk in front of the shop. I pushed open the door and stepped inside.

The interior exuded a peppery punch of staleness, and was littered with out-dated furniture and display shelving, upon which was strewn an odd assortment of glassware, long-forgotten toys, costume jewelry, figurines, and other useless junk that few people would want. Several items I recognized from the old houses of youthful friends, from my own home, and from my mother's collection—toy metal cars and WWII bombers, worn cricket bats, and Depression-era glass. I made my way toward the scuffed glass counter at the rear of the shop. The bloke behind it sat on a chrome and plastic chair, doing his best to ignore me in favor of a movie magazine from the 1960s. He wore his hair greased and slicked back.

"Wot you looking for?" he asked, without looking up.

"I've come for a box of goods that you picked up from a home in Linton a few days ago; yesterday, I think it was, or the day before."

"Yeah? Changed your mind about giving it to me? People do that. I've got a policy though. No give-backs." The storeowner—Hugh, I assumed—paused to pull a cigarette out of a Lucky Strike pack, put it to his lips, and lit the tip, at last making eye contact through half-closed lids.

"No, I don't want the box back; I'm looking for just one specific item from it. It was put in the box by mistake. It's of historical value, you see."

"Look round, everything in here is of historical value, mate." Hugh chuckled, pulling the cigarette from his mouth and picking something off the end of his tongue.

"Of significant historical value. It's a book, a ledger. Did you run across it when you unpacked the boxes?"

"Oh, of *significant* historical value," Hugh repeated in exaggerated tones. "I don't know what you're on about. I've seen nothing of the sort."

I took a breath, attempting to maintain my composure. "Do you remember picking up a few boxes from an older woman and her adult son? They live on Granta Leyes—"

Hugh blew out a stream of smoke and tacked the words on at the end, almost choking them out: "Of course, I remember. I'm not daft."

"And was there a book included with the other items?"

"Look, mate, I haven't even got to the boxes yet; they're still round back."

"Brilliant. Where? Through here?" I headed for a curtained doorway at the back of the shop.

"Wait! You can't go in there." The man rose and flew round the counter after me. Shoving his cigarette between thin lips, he yanked my arm. I jerked it free.

"Look, I don't mean any harm, it's just really important to my anthropological research that I find that ledger. I'm a lecturer at North Roads University." I pulled a card out of my wallet.

Hugh squinted at my card as the smoke circled his face. He handed it back to me. "Look, I ain't no professional. Just a guy running a shop, trying to make a living. If I go make a run, help people rid themselves of their unwanted junk, spend the petrol and the time, and they come back here and take back their stuff, I lose money. I end up a bloody fool with nothing for my trouble."

"Oh, I see." I reached for my wallet, withdrew a twenty-pound note and slapped it into his palm. "Will this do, for your troubles?"

"I guess it will have to," he said with a grunt, and pulled back the curtain to let me pass. "Just the book, Doctor, nothing else."

66

"Just the book," I agreed and ducked through the curtain.

The small room was filled with stacked boxes, each forming unwieldly towers that completely obscured the walls. The sight of it caused my chest to tighten and my pulse to race. Taking a deep breath, I pushed the anxiety down. It seemed logical that the Walkers' box must be closest to the door, assuming it was brought in recently, and so I started there. The first box held nothing but old linens and dishes; the second and third were similarly disappointing. Pulling apart the flaps of the fourth cardboard box—I hit the jackpot. Lying on the top was a dusty black leather-bound ledger, and inside, written within in faded ink—

Edward Walker

Acquisitions and Sales, 1850—

Yes! With a surge of triumph, I cradled the book, lifting it from the box. Underneath, I caught sight of another old book, tucked it into my coat and exited through the curtains again. Holding up the ledger, I gave the storeowner a relieved smile. "Found it. Thanks."

Hugh gave a downward jerk of his chin in reply.

Sitting in the driver's seat, I pulled the stolen book from my coat, and briefly examined the title, *Identifying Butterflies,* before laying it on the back seat. Carefully, I opened the pages of Edward Walker's ledger. It was formatted according to the conventions of a nineteenth-century accounting sheet—listing the items, the date of purchase, the trade price, and the price for which the item was subsequently sold. Two columns divided the page in half, one for the date of acquisition and another for the date of sale. A plethora of goods were listed, with page after page filled with the fine script of a meticulous hand. This accounting journal provided the critical means by which I could authenticate Walker's possessions. Closing the ledger, I set it on top of the book on butterflies in the back seat and started for home.

In the twilight, Linton looked positively gloomy. Indigo shadows fell across the facades of Victorian buildings. I wondered at Walker's view of a world where industry ruled, and all was enmeshed in soot and smog, when coal pollution billowed from smokestacks and all but blotted out the sun. The dirt and grime of Victorian London had once formed the subject of my favorite lecture. I wistfully recalled the students' expressions of disbelief as I regaled them with descriptions of the Victorian streets, of the stench of organic waste from horses and humans alike, fecal matter that pooled in the streets and clung to the boots and hems of trousers and skirts, following Londoners wherever they ventured. Then, it was a quick skip over to the horrors of homelessness, street crime, and prostitution, with a detour to the multitude of diseases that circled through the alleyways and sewers. Oh, I could paint quite a picture of the inescapable filth of London town. Then, I'd leap to the privileged classes, who escaped the dung and disease with a hefty glass of scotch and a lighthearted play in the evening hours.

I would then discuss the Victorian writers—early activists really—like Dickens who exposed and criticized the social injustices and moral abuses of Victorian society. The students would lean forward in their chairs, eyes fixed to mine as I came to the crux of the lecture: the Victorian writers' penchant to use pathos, shock, obscurity, and horror to reach their audience. The horror lay in the notion that an individual of strong character and high moral values might easily fall into a state of destitution, of starvation, and in turn suffer a grinding, miserable death.

A hush would fall over the lecture hall, as I explained, in a quiet tone—with students craning forward to hear!—how the Victorians had made considerable progress in medical science, which had given birth to its own complex set of moral questions.

Mary Shelley's *Frankenstein* demonstrated the tenet that whosoever shall attempt to depart from morality and play God shall wreak great havoc upon the world. Stevenson's *The Strange Case of Dr. Jekyll and Mr. Hyde* also explored the pitfalls of trifling with the mysteries of science. Jekyll tried to cure himself of a disease and, in the process, transformed himself into a monster. Wilde examined this theme in *The Picture of Dorian Gray*. Dorian made a deal with the devil in order to stay eternally young; a bargain that ended in tragedy. There existed a strong theme in Victorian literature that suggested playing with science could be ethically and physically dangerous, and that when man presumed to play God, he would suffer greatly for it.

Even as life imitated art, the Victorians would strive to create morals from random tragedies—concluding, for example, that the murders perpetrated by Jack the Ripper were a punishment from God for mankind's immorality. The Victorians feared that one misstep, one poor decision could render them a derelict, doomed to a life of poverty, corruption and, perhaps, insanity.

As I left Linton, revving the car engine a little on a straight section of road, my heart sank at the realization that it had been some time since I had so delighted in giving that lecture. What had happened? When had I made the transition from enthusiastic young lecturer to complacent old curmudgeon? Little things had occurred along the way, I realized. The moment when I understood that most of the students didn't share my enthusiasm for anthropology, that drumming up the proper appreciation for the past in a world of cutting-edge technology was analogous to flogging a dead horse. And it was probably the big things, too, like realizing that someone who had promised to be with you all your living days suddenly didn't love you anymore, didn't want to keep putting up with your less-than-perfect idiosyncrasies.

From out of the darkness, a large shape cut across my field of vision, and my focus leapt back to the road in front of me. I slammed on the brakes and my car slid past the stop sign and into the intersection, narrowly avoiding bashing into the other car. The driver shouted at me and drove off, shaking his middle finger through the window. It was a few moments before I was calm enough to leave the scene.

Upon reaching home, I laid the ledger and the butterfly book in the typewriter box with the journals, checked the traps, exterminated a victim in the killing jar, and threw the dead mouse in the bin outside the backdoor with the accumulating carcasses.

Feeling peckish, I made a quick salad and pulled some bangers from the freezer to cook up in the saucepan. When we were married, Diane had always prepared the meals, but since the divorce, I had discovered that I rather liked cooking for myself. I was looking forward to making the rabbit stew for Clara and her family, although I felt a pang at being alone on Christmas Day. This would be the first Christmas without Clara, Stan, and little Tommy.

After the washing up was done, I ducked out to the woodpile in the back garden, lit by a meager yellow porch light, and retrieved a few pieces of wood for the fire. I built up a fire in the study and, with a crackling blaze warming the room, I set about the business of wrapping the presents with old Christmas paper from the cupboard. Admittedly, wrapping gifts wasn't my strong suit but Tommy would be tearing open the paper anyway. And Clara would simply be impressed that I had made the effort.

The successfully concluded Christmas preparations called for a glass of sherry. Selecting a liquor glass from my mahogany cabinet, I topped it with a generous dose from a ten-year-old bottle of sherry that I saved for special occasions. Impatient to resume my reading of Walker's journal, I slipped on my gloves and pulled the journal out of the box. Opening to my bookmarked page, sherry at hand, I began to read where I had left off earlier that afternoon.

Chapter Ten

I set to the task of sorting my luggage, separating the ones intended for my study from the ones that contained my personal effects. The latter, Mr. Turner brought to my room, where they could be unpacked, and my clothing sent for laundering. I instructed Mr. Turner to carry the crates containing my new acquisitions to the basement and set them outside my study door. Mrs. Butterfield, the housekeeper, had taken over the tea preparations and I followed Betsy up to the nursery to meet my first-born child. Our arrival roused the baby from his nap. He was a striking boy; his sleepy blue eyes smiled up at me.

"Charles," I said—the name we had selected before his birth—as Betsy lifted him from his cradle. The infant took great interest in me; it was quite apparent he knew me to be his father. I reached out a hand to smooth his head but drew back, at once aware that I had not washed up since leaving the ship. What diseases might I carry on my person from that filthy steerage berth? Begging my leave, I hastily departed from the nursery. I was sorry to cut our reunion short but was anxious to check on Henri. Scrubbing up at the washstand and changing into a clean shirt, I buttoned my waistcoat and transferred my study key to my trouser pocket. Retrieving a glass of milk from the icebox, I stirred some black treacle into it before continuing on to my basement study.

Mr. Turner had left the stairwell gas lamp burning and it provided just enough illumination to light my way down the stairs. Sliding the key into the lock, I entered the study, dragged the crates in from the hallway, and locked the door. An unpleasant smell permeated the room and I reached for my handkerchief to cover my nose. I lit three lamps and placed them, in turn, as near to Henri as I could, careful not to set them too close to the bedding lest it catch fire.

Wrinkling my nose as I bent over the boy, it was clear that his state was largely unchanged. The struggling rasps of his breath came slow and deep, and his eyes gazed vacantly at the plaster wall. Grasping his wrist, I timed his pulse by the clock hands that ticked rhythmically on my desk. His pulse was no more than thirty beats per minute, slightly slower than when I last checked, and roughly a third the rate of a healthy child his age. I lifted his thin cotton shirt to conduct an examination of his physical condition. The skin color maintained its ashen grey appearance; his backbone protruded under his skin, and the unmistakable pattern of his rib cage narrowed into his hollow pelvis. The suppurating wound on his arm looked no better or worse. Returning Henri to a supine position, I continued my examination. His limbs were bony, the skin still reptilian in nature—dry and slack. I lifted Henri in my arms, carrying him over to my platform scale and laying him upon it. The boy weighed a meagre forty-five pounds.

Fortunately, his linens were unsoiled. With his entire system apparently slowed, whatever nourishment he may have consumed shipboard may not have yet passed through him. Nevertheless, with a baby in the house, should Henri soil his nappies, they could be easily assimilated with the nursery laundry, thereby avoiding arousing the suspicions of the housekeeping staff.

Having lit a robust fire in the hearth, I set about attempting to feed the boy. I retrieved the syringe from my luggage and filled the metal instrument with a concoction of milk and treacle. Kneeling on the floor, I braced Henri against my side and pried open his jaw, rapidly releasing the liquid down his gullet. He choked slightly in advance of swallowing, before, in one convulsive movement, ejecting the liquid into my lap. *Damnation!*

The boy moaned in my arms—a low, hollow wail that sent a

rushing chill through my soul, and I almost released him at the shock of it, but I hung on. The sound had scarcely escaped his lips, when his fixed stare broke, his eyes rolling back in their sockets. His lips twisted into a grimace, exposing even ivory teeth, as I struggled to brace him tight against my chest, guiding him through the convulsion. For two and a half minutes, Henri tremored and jolted in my arms before his frail body finally relaxed. At the conclusion of this event, I found his pulse to be abiding still at thirty beats per minute, and his breathing had resumed its rhythmic laboring. Uncertain as to what else could be done, I returned him to his bedding and enfolded the blanket around him.

Henri seemed to hover in a perpetual state of starvation, without succumbing to it. I wondered as to the number of days that had now elapsed since his poisoning. The boy had been in my care for just short of two weeks and had made no detectable improvement. I felt sobered, too, by this convulsive fit. Dare I admit to myself that I had no foresight, no instinct that would allow me to rescue this boy from the precipice of the grave and restore him to life? I cursed myself for thinking only of the science of the matter and not of the soul; and the distinct possibility that I might bring about this boy's demise by my self-indulgent experiments.

Increasingly desperate, I sought the medical journal that I had acquired from the estate sale of a former physician. My hands found the cracked leather binding and I slid the book out from its companions. Therein, I found a remedy to treat a poisoning: calomel as a purgative, to induce vomiting and diarrhea. Although Henri had already experienced an episode of vomiting, it had done little to restore his wellbeing. Perhaps more was needed.

Flipping to the glossary, I located "calomel" and discovered its role as an aid to teething infants. On a hunch, I locked the study, sprinted upstairs to the nursery and sorted through all the elixirs, medications, and tonics until I found the amber bottle I was looking for. I also grabbed the iodine—useful, no doubt, in the treatment of Henri's wound. I took the opportunity to change out of my vomit-soiled trousers.

Hurrying down the stairs, I ran headlong into Betsy who was rounding the corner from the kitchen. I stopped short, narrowly avoiding a collision; Betsy drew back, clutching our son to her breast and proceeded to reprimand me for startling her, demanding to know why I was racing around the house. I stammered, having no excuse at the ready, only to have her silence me with a sharp toss of her head.

"Well, you *are* joining us for tea, are you not?"

"Yes, my love."

"Good." Betsy preceded me into the parlor with a sniff of displeasure. I dropped the medicine bottles into my trouser pockets, smoothed my waistcoat, and followed.

The tea tray was laid out with a multitude of sandwiches and biscuits, for which I was most grateful, having worked up an appetite on my long journey from Liverpool. However, before long, guilt began to nag at my conscience as my thoughts drifted to Henri, recumbent on the floor of my gloomy study in the belly of the house, possibly perishing as I sat enjoying pleasantries with my wife.

I could not withdraw without arousing her vexation and so I spent the next long, drawn-out hour listening to Betsy's nauseatingly dull stories of her mundane household routines—which servant ruined what finery, the details of meals that Cook had prepared, as well as the gossip amongst our friends and acquaintances. I found it insufferable—so disinterested was I in domestic affairs, and Betsy had very little interest in my travels. She was not as enlightened as I and felt that the citizens of other countries were beneath her notice and dignity. At last, I seized the opportunity and excused myself to attend matters in my study.

Retrieving a bucket and some linen rags from the kitchen supply cupboard, I descended once more to the study and locked the door behind me. Henri lay placid on the floor where I had left him, and so I set to work preparing for his purging. I cut the rags into squares, setting some aside for the inevitable clean up. Peeling away the old bandage from Henri's arm to reveal the festering wound, I swabbed it with iodine and dressed it with clean linen. Then, I administered a single dose of the calomel—just enough to start the evacuation of stomach and bowels.

It was not long before the boy started into a paroxysm of heaving and vomiting. I held the bucket under his chin and he promptly filled it with bile. I sat with him in the dank room, guiding him through the ordeal. Upon the cessation of the fit—when the spasms of Henri's body at last released him—I laid him gently down and set to tidying the mess. The vomit pail, with dirtied linens stuffed inside, I set by the door for later disposal.

As the boy convalesced, I grasped his wrist and felt for a pulse, which was barely perceptible—the trial had taxed him so. I spent the next several hours monitoring the child, keeping a close account of his breathing, and examining his pupils for any signs of awareness. The calomel, it seemed, had done little to aid him, and I was loath to administer another dosage, for fear it would lead to mouth ulcers—or worse. Consulting again the medical journal, I came across a promising remedy that was within my power to administer: bloodletting.

Although repulsive to me, bloodletting has been in common practice for hundreds of years, and the medical journal detailed numerous pronouncements as to its efficacy. I had previously procured a bloodletting kit for resale and a search of my study produced a wooden box that contained the phlebotomy kit. Within the gold velvet lining, I found a scarificator, a number of collection cups, several blades, and a rubber suction bulb. Seizing a bottle of gin from my desk and a strip of linen, I sanitized the equipment before consulting the journal for complete instructions on how to perform the phlebotomy.

Henri would need to be secured to a chair to prevent him from slumping forward and to ensure his arm remained immobile. I lifted the body of the boy to my desk chair and fashioned a restraint around his waist with the cord from my smoking jacket. Stretching out Henri's arm, I bound his wrist to the chair's armrest with a spare strip of linen. During these ministrations, the boy's head lolled sideways, and his eyes continued their sightless gaze.

Steeling myself for the task ahead, I prayed that the bloodletting would not be too taxing to Henri's frail system. I had read of a man run through by a sword during the war; bloodletting had been essential to his recovery. Strengthening my resolve, I held the instrument against Henri's thin arm and popped the blades into his young flesh.

The boy never flinched. Withdrawing the device, I held the glass cup to the wound; his blood flowed weakly into the receptacle as I pumped the bulb. Henri continued in his oblivious state, despite the steady *drip, drip, drip* of blood—surprisingly loud in the quiet room. I wondered if the poison had also affected his nerves, if he were, perhaps, unable to experience pain. There was little blood to let, probably due to the reduced heart function and the slowing of his bodily molecules. I worried, of a sudden, that on the heels of the calomel treatment, the bloodletting might do him in. Or would it prove his salvation? My very uncertainty caused my stomach to roil in vexation. Removing the cup, I pressed a cloth to the lances, applying a firm pressure. Then, I bandaged Henri's arm and released it. With a trembling hand, I poured myself a generous glassful of gin and belted it back. The alcoholic warmth coursing through my veins helped to steady my nerves.

Now, how to dispose of the blood collected in the glass? Through the high window, I spied an azalea bush, its spent buds lying in a rust-colored litter around the base of the plant. Reaching up, I opened the window a fraction and poured the cup of blood into the soil. A summer rain had begun, which cast a coolness to the July air. I closed the window so as not to lose the warmth of the room. It was imperative that Henri did not catch a chill, as that would surely end his life.

I was startled by a sudden knock at my study door, followed by Betsy's squalling complaint of "Edward? Where did you disappear to?"

The handle turned and then halted when it reached the limits of the latch. In shrill tones, Betsy demanded to know why I had locked the door. I asserted that I was otherwise engaged and could not, at present, attend her. She demanded that I grant her entrance and inquired as to whether I was hiding anything in the study for *her*—so accustomed was she to receiving exotic treasures from my journeys.

"Well, now, perhaps it *is* a surprise. Perhaps something will reveal itself after a few days," I replied, without thinking.

Betsy persisted, with the demeanor of a spoiled child, demanding to see the surprise immediately. She was relentless in her entreaties, sobbing about the pains of childbirth and delivery that she had had to bear alone, and the sufferings she had endured at my expense and in my absence.

Finally, Betsy had tried my patience to its limit and I turned her away with a harsh reprimand. "You shall *not* see it until I am ready to show you. You will *not* come in, and *that* is *that*. Now, if you want it, be a good girl, Betsy, and *go away!*" It was cruel, I knew, but it was for her own good, and mine.

"Oh, Edward!"

Through the study door I could hear the poor girl bursting into tears. I listened for her soft footsteps making their way upstairs again before I wearily completed my cleaning. Untying the boy, I laid him in his bed on the floor, covered him with the blanket, and exited the study, making certain to lock the door again behind me.

At supper, I had to endure a sulky Betsy. When I did not respond with tender supplications, she attempted to elicit information about her gift with a renewed effort. Tomorrow, I would pay a visit to my friend James, the curiosity dealer. I had some belongings to sell and perhaps he could trade me something suitable as a gift for Betsy. Having no knowledge of what he might possess in inventory, I could not give Betsy any hints about her intended gift. And so we played a cat and mouse game in which she proposed an exhausting number of questions and I remained tight-lipped and silent. Finally, I was pinched and slapped for my insubordination, and she went to bed in a huff.

Now, at last arriving at the day's end, I am able to make this journal entry. It has taken me some time to write—so eventful was my day— and now I am ready to collapse in a state of utter exhaustion.

It is now clear that the scientific nature of my study of this *zonbi* phenomenon will require strict notation of my observations. I resolve to keep exact and meticulous notes regarding Henri and his treatment, so as to present all scientific evidence at the conclusion of my study.

The child's condition has not, as yet, improved, but neither has it deteriorated; he is the same huddled lump that waits, poised somewhere between life and eternal slumber. His transfixed eyes speak of his bondage to this in-between world. His captor—be it *bokor* or common poison—will not release him.

My suspicion is that the poison has caused a cessation of the molecules in his body, thereby altering the motion that keeps them at their natural distance, gives them flexibility, and limits their combinations, one with each other. The once flexible and quavering tissues have now set like stone, forming one compact mass. Therefore, I must strive to set the life force again into motion.

But, this is a task for the morrow. Now I must retire to bed. I have lit a fire in the woodstove and shall leave Henri in its glow and warmth as I lock him in for the night. With the staff retired to their rooms, I shall wash out the bucket and dispose of the linens in the refuse pile in the rear yard.

Note—I must come up with a more suitable bed for Henri; it is dreadful for his health to lie on the cold, damp floor.

CHAPTER ELEVEN

The obligation of the full day ahead—cooking, cleaning, and mouse murdering—weighed heavily on my mind as I rose from a fitful sleep. Frying some bacon and eggs for breakfast, I thought about the contents of Edward's journal. If memory served, calomel was another name for mercury. Walker had continued to poison the child, even while attempting to save his life. It wouldn't be long, I was sure, before I would read of Henri's death. And the bloodletting would not have helped; although Walker's use of it had not surprised me—this common Victorian-era practice purported to be a curative for all kinds of ills, like cancer, diabetes, high blood pressure, even fever and madness.

I circled between stove, cupboard, and sink, eating at the counter then rinsing my breakfast dishes, thoughts elsewhere. I noticed with a start that it was sunny outside and the frost had begun to melt from the branches outside the kitchen window. I needed to get that stew started, and I would, soon enough, but I was anxious to compare the contents of Walker's crates to the lists inscribed within the ledger.

Donning my cotton gloves, I retrieved the ledger and flipped to the first page. The entries began in 1850. Walker must have been a young man at that time. These early purchases had been made mostly in London, with some along the Kent coast, no doubt shipped from abroad. By 1852, acquisitions were increasingly made in Paris and Frankfurt. Skipping ahead to the mid-1850s, I saw Walker's travels had expanded to encompass the far reaches of Africa, South America, and even the West Indies. His handwriting remained elegant throughout, demonstrating the care and attention that he had devoted to his work. It soon became evident that this list was compiled from almost ten years of scouring the world, amassing the strangest of life's curiosities. The records ceased after the final entry of July 14, 1865—the Haitian carved idol given to Walker by Emmanuel. Ruth said Walker had died suddenly from a tropical disease that he must have picked up in the Caribbean during his final voyage, which would explain the lack of subsequent entries.

I noticed in the pages several scientific names with which I was unfamiliar. I would need to systematically go through these catalogued items and find the ones that were currently in my possession.

Only the jars were numbered, so I began with these. I cross-referenced the catalogued numbers and descriptions against the jarred specimens until I came across a match, then arranged the jars in chronological order. With the collection spanning so many years, and with items being added and subtracted from the inventory, this was a complicated task. Once I had matched all the jars in my possession to the record in the ledger, I jotted down in my notebook the ledger's page number, item number, name, and description as recorded by Walker. Loading a fresh roll of film in my camera, I took photographs of the jars, and recorded the sequence of the photos in my record book, in case anything happened to the objects—heaven forbid!—before the film was developed.

After the jars has been thoroughly recorded, I lifted the individual boxes from their crate and set them on the desk. These items lacked identifying numbers and were recorded in the ledger by description only. I documented these in the same manner as the jars and photographed them accordingly.

I left for last the phlebotomy kit—the gold velvet lining suggested it was the same one that Walker had described in his journal; the one that he had used to bleed Henri. I lifted the brass scarificator from the casing with care. It felt cold and heavy in my hands. Examining the front plate, I could see how the device functioned: one would wind the handle to spring load the blades and then, holding the instrument to the patient's arm or leg, press the release button, and the blades would dart out, piercing the patient's flesh. This particular scarificator sported eight blades, a smaller unit than the twelve or fourteen-bladed devices used for maximum bleeding in severe medical cases. Upon testing the mechanism, the blades sprung up with a sickening snap. I photographed the instrument and returned it to its case.

I felt a curiously strong connection with Walker, I acknowledged. He seemed my counterpart 125 years in the past—preserving history, investigating peculiar phenomenon, and leaving integral clues for the anthropologists of the future to follow. I felt a quiet sense of privilege, to be in possession of his collection and journals, and to gain entrance into his world. I rather fancied—although would, of course, admit this to no one other than myself—that Walker were somehow communicating with me alone, as if he had deliberately left these things for me to find.

Looking over my notes, I realized that these artifacts represented only a small portion of Walker's original collection. There were a significant number of items listed in the ledger whose fate was unaccounted for. The fetish doll carving, in particular, was not among the items Ruth had given me, and I wondered what had become of it. Perhaps Betsy, or subsequent family members, had sold parts of Edward's collection after his death.

Walker's ledger listed a number of animals with genetic anomalies that he had sold to sideshows, circuses, and private collections. In the later years, his tastes seemed to focus predominately on abnormalities of the human body. Clearly, this macabre fascination with the strange and unusual had fueled his decision to bring Henri back to England. I longed to get back to Walker's journal, but I had a great deal of cooking and cleaning to do before Clara, Stan, and Tommy arrived.

I chopped vegetables while munching on handfuls of granola straight out of the box. Within half an hour the kitchen was filled with the heady aroma of sautéed rabbit, fried bacon, and warmed wine. Having layered the stew into a casserole dish, I popped it into the oven. The three hours of cooking time would allow me to tidy. Mindful of Clara's distaste for mice, I checked the snap traps and found one occupied. I could hear the little bastards scratching and rustling inside the walls as I removed the dead mouse, which I added to the bin of corpses outside.

After an hour of vacuuming and dusting, my back began to ache. I needed to get horizontal, if only for a few moments. Perhaps I could fit in a little journal reading before Clara and the family arrived. Retrieving the journal from my study, I climbed the stairs to my bedroom. I was struck by the starkness of the walls as I went by, only now noticing that Diane had stripped them bare of the artwork and framed photos that used to hang there. Clara's school photo montage had gone, depicting her transition from an adorable child to an awkward preadolescent and then into a teenage beauty. *Damn Diane. Could she not have left me one?*

I had stripped down to my drawers, crawled under the covers, and was plumping my pillows when the phone rang. *Bugger.* In a fit of annoyance, I leapt out of bed, crossed the room and snatched up the receiver.

"Hello, Dad."

"Hello, Clara darling, how are you?" My irritation evaporated at the sound of my daughter's voice.

"Just smashing, Dad, and you? You *are* recuperating, I hope, and not working yourself into a lather about your job?" Her tone was alive with the energy of love and concern.

"No, I mean, yes, I've been relaxing...mostly. Did some Christmas shopping yesterday and making rabbit stew for dinner tonight. I was just hopping into bed with a book while it's roasting in the oven."

"*Mmm*, my mouth is watering already. What time shall we pop round?"

"Oh, say five?"

"Brilliant, only don't let on to Tommy. I don't think he'd eat the stew if he knew what was in it. His favorite book right now is *Peter Rabbit*."

"Mums the word then," I replied with a laugh.

"Oh yes, speaking of Mum, that's why I'm ringing. She asked about you." Clara hesitated, and I could tell what was coming.

"Come now, out with it. What does she want now?" I sighed wearily.

"Sorry, Dad. I don't like to ask, but the mantel clock in your study was her grandmother's. Because of that silly house rule that your study is off limits under pain of death, she didn't check it." Clara laughed nervously.

"You can pick it up tonight when you come for supper, and next time, tell your mother to ring me directly. It's not fair of her to put you in the middle of things."

"I think you'd better tell her yourself, if you don't want me in the middle of things."

"See you all tonight, my darling, and if you're so inclined, bring a sweet. Even with my newfound gastronomic flair, you remain the Queen of Desserts."

"Will do. Bye, Dad." Clara hung up.

Climbing back into bed, my thoughts returned to Walker. Having been entrusted with his journal and likely the only one to have ever read the entries within, I felt a strong sense of duty and responsibility to treat his possessions with the utmost care and, somehow, to do them justice. I found my place, and wondered—had the calomel and bleeding finally done the poor boy in?

Chapter Twelve

Tuesday, July 25, 1865

It was revitalizing to sleep in my own bed the first night of my homecoming. The down-filled mattress felt like a cloud in heaven compared to the rickety camping cots I had endured during my excursion in the West Indies. Despite Betsy's obstinate manner, my wife possesses a sweetly demure side that presents itself at my mollycoddling. Our marital reunion, after months of abstinence, has been quite pleasant, so much so that Betsy felt it difficult to allow me to return to my study, and again inquired after her surprise. Her large brown eyes moistened with tears and her plump lower lip pouted as she begged me to present it to her. If her cheeks had not been fresh with the blush of passion, I would have been able to resist her yet a few days more, but what man can deny anything to a woman who has just given of herself? I had some important business to attend to with James, my associate, after which I promised her she should have her gift. My business was necessarily two-fold. In addition to acquiring a gift for Betsy, I had some trading to do.

We breakfasted in a lavish style, with all manner of pastries and berries, clotted cream, crisply roasted bacon, and coffee imported from Italy. I could scarcely move after indulging in such fine cuisine, the likes of which I had not been accustomed to these past months, so had to recline another hour on the divan before I could return to my study to assess Henri's condition. I had an experiment in mind.

Plucking the remaining pieces of bacon from the serving plate, I took my leave with a gentle kiss to Betsy's cheek. It was already eleven o'clock in the morning, and I was struck by guilt when I realized the length of time I had left the boy unattended. With growing trepidation, I reached for my key. Had the phlebotomy helped to restore motion to his molecules or was he ever nearer death's door? Worse yet, had the terrible event already occurred?

Turning the lock, I pushed the door open. Immediately upon entering, my senses were assaulted by the iron tang of dried blood, the lingering smell of vomit, and that unidentifiable stench that had been peculiarly associated with Henri since the beginning. How concentrated it now seemed in this small space! I held a handkerchief to my nose and approached the child where he lay on the floor beside my desk—exactly as I had left him. I placed a hand under his nose and felt the faint stream of breath across my knuckles.

With two fresh strips of linen, I redressed the lancet wound created the night before, as well as the one left by the *bokor*. Neither looked to be healing. I prised Henri's mouth open and slid a piece of bacon between his lips, clamping his jaw together in an attempt to induce swallowing. When my efforts were clearly in vain, I removed the bacon from the well of his cheek. The treatment of the previous night seemed to have done nothing to improve the boy's state. Reasoning that a second course might prove beneficial, I prepared another dose of calomel and administered it, bucket at the ready. Henri went through the motions of heaving but left only a trace amount of bile in the bucket. Thereafter, I cleaned the scarificator and prepared Henri's arm for the blades. This time the blood was even slower to fill the cup. Perplexed, I terminated the procedure.

I returned Henri to his bed on the floor, covered him with the blanket, and disposed of the blood out the window. The late morning air was warm, so I left the window open to disperse the dreadful smell that had accumulated in my study.

Next, I selected suitable curiosities to sell to James, arranged them in a crate, and nailed it shut before pushing it outside the door. Henri remained as before, his gaze vacant and sightless. Perhaps during my absence, the administered treatment would take effect and he could be induced to take some broth. Surely, if he did not take sustenance soon, he would die—and yet he had gone so long without. I was vexed beyond measure.

Locking the room, I proceeded to wrestle the crate up the stairs to the foyer, and out of doors, where Mr. Turner assisted in lifting it to the back of my wagon. I concluded that it was best that the butler, who tended to inept fumbling, be absent from the house when I returned with Betsy's gift from the "West Indies." Therefore, I sent him on an errand—to procure for my wife the most ostentatious bouquet of flowers he could find and return with them in time for my presentation of Betsy's gift, at precisely six o'clock.

Instructing my driver, the young Master White, to take me to The Curiosity Shoppe, I climbed into the carriage and we rattled away.

The air had grown insufferable as morning shifted toward noon, and the stench of the city percolated in the summer heat. The smell of excrement mingled unpleasantly with the blood and offal that emanated from the butchers' shambles. Shouts of the fishmongers, the bells of the muffin men, and the incessant whines of the street musicians and organ grinders assaulted my ears. Clenching my teeth, I set my mind to complete my business expeditiously, so I might, with haste, return to the sweet suburban air.

Finally, we arrived at The Curiosity Shoppe on Leman Street. I leapt down from the carriage, leaving Master White to follow with my crate. The ting of the brass bell announced my arrival, and James appeared from a back room. I was delighted to be reacquainted with my old friend, and we exchanged exuberant greetings and hearty handshakes.

White deposited my crate on the counter and returned to the carriage, while I perused James's latest offerings. Wedgwood plates formed a neat line on a wooden rail that ran the length of the room, below which hung an assortment of oil paintings procured from estates and private collections. Antique furniture, arranged to allow a narrow path through the shop, clustered here and there; and, on every desk, dresser, and table, exotic pitchers and figurines of fine china were situated. A magnificent stuffed specimen with a ruddy coat and striped markings that cut down its back caught my eye.

"A *thylacine* acquired from Tasmania," James said. "Isn't he a beauty?"

"Indeed he is. I will have to take him. However, I have another matter upon which I will require your assistance."

I explained my predicament regarding Betsy's present and asked James if he possessed an artifact from the Caribbean that might suit.

"That could be arranged," he grinned. "Let's have a look at what you've brought for me today."

James locked the door and drew down the shade—my curiosities were not for mixed company, but were the chattel of back rooms, black markets, and secret trades. Opening the crate, I brought out the six monkey pelts I had acquired in Jamaica and slung them over the back of a nearby chair so that James could admire them.

"These are exquisite," he said, running his hand through the inky fur. "Too bad there aren't more. They would make a handsome rug."

"Or perhaps a woman's shawl? They would appeal to a taxidermist, too, since the heads are intact."

"True, true. On to the next."

I deposited a glass jar containing a teratoma tumor on the counter. This monstrosity—a fist-sized knot of flesh and hair, from which protruded a small collection of teeth jutting out at awkward angles—had been excised from the stomach wall of a twenty-five-year-old Cuban man.

James's eyes grew wide as he beheld this extraordinary curiosity. "What is it exactly? Why, are those teeth?"

"It is a teratoma tumor, probably an undeveloped twin."

"Brilliant. I've a customer who has a penchant for particularly gruesome items."

"Here's another." I brought out a slender vial that contained a charred finger bone. "The only remains of a Dutchman captured and devoured by a cannibal tribe."

"Excellent."

"Now, do you have something that might be appropriate for my wife?"

"I know just the object," James replied, retreating to the back of the shop where he tugged open a large folded screen. Intricately carved in polished mahogany, the screen depicted a scene of small birds nesting among flowering vines, some with wings spread, others with wings folded contentedly. Mother birds were interspersed throughout the piece, bending over the open beaks of demanding fledglings.

"Outstanding!" I exclaimed. "Perfect for Betsy's dressing room."

We placed a value on all items traded and arrived at an agreement that pleased us both. James wrapped the *thylacine* and screen with care, and, after parting with a handshake, I loaded the goods, with the assistance of Master White, into the wagon and started for home.

Arriving at the house, I ensured the coast was clear before helping White carry the screen into the sitting room. Sending White back for the *thylacine*, I instructed him to place it in my smoking room, then, raced upstairs and tapped on the nursery room door.

"Darling, are you in there?"

"Just finishing up with Charles, dear," came Betsy's soft voice from within.

"When you are done, there is a surprise for you in the sitting room."

A squeal came from within the nursery—whether originating from Charles or from Betsy herself, I could not tell.

From the linen cupboard, I obtained one of our best silk linens, and draped it over the screen. As I did so, Mr. Turner stepped through the door, his countenance partially obscured by the tremendous bouquet he held.

Grinning, I stood proudly before the offerings—a smile born more from a heist well-executed than the joy of bestowing gifts.

At last, I had addressed my responsibilities, and there would be nothing to interfere with my care of Henri and my scientific pursuits. The published study that would result from such an enterprise would doubtless afford me significant fame and fortune, ensuring that Betsy would readily forgive any necessary deception that preceded it.

Soon Betsy was descending the stairs. Her hair was freshly coiffed, and her blue silk skirt was crisp, as she danced into the room.

"Oh, my darling Edward! Oh, my word!" Betsy exclaimed, as she rushed to me, throwing her arms about me, and smothering my cheeks in kisses. "I do so hate when you are gone, but I console myself with the thought that I will soon be graced with your return and that of your wonderful gifts from exotic lands. I do so cherish them." Betsy pranced up to the covered screen and tugged on the sheet until the screen was revealed.

"Oh, Edward, Edward!" she gasped, hands flying about her face in exaltation. "It is simply exquisite."

"For your dressing room, my love. A little old man carved this by hand over the course of the past two years," I said with greatest earnestness. Betsy nodded solemnly.

"I don't know what to say…words cannot express…oh, darling." Again, her arms wrapped around my neck. "How I love you so!"

"My dear," I said, removing her hands from around my neck and turning my lips from her kisses, "hadn't we better have tea now? I'm ready for a bite, and then I must return to my study."

"Yes, let's." Betsy returned to the screen, running her fingers over the carved vine. "The likeness is simply extraordinary. You must tell me the names of the birds, Edward."

"Later, darling. Best inquire as to when supper will be ready—if you can tear yourself away from your screen long enough, that is." I winked at her. Betsy feigned a strike at me before she laughed and carried off down the hall.

CHAPTER THIRTEEN

My empty stomach rumbled, coaxing me to give up further reading in favor of a late lunch. The stew required my attention, and I needed to finish cleaning the house. A stuffed *thylacine*? That now-extinct creature would have been infinitely more valuable than the two-headed rat and deformed kitten that now stared down at me from my fireplace mantel. Neither the *thylacine*, nor the carved screen were recorded in the ledger. Perhaps Walker did not make note of items he kept as personal possessions.

Rummaging through the fridge, I pulled out the fixings for a sandwich. I still had an hour before the kids would arrive—time for some last-minute tidying up and trap checks. The trap behind the couch contained a live captive. I disposed of it in my usual manner, hid any traps that might be visible to my guests, and returned the bottle of chloroform to the medicine cabinet in the bathroom. The turds scattered alongside the baseboards and across the pantry floor suggested a veritable horde of mice breeding within the walls. I hoped to God they stayed there while Clara was in the house.

I selected a bottle of French Bordeaux from my wine collection and, as I was warming a baguette, Clara, her husband Stan, and little Thomas arrived, rosy and chilled from the cold. Clara greeted me with a kiss to the cheek, balancing a pie plate in her hands.

"Mince pie," she announced with a grin, "made fresh this afternoon."

"Darling, you're amazing." I squeezed her shoulder affectionately.

"Not really—I had the pie shell in my freezer." Clara smiled as I took the pie from her.

Stan removed Tommy's boots and wet socks and placed them on

the heat register as Clara peeled Tommy's coat from his trailing arm.

"How are you, Dad?" Stan asked, clamping one hand on my shoulder, the other pumping my hand up and down.

"Hunky dory," I replied, smiling. Stan was a fine match for Clara, and I generally approved of the man. He clearly loved Clara and Tommy and made a decent living working for the BBC. What more could a father wish for?

"Grandpa!"

I knelt down as Thomas leapt enthusiastically into my arms. He smelled like sugar and winter air. I tickled him under the chin and poked his soft belly, and Thomas rewarded me with childish laughter as he twisted in my arms.

"I'm going to get you back, Grandpa!" he squealed gleefully.

Glancing up, I caught Clara smiling as she said, "That's probably enough for now, before you get him too riled up to sit for dinner."

I released Thomas and he raced to the lounge to raid the toy box. I removed the stew from the oven as Clara got to work setting the table. It was a cold night; the frozen rain had started again, drumming noisily on the walkway and rapping on the window panes.

"Perfect night for a stew," Stan said.

"Yes, quite." I uncorked the Bordeaux and poured three glasses, handing one to Stan and one to Clara as she returned to the kitchen. "Happy Christmas."

Retrieving Tommy from the lounge where he had been playing with his cars, I secured him into his booster seat as Clara ladled out the stew.

After we had taken the edge off our hunger, Clara said evenly, "So, Dad, tell us about your work. I mean let's not kid each other, you are working on something while you are supposed to be resting, aren't you?"

I raised my eyebrow but understanding that she had no intention of letting me escape, I confessed, "Well, yes, there is something…"

"Tell us about it," Stan said encouragingly.

"All right, then. It's fascinating, really—I have acquired a nineteenth-century journal, and a number of crates, that belonged to a seeker of curiosities who traveled the world searching for oddities to buy and sell—"

"But aren't you are supposed to be taking a break from this kind of stuff, Dad?" Clara leaned across the table, looking me squarely in the eye. "So, you're not taking a leave of absence, are you?"

"I haven't decided yet. And it's not work, exactly, it's just a little side project, for myself," I mumbled defensively.

"Dad, what about your health? The stress is clearly getting to you. Look at him, Stan. You can see he's looking quite frazzled and pale, right?"

"Clara, please," Stan protested. "Let's just enjoy dinner, shall we?"

"Well, I can see it," Clara insisted. "You are not looking one bit better since I saw you the other day. You need to take care of yourself and sometimes that means putting work on hold."

"Oh, for heavens' sake, Clara, I'm only reading a bloody journal. What would you have me do? Lie comatose on the couch and stare blankly at the ceiling?" I took a hearty swig of my wine, trying to quell my irritation at Clara's attempts to run my life.

"So, what's the journal about?" Stan asked into the silence.

"Well, it is more of a registry, really, a ledger that the curiosity dealer used to track curiosities that he bought and sold."

"Curiosities? What kind of curiosities?" Stan asked, filling his wine glass.

"Not items I would want to describe over dinner." I nodded at Tommy, who was chasing a carrot piece around in his bowl.

"Sounds intriguing," Stan remarked.

Having speared his carrot and lost further interest in his food,

Tommy began to fidget in his booster seat. Clara undid the strap and helped him to the floor. He was off like a shot toward the lounge where his cars waited.

"Now can you tell us what was in the crates, Dad?" Clara asked.

"They are what I would describe as oddities."

"Oddities? How so?"

"For the Victorian gentleman, they were thought of as scientific specimens; most people today, however, would find them quite grotesque."

"Specimens of what?" Stan asked.

"Humans."

Clara grimaced.

"Well, fetuses, really, and a few stillbirths."

"Ugh, really?" Clara shivered.

"And you have these here, in your home?" Stan asked.

"A few."

"Fascinating. What would a fellow want with these sorts of things?"

"Buying and selling curiosities in the Victorian era was a lucrative business. The Victorians, in general, had a fascination with the strange and macabre. Human bodies, in particular, were in high demand. Medical students dissected corpses to further their understanding of anatomy. Medical museums began to crop up all over London, which were intended to showcase the human body and demonstrate the consequences of neglecting one's health. In the 1850s a Dr. Khan founded The Anatomical and Pathological Museum, the most popular of the anatomical museums, but it became a front for selling quack cures for venereal disease. As a result, The Obscene Publications Act came into existence; legislation which denounced all public displays of anatomical specimens as potentially obscene.

"Afterwards, the trade went underground and dealers sold goods on the black market to medical schools, sideshows, and private collectors of the peculiar. It's possible that much of the collection I have in my possession originally came from a medical museum but—"

The sound of shattering glass came from the hallway, followed by high-pitched, frantic crying.

"Thomas!" Clara exclaimed, running from the room. Stan and I scrambled after her, the pungent odor of formaldehyde emanating from my study. I knew immediately what had broken.

We converged in the room, staring in shock at the wailing child on the floor amidst broken glass, blood, and a pool of amber liquid. In the middle of the wreckage was the little two-headed fetus, rubbery and exposed after 125 years in the jar.

"Jesus!" Clara seized Thomas and plopped him on my desk, frantically checking his bloodied feet for glass shards.

"Goddammit, Thomas! What were you doing mucking about in my study? You *know* you are not allowed in here." I could not help my fury. The jar had been destroyed and who knew what damage had been done to the fetus—after I had been so careful to protect it.

Thomas choked between sobs, "I'm s-sorry, Grandpa… I wa-wanted to see the little doll, but it's so scary. I-I dropped it."

"Well, you ought not to have touched it. Do you see what you've done? Do you understand now why Grandpa has always told you not to touch his things?"

"Dad, that's enough. Can't you see he's traumatized? What's got into you?" Clara snapped, glaring at me.

"He's old enough to know the rules."

"He's a *child*, Dad. You're the adult. You shouldn't have left that horrible thing out, knowing we were coming over. Don't you usually have this place under lock and key?"

"Usually, yes, but I was distracted with all the cooking and cleaning.

It's your responsibility as a parent to—"

"Take it away, Grandpa, please. I don't want to see it anymore," Tommy sobbed, hiding his face in Clara's blouse. I retrieved a vodka bottle, a Mason jar and a soft dishtowel from the kitchen. Grabbing a cereal box, I pulled the bag of cereal from it and collapsed the cardboard flat. Returning to the study, I spun off the bottle lid and filled the jar with vodka. Using the towel to edge the fetus onto the cardboard, I slid the fetus into the jar and sealed the lid.

"Let's get him to the bathroom, Clara, where the light's good," Stan suggested. Clara scooped up Tommy and the three of them headed down the hall.

I placed the jar up high on my bookshelf where it would be safe from small hands and followed them into the bathroom.

Clara held the boy and comforted him while she shot me smoldering looks over the boy's head. With a pair of tweezers, I pulled two small pieces of glass from his feet, cleaned the wounds and covered them with Band-Aids.

"Look, I'm sorry. I overreacted," I admitted.

"Yes, quite," Stan said, hugging Tommy to his side.

"And this is exactly why you need to take that leave of absence. Yelling at a poor child who is clearly in distress is not a sign of a well man," Clara said sharply. "I am going to sit with him awhile." She carried Tommy into the lounge where they both sat in the rocking chair.

I returned to my study to clean up; the smell of formaldehyde was overwhelming. A few minutes later, Clara poked her head into the room with Thomas limp in her arms.

"Tommy's asleep. I think it's time we left. I've got a headache building."

"I'm terribly sorry, darling, but please don't go, we haven't opened the presents yet."

"I'm sorry, Dad, but he's out like a light, and it seems cruel to wake him after what he's been through. He can open them at home tomorrow. We'll just leave yours here and you can do the same."

"Won't you take some pie home? We didn't even get to sample any."

"That's quite all right, Dad, my figure can do without it. You have it."

As Clara and Tommy made their way to the front door, I picked up the stack of presents, and handed them to Stan.

"Goodbye, Dad," said Stan. "Sorry the evening had to end on a bad note." He shrugged in an apologetic way.

Shame burned in my cheeks and I bent to plant a kiss on the sleeping boy's head. I kissed Clara on the cheek. "I'm really sorry, darling. I shouldn't have—"

"I know, Dad. Please, just get some rest, okay?" she said, with a frown of concern.

"I will. I promise."

Clara managed a tight smile and then turned to follow Stan out to the car. I stood on the step waving until the car backed out of the driveway and disappeared down the street. As I turned and stepped back into the warmth of my house, I realized that I had forgotten to give Diane's clock to Clara.

Chapter Fourteen

Tuesday evening, July 25, 1865

Quite some time had passed before Mrs. Butterfield announced it was time to come to table. We dined in lavish fashion on quail and roasted summer vegetables, and for dessert, a delicious blueberry pie with whipped cream. Betsy continued to chirp about the ornate screen and I was only half-interested in her praise. My thoughts naturally lingered upon Henri. I was eager to get back to my study and assess his condition, to see if the second course of bloodletting and calomel had aided in his recovery. I also had to compile my notes in preparation for the scientific report that I intended to submit to the Committee of Recommendations, which, if approved, would provide me with a grant to continue in my scientific research of the *zonbi* phenomenon. The next meeting of the British Association for the Advancement of Science was in September. I had only two short months in which to make some great discovery. Nevertheless, what could I do? The excitement of the household over Betsy's present kept me engaged so that I could find no excuse to steal away to my study.

My wife had become enraptured with me anew. I had become her little pet again, and she cooed and fussed over me incessantly, treating me more as a favored child than the family head. While it was difficult, at times, to cloak my irritation, I knew that as my presence once again became commonplace we would settle back into routine. Betsy would submerge herself in her feminine duties of childrearing and paying social visits, and I would have uninterrupted opportunity to further my own scientific inquiries.

Finally, duty fulfilled, I was able to detach myself and returned to my study and to my comatose ward. In the dim hallway, I fished the key from within my waistcoat pocket and rotated it in the stiff lock. A soft glow now shone through the high basement window, which did little to illuminate the room. The foul stench seemed to have magnified overnight and I crossed to the window to wrench it open a little further. Returning to lock the door behind me, I faced a most disturbing and inexplicable situation.

Should this journal be read by another, I wish to affirm most stringently that I do not exaggerate for the purpose of telling an expertly crafted tale, nor do I purport to be a rival of any contemporary novelist that can be so named. What I relate herein are a sequence of events to which I bear honest witness, without duplicity or embellishment, in my own home and in the presence of God. My hand, even now, is trembling as I write this.

I immediately looked to Henri's last place of repose, fully expecting to find him lying as he had always been, seemingly incapable of movement on the makeshift bed I had arranged on the floor. Now, only rumpled blankets met my bewildered gaze.

"Impossible," I muttered to myself.

A frantic search of my study yielded no clues to his whereabouts. I spun around, too overwrought to consider even lighting a lamp to aid in my search—as foolish as that now seems, when I put it in writing.

It was then that I felt something brush against my leg and my eye caught a shape bounding past in the dim recesses of the room. The body hit the bookcase with a thud, sending a bottle crashing to the floor. Henri, concealed by shadows, emitted a piercing animalistic scream.

With a trembling hand. I seized a lantern, lit it, and held it aloft in the direction of the child. The lamplight cupped one side of his body, illuminating a bent knee and bony thigh, a taut arm, and—

Oh, the horror!—his dreadful eyes! My heart jolted and seized inside my chest, and I cursed in fright, almost dropping the lantern in my backward stumble.

Strengthening my resolve, I raised the lantern again, slowly. The light shone across the boy's shoulder and burnished his lower jaw. His black eyes glinted like onyx, and a chill rippled through my innermost core and my blood cooled in my veins. Those eyes—which throughout my journey had remained fixed, divested of vision—now flickered in their sockets.

The boy was awake.

His former comatose state had at last given way and he was now able bodied, aware, and conscious. Had I successfully managed to expunge the poison from his system, and set his molecules again into motion? What other capacities had he regained? Was he able to comprehend words? Could he speak?

The boy's eyes fixated on me, as though Henri's penetrating gaze was surveying the depths of my very soul, thought by treacherous thought, deed by terrible misdeed—my sins and sorrows alive for him to view.

I stood frozen in the room, amid the books, the clutter, and the curios and yet all seemed to have fallen away and there was nothing, nothing but this enigmatic child and me.

"Henri..." I began, but at the sound of my voice, the child clambered over the table, overturning the chair, and causing me to drop the lantern, which smashed on the floor and, in a fury of flames, ignited Henri's bedding.

The shock slowed my reaction so that my study was filled with smoke—which burned my eyes and raked my lungs—before I had stamped out the flames. Searching through the gloomy haze, I made out Henri's crouched shape, cleaving to the door—thankfully locked. No telling the calamity that would have ensued had the frenzied boy slipped upstairs. Henri pawed at the door handle and, when it would not yield, began to tear at the door with his nails, frantic to make his escape. I recalled with sudden panic that the window behind me was half open.

I sidled toward the window. Under my slippered feet, the sharp edges of glass crunched disconcertedly loud in the quiet room. With my gaze fixed on the boy, I held a hand aloft and felt for the window lever. Henri watched me with an intense stare but moved not. In the thin filtered light, I could discern the rapid rise and fall of Henri's small chest, fueling his now stronger, deeper breaths.

My own breath was short and shallow as my heart skipped in my chest. Where was that lever? As I groped along the edge of the wooden pane, a sliver stabbed at my fingertip. Raising my hand, I felt the cool glass—too high! Lowering my hand slightly, I hit upon the curved brass handle, gripped it, slammed the window closed with a bang, and slid the lock home.

Henri's gaunt body jerked.

I heaved a sigh of relief, content that he could not escape now.

I stood for several moments trying to harness the runaway horse that was my frantic heart. Henri never ceased glowering at me, and I felt pinned, like a butterfly in a specimen case, under his black stare. I was painfully aware of the prolonged lapse of time and knew I had to make a move. Taking a tentative step to the left, I reasoned that a circuitous route—around the room and advancing from the side— would calm the boy more than a direct approach. Moving furtively, I eased myself along the windowed wall. Just as I was within reach of the corner, my foot sank into something soft and pliable, and I heard a distinctive snap—the very sound one hears when one breaks the neck of a bird just wounded on the hunt.

My stomach twisted and, stepping back, I looked to the floor where a dim shape lay shadowed in darkness. Of a sudden, the metallic odor of blood was strong in my nostrils. Of Henri—his visage was yet turned to me, tracing my path to the desk, ever watching as I seized another lantern and struggled to light it. This time he did not recoil from the light. Lowering the lantern, I studied the object that lay upon my study floor.

In life it had possessed chocolate brown fur, now blood-soaked and glistening with wet entrails that oozed from the gash in the animal's flank. The angular snout, the masked face—it was a polecat. I choked back the vomit that rose to my throat. The animal had been eviscerated. Something metal glinted by my foot. It was the scarificator, blades extended and saturated with gore.

With one vigilant eye ever cast in Henri's direction, I seized the letter opener from my desk and inserted the blade into the gash in the polecat's hide, using it as a lever to get a better look at the animal's innards. Henri had apparently—in a frenzy of strength, the like of which I could not imagine—used the scarificator blades to rip through the weasel's hide and musculature both.

The intestines and internal organs were torn in a ragged fashion, the innards strewn about, yet missing from the mess of tangled viscera was the heart of the beast.

Harnessing my fear, I approached Henri cautiously, my lantern raised high and the letter opener held before me—a desperate weapon should he, perchance, decide to leap. He did not, but watched me with wide black eyes, breath racing, and fingers gripping the door.

When I drew near enough to see, I halted in horror. Dripping from his protruding jaw and on to his shirt, soaking through to the skeletal chest beneath, was the wet crimson of fresh blood. The boy had finally feasted.

The vomit could no longer be contained, and I doubled over and heaved up the contents of my stomach into the burnt and ruined bedding on the floor. Acid burned my throat and nasal passages as my expelling continued unabated until I had purged myself utterly, contributing to the general stench and ruination of my study.

After which, I rose unsteadily to my feet—I needed to somehow regain control of the situation. Caution was critical; the boy had just felled a rather vicious weasel and devoured its heart. I recalled the actions of an Amazonian caiman, springing to sudden life when a peccary ventured too close, snapping it in two with powerful jaws. Had this hapless polecat pawed his way in through the window only to be assailed by Henri in like manner?

I wanted to cry out as something unwound within me. *What was this madness?* I shook my head in an attempt to clear my mind of panic. While I was not undone by strange rituals, by mutations of nature and foreign cultural practices, I had never come across a child such as this.

With what, on God's earth, am I dealing?

The bloody shambles needed to be cleaned up, but I faced the pressing issue of what to do with this wild boy. I had not expected such a violent reaction upon his awakening and I had not had the time to prepare. It was best for me to sedate him; subduing him would limit the danger to me, as well as himself, until such a time as I could discover the cause of his vexation.

Given my successful recent movement along the wall, I felt that I could move to my cabinet without causing him undue agitation. Setting the lantern down upon the desk, I rummaged around until my fingers closed over a bottle of ether. Given that its vapors were highly flammable, I reluctantly extinguished the lantern, plunging the room into shadow. Tipping the bottle liberally on to a spare linen strip, I turned my head so as to avoid breathing the fumes. The evening light receded as the sun sank to the horizon, but enough light remained for me to complete my task.

Groping through the gloom, I drew nearer to the dark shadow that pressed itself against the closed study door. My steps were deliberate, imperceptible. I dared not even whisper his name for fear that he would again bolt like a cornered horse. His slow breathing whispered like a draft under the door, the sound of which led me to him, until the feel of it on my outstretched hand declared I was within reach. I lunged, with the intent of knocking him off his haunches. Henri screamed—a shrill, primal noise that pierced the silence. I shoved the cloth against his open mouth while locking fingers around his narrow forearm to hold him immobile. He thrashed in my grasp, but I held him fast. Henri's mouth strained against the cloth, gulping ether into his lungs. Soon—although it seemed to me an eternity— his thrashing grew weak, uncoordinated, and he collapsed in my arms.

CHAPTER FIFTEEN

"What?" I blurted aloud. It was a little after nine a.m., and I had woken early and fetched the journal to read in bed. I had started to doze again when Walker's words had jolted me like an electric shock.

I could scarcely believe what I had been reading—the child snapping out of his coma and eviscerating a polecat! Certainly, the journal must be a gaff, after all—a literary sideshow attraction. The Victorians' fascination with gothic literature only fueled their interest in the macabre, including artifacts such as those that remained of Walker's collection. Perhaps this journal played some part in Walker's business, like the narrative of the watchstrap braided from the hair of a murderer, a story Walker himself delighted in telling. It seemed likely that Walker had fictionalized this account of Henri to encourage a sense of the mystique, furthering sales and providing fictional fodder to his "scientific" inquiry.

Recalling the gold velvet-lined bloodletting kit, I leapt from my bed, raced down the stairs to my study, and flicked on the desk lamp. The filament popped and went dead. *Damn.* Stealing a bulb from one of the lounge lamps, I returned to my study and replaced the burnt-out bulb; the room filled with light. I rifled through the crate until I found what I was looking for.

Nestled within the heavy wooden box, the scarificator glinted in its velvet bed, somewhat sinister in the lamp glow—a device of torture. Seizing my magnifying glass from my bookshelf, I lifted the scarificator from its box. Tiny screws dotted each side, presumably so the device could be dismantled for cleaning and blade changing. From my desk drawer, I retrieved a small screwdriver from a jewelry kit. With some difficulty, I managed to loosen the screws and lift the plate away from the blades to better examine the inner workings of the instrument. I searched for any remnants of blood that might have seeped down the cracks between the blades but detected nothing. Walker had either been scrupulous in his cleaning of the contraption, or he had lied about its usage.

There was nothing by which I might validate at least part of Walker's story. No blood to run a DNA test—not that the detection of blood would really prove anything. Walker could have killed the animal himself for some devious purpose, perhaps for the benefit of securing his grant for a scientific study? But in the absence of other proof, I might learn whether a polecat's blood remained on the instrument. I could trust none of Walker's account without some sort of measurable proof. For now, I planned to continue reading the journal—it was entertaining, at least!—and see what else could be gleaned.

Assuming, for a moment, that Walker's account was true—I could not help but consider such a fantastical notion, so dreary had my own life become!—that the combination of calomel and bloodletting had revived the boy, the process itself would have introduced a dangerous level of mercury into the boy's system. Surely the mercury combined with the bloodletting would have been enough to kill the child. And the weasel's heart? Oh, it was an entertaining tale, indeed. But, gaff or not, Edward Walker's journal was undoubtedly a rare historical document that I was ecstatic to have found.

I went upstairs, intending to shower but the phone rang. Picking up the receiver, it took me a moment to recognize the voice—Joe.

"Dunny, happy Christmas to you, brother." His speech had a roll to it, something he'd picked up from his years of living in Scotland.

"Happy Christmas," I said in return, noticing the dismal, insincere tone in my own voice. A moment of silence followed. We never did quite know what to say to one another. Our lives were so different. Joe had never been settled, never been responsible—he had spent his adult years littering the countryside with broken love affairs and broken bar stools.

"How's bonny old Scotland?" A safe topic of conversation.

"Used and abused. I've been back in England since sodding July, Dunny boy. Where you been?"

"I've been here, the usual, working—" I looked at the journal, allowing my thumb to brush across its pages.

"I've been making loads of money, got a wife now, a baby on the way. She's got me, she has; I'm giving up my wild ways. Never thought I would, but Brandi has my heart, and now that I'm going to be a dad…well, she made an honest man out of me." I heard a female voice in the background, and then laughter.

"Congratulations," I said, politely but without feeling. I'd heard this story before, of course, with former girlfriends. The fact that he'd finally married one seemed doubly tragic.

"So, what'd ya get me for Christmas, Dunny?"

"Christmas?" I stammered. We hadn't spent Christmas together since Mum died eight years ago; there didn't seem any point. Phone calls on Christmas were sporadic. I hadn't been anticipating his call and whenever I had tried to call him, I inevitably got a "this number is not in service" recording.

Jeering laughter tumbled through the receiver. "I'm just taking the piss, Dunny. I know you got me bugger all. Just wanted to let you know I was alive, in case you got to wondering." The unsaid portion floated between us like a ghost: *not that you would be wondering.*

"Thanks for telling me. I'll have to send a teddy bear for the new baby." I tried to smile, but my voice sounded flat and tired.

"You still living in Dunmow?"

"I am."

"Great, I'll swing by one of these days." Joe laughed again. "Gotta go now, mate. Say hello to the missus." And he hung up.

I felt empty. This was the brother I'd known all my life, but yet didn't know at all. We had shared the same beginnings, but I knew as much about his life as he did about mine. There was an underlying understanding that we shared a mutual disinterest in each other's lives. Yet, something bound us—some sort of duty, or perhaps an unbreakable familial cord that strung us loosely together. I wondered what life would have been like if we'd been close, like Diane and her sisters, who shopped together, had dinner and drinks together, and looked after each other's kids. No, I wouldn't have looked after any kids, I scoffed to myself. I hadn't looked after my own. I was alone on Christmas morning, quite by my own doing.

I *was* alone on Christmas morning, but that meant I had all day to read Walker's journal. Picking up the journal, I settled back against the headboard, and had just started to read when a movement caught my eye—a brown mouse was scuttling across the floor! I leapt from my bed, yelling a string of profanities, and tried to trap the mouse in the corner, but it bounced past me, squeezed behind the dresser, and disappeared through a new hole in the wall next to an empty trap.

"You hateful little beast!" I hollered, batting the trap across the room.

Sod it. My life was just about disappointments and failings, about being alone and unworthy. *Fuck these mice.* If I could set the damned house on fire, I would. Maybe Clara was right—I should give up all this nonsense and go to counselling. Call the exterminator and be done with it. What was I trying to prove anyway? And where had it got me? Alone on Christmas. Crikey, I needed to stop saying that. I was getting on my own nerves.

Flopping down on my bed, I stared at the ceiling trying to quell my growing despondency, the overwhelming sense that my life lacked direction. I felt like a right dolt for yelling at poor Tommy last night. I must have looked like a bloody lunatic. I'd be surprised if Clara and

Stan ever brought the boy round again. *Duncan, you are a stupid fool.*

With a sigh, I forced myself to get up, to make the rounds of the mouse traps. Two discovered in the pantry trap, I killed in the chloroform jar and dumped in the bin.

Rummaging in the kitchen for breakfast, I found nothing appealing, and settled for coffee and a hard-boiled egg. The day was dark—the sky the color of drawing charcoal—and I felt a heavy weight settle upon my shoulders. The coffee did little to revive me, and shuffling restlessly into the lounge I saw the present from Clara and Stan on the coffee table. My little Christmas tree sat unlit in the corner, its trinkets and ornaments hanging limply among the dark, drooping branches. I had forgotten to water it and the trunk leaned like a decrepit beggar. Plugging in the lights did little to improve its appearance.

My Christmas gift was a grey hand-knitted sweater made by Clara, or so the tag said. My throat tightened as I ran my hand over its soft wool, and tears welled up in my eyes. As I lifted the sweater out of the box, a book fell into my lap. *Meditate Your Way out of Depression.* Clara. Always the practical one, the only one who seemed to believe in me—to care whether I succeeded in this damned life. Yet, I just constantly pushed the limits.

I lay back on the couch, pulling the sweater up over me, and resting the book on my chest. I watched the lights of the Christmas tree blur under the watery screen of my tears.

It was half-past seven when I woke again. Good Lord, how was it possible that I had slept that long? My body felt terrible—heavy and stiff. Rubbing the crust from my eyes, I pushed my arms through the sleeves of the sweater. The fit was good. At last, I felt semi-normal. I was certain to be up all night now. I sighed. It would be the journal and me, depression be damned.

Chapter Sixteen

Once Henri had succumbed to the ether, I placed his limp body in the desk chair and looked around for some means to secure him. In light of the boy's newfound strength, I required a rope, strong and thick—and would find just such a one in the stables. I had little notion of how much time I might have at my disposal, not being in the habit of sedating humans, let alone *zonbi* children of uncertain temperament.

Stealing out through the back kitchen door, I cut across the grounds to the rear west wall. The horses whinnied, startled at the squeal of metal on metal, as I threw back the dead bolt and slipped inside the stable. No sign of anyone; the groom, I was certain, had retired hours earlier. A thick loop of rope hung on a hook beside the bridles. Shouldering the rope, I retraced my steps back to the house.

The linen cupboard afforded additional cloths and a quilt, and with arms loaded down, I stumbled to my study, locking the door again behind me. The stench was almost unbearable—a pungent mixture of animal carcass and vomit, the bitter smell of smoke and the sweet reek of ether, and the ever-present stench of Henri himself. The boy slumped in the chair was a dim silhouette in the shadowy room. I dared not light the lantern with flammable vapors about. Feeling for my hunting knife, I cut two long pieces of rope, and fastened Henri's wrists to the chair; another, I wrapped around his waist and knotted through the back of the chair. The boy's deep breathing was the only sound in the quiet room.

I wedged the window wide open in an effort to rid the room of the noxious effluvium. Then, behind me, I heard the moans of Henri regaining consciousness. How quickly the effects of the ether had worn off! The choices were before me—administer more ether to keep Henri quiet while I worked to clean the study or allow him to recover himself and endure whatever outburst he might unleash. Subduing the boy would result in additional flammable vapors within the room, which would prevent me from igniting a lantern, and as it was impossible to tidy the room in the dark, I opted to let the boy recover.

When the vapors had dispersed, I lit a lamp and passed it over the boy. Henri's eyes flickered open, his limbs twitched, and his mouth twisted and unleashed a high-pitched, hysterical bout of laughter. Shuddering with horror, I turned from this unnatural child to address the study.

The desecrated polecat made a dreadful mess on the floor. I wrapped the gruesome carcass in the burned bedding, along with the shards of glass—slicing my finger in the process. The strips of cloth, I used to sop up the blood splattered about my study but it was evident that a bucket of soapy water would be required to adequately clean the floor.

Again, I stole furtively upstairs, filled a bucket at the sink's pump, and returned downstairs to my study, striving to prevent water from slopping on Betsy's polished parquet floors. My arm ached from the weight of the bucket, as my body, exhausted from recent physical demands, groaned against the strain.

Stooping before Henri, I wet a cloth and wiped the polecat gore from his mouth, chest, and hands. Though still lethargic from the ether, Henri jerked his head away from my ministrations. Baring his teeth, he emitted a low groan, which caused me to pull back in fear, imagining how Henri had torn the heart from the body cavity of the slaughtered weasel.

With a grunt of effort, I hoisted the burnt blanket with its gruesome contents up over my shoulder and shoved it out the basement window into the garden. Easing the window down, I slid the lock back in place.

I wiped the blades of the scarificator with a clean cloth and sterilized them in spirits as I had done before. Placing the instrument back in its case, I locked it in the cabinet—safe from Henri. Thereafter, I set to the task of washing the floor and squeezing out the bloody cloth until the water turned ruddy in the lantern light. I discovered the fetish doll Emmanuel had given me knocked to the corner and spattered with blood; I wiped it clean and set it high on my bookshelf. Utterly exhausted, I held a lamp aloft, scrutinizing the stone floor for any further signs of the evening's furor. All appeared, finally, in order. By my pocket watch, it was shortly after eleven o'clock in the evening, and as much as I yearned for bed, I needed to bury the carcass.

Taking the rags and bucket of bloody water, I crept upstairs, groping through the gloom to find my way out the kitchen door to the back garden and the basement window. Dumping the water under a bush, I threw the rags on top of the gory bundle and dragged it to the tool shed. Within, I found a shovel, and began to dig a hole to the rear of the structure, hidden from view of the house.

The moon was but a sliver and the garden tomb-dark. I felt my way through the task, kneeling in the dark and periodically thrusting my hand in the hole to test its depth. When the hole was approximately two feet deep, I leaned the shovel up against the side of the shed, and retrieved the bundle containing the dead polecat. The pungent richness of raw earth mingled with the night air as I filled the hole, burying the barbarity. I stomped on the grave and levelled out my footprints with the blade, hoping the grave would not rouse the suspicions of the groom come morning. Making my way back to the basement, I returned the bucket to the kitchen before conducting a final check on Henri.

Entering my study, I discovered that Henri had regained all his newly found strength and vigor. His eyes, wild with demonic animation, locked on mine. The intensity of his stare disarmed me and a rush of emotions—fear, guilt, vulnerability—overwhelmed me and, for a moment, I closed my eyes. When I opened them, the boy was tugging and jerking his wrists, struggling violently to free himself from his bonds.

I could scarcely believe that this was the same boy I had brought across the Atlantic in the hold of a ship. That boy had been too weak, too mentally vacant, to move or cry out. Now, he was as robust as any other healthy twelve-year-old child. Henri's eyes were beseeching as they darted from me to the bonds around his wrists.

"I can't release you, my dear boy," I said, shaking my head. "It's for your safety, as well as my own."

Henri moaned, low like a cat's growl, and thrashed in the chair, raising his feet off the floor and stomping them down. He set the chair a-rocking until he had gathered sufficient momentum to lift himself up off the floor. I watched, horrified, as Henri began to walk the chair toward me. Seizing the back of the chair, I forced it down again, and, with my other hand, grasped the rope from my desk and lunged at his left leg. Henri jerked it from me. I managed, however, to get a grip on his ankle, and held it to the chair leg with one hand while I tied the rope around it with the other. The boy kicked out at me with his free leg, but I caught that foot too and secured it in the same manner as the first.

Henri growled again; a noise which escalated by growing degrees into a full-throated roar, eyes thrashing in their sockets. Anxious to quell his clamor before it roused the household, I hastily tied my handkerchief over his mouth. Henri's muffled grunts ceased as he struggled to suck air through his nose, yet he kept up his flailing fit. The child was fierce with rage. The poisoning effects of the *bokor* that had kept him comatose were assuredly abating, setting his molecules into motion again but I could not properly evaluate whether this erratic behavior was a temporary side effect of the sudden withdrawal or something more insidious. Emmanuel's description of Henri before the poisoning had been of a boy given to laziness, obstinacy, and theft. Were these tendencies indicative of a temporary phase of childhood or a natural propensity for wickedness?

I do not know how to proceed, at present, but am determined to maintain a record of my observations to present to the British Association for the Advancement of Science. And although weary from lack of sleep and the evening's vexation, I now take to my desk to put pen to paper.

The boy is frantic, angry, and possesses an unexpected strength. His writhing continues unabated into the night; he stomps and thrashes against his bindings; his voice a muffled protest beneath the gag. I am near ready to collapse from fatigue but dare not leave the child alone until he exhausts himself. It is clear to me that something has electrified his life force into activity again, but, ignorant of the cause, I must let these influences diminish before the effects of any one substance can be made apparent.

Henceforth, I shall use the ether only when strictly necessary. These recent events prompt the question as to what manner of delinquent I have bound in my study. What would have possessed the boy to attack and feast on a live animal? Such behavior is not only beyond the realm of normal behavior, it is deeply disturbing. It is my theory that past attempts to feed Henri with milk and bacon failed because the boy craves only one thing—live organs. In the name of science, I shall have to prove or disprove my theory. But how?

This child is more than I bargained for, but, for the benefit and advancement of science, I must proceed apace. The scientific community needs to know of this boy, of this *zonbi* medicine and its effects, and who else but I can be such a messenger of discovery? If there is some financial gain to myself thereby, it will not be unearned. And if there is any humanity left in the child, does it not fall to me to make some attempt to save him from himself? I shall now leave off writing to try anew to calm him.

I approached the child, speaking in low and soothing tones. Henri paid me not the slightest attention—he was making such a racket rocking the chair and growling through the gag that I did not think he could hear me above the clamor and I dared not shout. My basement study was walled in stone—far below the second-story bedrooms, and the window was firmly shut, yet I worried that the sounds of Henri's distress might reach the upper floors. Using ether to subdue him would again fill the small space with flammable vapors, requiring me to extinguish the lantern. It would be impossible to record my observations in the dark, so it seemed that I had little choice but to see the boy through whatever demons his convalescence would present.

Oh, how I fought to resist the weariness of a body begging for sleep, my eyelids weighted as with iron over gritty, tired eyes, my body aching and my mind slow with rebelliousness. Henri's incessant clamor was unnerving, and I braced myself for a knock on the door from Betsy, demanding to know the origins of this dreadful noise.

From my desk drawer I took out a piece of drawing paper and a pencil and sketched the boy, capturing the wild panic in his eyes, and the pull of his mouth as it stretched around the gag. I traced the chair around him and the bonds, which held fast against his frantic onslaughts. I labeled the drawing *Specimen Zonbi*, for in my agitated state I could view him no other way—so unearthly was his manner that he seemed an aberration, a formidable and most peculiar curiosity.

Another hour passed before Henri's frantic movements began to subside and another fifteen minutes before they ceased altogether and the boy's head, at last, slumped forward.

I have remained to ensure that he does not re-awaken, but now I feel that I can finally creep to bed, and let this horrible night drain from conscious thought.

Wednesday, July 26, 1865

I roused with difficulty from a heavy slumber—so weary was I still—to the happy gurgles of baby Charles, cooing from across the room. The sun streamed in the window, illuminating the yellow wallpaper and making the room glow like the center of the sun. Betsy was settled into the rocking chair by the window with her back to me, nursing the child.

Rising from the bed, I could see, between the fluttering lace curtains, the back garden, where late last night I had buried the polecat behind the shed.

Reaching into the wardrobe for fresh clothing, I explained to Betsy that I would require another full day in my study. She protested, just as I had anticipated, lamenting that we had not spent any time together since my return from the West Indies.

"Now, darling, you know that isn't true," I gently reprimanded her.

"But we haven't been *out*. There are endless luncheons and soirées to which we have been invited and we have not been to any in simply forever. People are starting to talk about us. They think we must be ill, or worse—"

"Certainly they are aware of my travels, my dear," I interrupted irritably. "Travels—must I again remind you?—in pursuit of the trade that pays our bills." I had such little time to record my observations of Henri and formulate my theories in advance of the committee meeting!

"Yes, Edward, but they are impatient. More than a few of our acquaintances have seen your carriage around town and know that you have been back for several days. They are expecting to see us out now and it appears that we are being rude. There is propriety to think about and the consequences of our inattention to our social responsibilities."

There was a pout in her voice.

"I simply cannot. I'm sorry." Leaning down, I kissed Betsy's cheek and left the room.

"Edward!" Betsy protested behind me, stretching out the *a* in my name, in a waspish, demanding fashion. I proceeded down the stairs to my study, pausing in the kitchen for bacon and a croissant.

Turning the key in the lock, I pushed on the door, only to find that it would not budge—something was apparently blocking it from the inside. Shoving myself bodily against the door, it gave way a little. I gave the door another hard push, effectively sliding the object across the floor. Forcing my way into the room, I realized that the obstruction was Henri, seemingly sleeping, head lolling over his chest, his thin ribcage moving rhythmically with shallow breaths. My eyes fell to the scrape marks on the stone where inch by inch, the boy had worked the chair across the floor. Deeper scratch marks had been gouged into the back of the door, where Henri had fought to free himself. The boy's fingernails were bloody and broken, and his mouth—where the ether had made contact with his skin—was dotted with red eruptions.

Sinking to my chair, I thought again about what I was to do with the boy. Henri's eyes fluttered open and I observed that the consciousness, that had been present before in such angry flailing and shrieking vocalizations, seemed weaker now, his expression cloudy.

Henri exhibits a continued disinterest in the bacon, and I have arrived at the inevitable conclusion that live organs are the only foodstuff that will rouse him from his somnolent state.

CHAPTER SEVENTEEN

It was a thrill to have discovered the circumstances in which Edward Walker had drawn the pencil portrait of the boy that even now sat on my desk. I felt increasingly connected to Walker, connected in a way I had not felt before. What an extraordinary situation—perhaps a little *too* extraordinary. After all, some crafty opportunist hoping to dupe the scientific community out of a sizeable grant could have fabricated the drawing. But perhaps, as with many dubious an account, there existed a kernel of truth. My task, as a scholar, was to separate truth from fiction.

Heart-eating *zonbis* aside, if I had been a Victorian man who had witnessed Henri's awakening from his trance-like state, I, too, would have concluded that the child had come straight from the devil; but, as a twentieth-century scholar, I knew there had to be a scientific explanation for the boy's erratic behavior. Was this bizarre fetish for live organs a byproduct of tetrodotoxin withdrawal? With the regional variances in zombie potions, it was impossible to know the exact nature of the substance that had caused Henri's symptoms. A *bokor* frequently used, or so I understood, an antidote of some description to restore his victim. Perhaps this antidote served to prevent the very reaction that Henri had experienced. Searching my bookcases, I located the black spine of Davis's *Passage of Darkness*.

Pouring myself a glass of scotch, I perused Davis's book, seeking information on the withdrawal effects of *bokor* poisoning. Little immediately revealed itself. I assumed the existence of a *zonbi* boy and had no way of knowing whether he had actually existed without some kind of proof. What of the scratch marks on the back of Walker's study door? Would they still exist after more than a century?

Was Walker's house still standing? In the journal, Edward Walker had written that his house was located on Berkins Road but had not provided a house number. Ruth Walker might know—but what reason could I give for asking for the original address of the estate without arousing her suspicion? Leafing through the ledger, I found what I was looking for. In neat script on the front page, Walker had recorded his address as 21 Berkins Road.

Jogging to my car, I consulted the road map I retrieved from the glove box. The unit block of Berkins Road was located on the south side of London, in Brockley. There was a fair chance that the house was still standing—Berkins Road and the surrounding area had been the residence of choice for the Victorian elite and many of their large estates still remained; some, however, had been converted into flats, and others, I recalled—with sinking dismay—had been destroyed in World War II during The Blitz. And if Walker's door had been damaged, it was likely to have been swapped out or repaired sometime over the last one hundred years. It was a long shot, but I had little else to go on, and little else with which to occupy my time.

I jotted down the address on the map page and checked my watch. It was just after ten p.m.—my excursion would have to wait until morning. Returning to my study, I picked up *Passage of Darkness* and poured another glass of scotch.

I woke on Boxing Day with a grinding headache, and groaned when I discovered the empty scotch bottle on my dresser. My mouth felt fuzzy, my body heavy, and my brain slow. What time had I fallen asleep—three, maybe four a.m.? I brewed a cup of tea, ate some unbuttered toast and scrambled eggs, then grabbed my coat and boots out of the hall cupboard and was once again behind the wheel—driving myself into who knew what!

I hadn't even had time to think about what I was going to say to whoever opened the door at Walker's old address. I ran my tongue across my teeth; they felt thick and fuzzy from the sugary tea. Peering into the rear-view mirror, I observed that my bushy eyebrows were grossly unkempt, as was my tangle of grey hair. A haircut had been scheduled for the previous week, but it had slipped my mind. I balanced the steering wheel between my knees and used my shirttail to scrub my teeth. I wet a finger and smoothed down each eyebrow, then fingered my hair into some semblance of neatness as I drove through the crowded London streets.

I needed to work on my script; what was I to say if someone opened the door?—that I was an anthropologist who needed to investigate their basement? For scratches in a door? They would think I had escaped from a loony bin! Perhaps I could say that I had reason to believe there was forensic evidence in their basement. No, that would require a special crew to come and carefully extract it, and besides, I didn't really want to identify myself. Could I say I was the gas man? Or the furnace inspector? I had no tag identifying myself and was hardly dressed for the part. Still, maybe I could get away with it. People were gullible, weren't they?

Perhaps if one is convincing enough, authoritative enough, one can override a person's good sense. I had to try it. I pressed down on the accelerator, and the Volvo lurched ahead as I weaved in and out of the slow-moving traffic, leaving trucks and elderly drivers far behind. On the next straightaway, I rechecked my route and took note of where I was to turn. I needed to take the roundabout and, in two kilometers, turn on to Shooter's Hill Road. Weaving my way through the city streets, I narrowly avoided colliding with a double-decker bus. *Bloody tourists.* I passed through the eclectic mix of century-old houses and newer apartment buildings in Lewisham, before finally turning on to Berkins Road.

Slowing the car to a crawl, I began an intensive search for house numbers. The street was quaint, with most windows lit up with Christmas lights. The properties, predominately brick Victorians, were enclosed by wrought-iron gates, ivy-covered retaining walls, and neatly trimmed hedges. I passed a house that was almost completely engulfed with overgrown shrubbery, its number obscured. I kept inching forward, my head swiveling from one side of the street to the other, locating numbers twenty, nineteen, eighteen, then seventeen. The numbers were getting smaller, indicating that the house obscured by the shrubs must be the one I was looking for. I maneuvered the steering wheel sharply to the left and steered the Volvo into an empty parking spot.

Assessing the property, I could see the high roof looming behind an unruly hedge. An iron gate emerged from the shrubbery, forming a barrier to the pathway leading beyond into the darkness. Decaying wet leaves littered the ground. My first thought was that the place was abandoned and that emboldened me to approach the house, feeling that I might not be required to come up with a story explaining my presence. The gate swung out at my push and I edged through.

The massive Victorian manor was in a state of neglect. The sorrel brick façade was dirty and crumbling in places, and the scaffolding, which rose on one side of the house, looked weathered and rusty in the winter mist. If no one had cared for the outside of the place, then perhaps no one had cared to repair whatever scratches remained in that basement study door.

Clearing my throat, I climbed the stairs and rapped hard on the front door. Nothing. Cigarette butts littered the ground, and a pair of work boots had been flung to the stoop. I knocked again, louder, and waited. After a minute, I descended the stairs and looked up at the façade. Two big windows overlooked the front garden, heavy curtains obscuring whatever lay within. It was impossible to tell if there was a light on inside. I wasn't sure if anyone lived here or if the

Victorian was a renovation project momentarily devoid of residents.

I began to walk toward the side of the building, trying to place the journal's description of the house with the one I saw before me. The decrepit house in modern London seemed a far cry from the proud and happy home described in Walker's journal.

Just then, the door opened and a young woman peered out. "Hello? May I help you?" she asked, eyeing me suspiciously.

"Oh, hello!" I trotted up the stairs toward her.

"What do you want?" she asked softly.

"Oh, well, I'm um… I'm…"

The woman had caught me off guard, just as I had come to the conclusion the house was empty. I promptly forgot everything I had rehearsed in the car. "I'm an inspector," I said hurriedly.

"The permit inspector? Oh, I wasn't expecting you till next week. You work holidays?"

"Oh, yes, we do, actually. This *is* 21 Berkins Road, ma'am?"

"Yes, you have the correct address…but I'm really confused because they said they couldn't send anyone over here until next week. Which permit office did you say you were with? Perhaps I have them mixed up."

"Oh, um… well…"

Over her shoulder I saw movement inside the house, and a tall, burly man in his thirties approached the door. Standing next to her with a hand on her shoulder, he addressed me: "Can I help you?"

"No, I don't think so. I think I'm mistaken," I stammered again, stepping back down a few steps.

"Mistaken about what, exactly?"

"He said he was an inspector, but we aren't expecting anyone till next week. I asked him which department he was from, but he wouldn't tell me," the woman stated.

"Right," I said, backing away further. "Sorry to have bothered you, I just remembered I *am* supposed to come here next week—which means I'm late for where I really have to be, which is across town. See you next week, then!"

Turning on my heel, I sped down the path, hoping the man would not pursue me, demanding to see my ID. I yanked open my car door and climbed inside. Damn my amateurism! I wished I were as proficient a liar as Walker had been.

Pulling away from the curb, I threaded back into the flow of traffic. The rain had started again, and the wind blew strong, making the Christmas lights over shop windows clatter against the facing. I did not want to go home, and drove in circles around the neighborhood, thinking about the scratches in the door. I simply had to find a way in.

Finally, unable to muster any kind of coherent plan, I headed for home. Once there, I jotted down a few ideas in a notebook. If I tried to return the following week, posing as the house inspector, I'd be sure to be caught if the real inspector showed up first, not to mention the suspicion I had already aroused in the homeowners by refusing to state which agency I was with. I could call the city office and cancel the inspector, but then I would have to actually step into the role of house inspector, stay there for hours and give them a full report. I didn't know the first thing about inspecting houses. I could never pull it off. It was likely that they had already called the authorities and reported me as a suspicious person. In which case, I should not show up at their door again.

I wracked my brain trying to think of another solution. I needed to see that basement room, and there was really only one viable option—*break in.* How else would I discover if those marks existed? Thieves broke into residences all the time without detection. I was better at stealth than I was at lying; I just needed a plan. Under the words *break in,* which I had scrawled in my notebook, I listed the following: *black clothes including wool hat, small torch, break-in tools.*

I felt as though I was playing a part in some two-bit clichéd detective movie, but if that was what it would take, then that is what I would do. I figured that two or three days would be enough to put the odd inspector visit out of the couple's mind—I did not want them making a connection between that and the subsequent burglary of their home. But what if they decided to replace the basement door in the interval—if it hadn't been done already? Would they be halting the renovations in order to wait for the inspector's approval, or would they be working overtime to get things ready for his arrival? In order to be sure, I would have to break in tonight.

I rented a car from my local Enterprise office, not wanting my Volvo to be recognized as the inspector's vehicle, should the homeowners have seen it. I chose a dark-colored hatchback—one that I thought would be difficult to spot in the dark—and returned home in the rental car just after sunset.

I thought I would practice by breaking into my own house. Trudging through the rear garden to the ground floor window, I worked my tools, trying to jimmy the lock through the narrow opening. It was difficult work and I returned several times with different tools until I discovered a pick/flat-head screwdriver combination that worked. I picked the window lock several times until I became adept at it. Once I had shaved my time down to five minutes, I felt confident enough to quit.

I would need to be able to creep down the streets unnoticed—to go through residential gardens without hesitation, even jump fences if need be. But how would my back hold up under such acrobatics? Logistics notwithstanding, I was increasingly excited at the prospect of such high adventure; I felt like a teenager again, sneaking into a London nightclub underage.

Wearing black beneath my winter navy blue coat, I pocketed the burglary tools, grabbed my penlight and hopped in the rental car.

Exhilaration gripped me as I started down the road. The wind drove hard, and the streets of London were dark; low clouds had moved in, blotting out the half-moon. I parked the car several streets away from the Victorian manor, planning to cut through the back gardens and approach the house from the rear to eliminate the risk of being spotted on the streets.

I waited for the brilliant headlights of a car to pass and then bolted for the foliage, allowing the trees' shadows to enfold me. Breathing heavily with excitement and exertion, I waited for my eyes to adjust to the dark windy night, heavy with dampness. Then I began my descent through the twist of connecting gardens, stealing across veiled lawns, climbing through shrubbery, and stumbling over tree roots. A dog barked in the distance and some small creature darted away through the scrub, startled at the invasion of his garden home. Mud and wet leaves squelched underfoot. Fences rose up in my path, sometimes low, slatted, and easy to scale, sometimes tall stone walls that were almost impossible to climb. The long drop to the ground jolted my ankles and reverberated through my lower back.

Gulping for air, chest heaving and hands trembling, I leaned against a tree in order to get a sense of my bearings. To my right, I spotted the high roof of the former Walker estate and the telltale metal scaffolding that ran the width of the house. Crouching heavily in the overgrowth, I mapped my path to the rear basement window— one that I assumed to be Edward Walker's former study. Under the drooping canopy of low-lying trees, I stole towards the silent house. The azalea bush that Walker had described in the journal was now an unruly hedge, partially blocking the window. Reaching through its twisted branches, I felt along the contours of the window in the dark where my fingers encountered a damp wooden surface. *Shit!* I hadn't anticipated that anyone would board up the window.

I forced myself further into the bush, breaking a few branches as I squirmed my way closer to the window. A quick investigation with my penlight revealed a weathered and rotten board anchored by rusty nails.

A gap existed between the board and the windowpane and I eased my screwdriver between the two and pulled back on the handle. The board readily gave way, pulling free with a sharp squeal. I froze, my heart thumping in my chest, my breath quick shallow darts that I had to fight to control. Had anyone heard? I paused for some moments, building trust in the silence, before continuing with trembling hands.

Wrestling the board up over the bush, I dropped it behind me, exposing the dirty window. Turning on my penlight again, I directed a beam of light over the windowsill where woodlice scurried and ducked into crevices. In an attempt to pry open the window, I jammed the end of the screwdriver between the sill and the glass pane.

Banging against the frame with the heel of my hand, I pressed down on the handle of the screwdriver, trying to provide the leverage I needed to raise the window. It vibrated in the casement but did not budge—perhaps it was nailed shut from the inside. I tried again, harder. A sudden noise sounded within the house: a single *woof*, loud and low. *Bugger!* They had a dog. Where had it been yesterday when I came to the door? Out at the groomers?

Light flooded the lawn behind me, streaming down from an upper floor window. The barking from within the house started up again, growing in intensity until a muffled stream of expletives silenced the dog. Pulse racing, I pressed myself into the tangled branches of the bush. From my immediate vantage point, I could not see inside the window of the bedroom, but I imagined that the householder would be searching the garden for the disturbance that had set off his dog. The light flicked off again. Should I wait and hope he went back to sleep, or should I take off running now, before he came out and set the dog after me? The dog would seize me in seconds—my only chance was to make a break for it now. I tried to step over the board, but I clipped the edge of it, slipped and fell to the ground, scraping the palms of my hands on the mud and debris. The dog, with his supersonic hearing, went mad again.

I picked myself up and ran for the rear garden, adrenaline surging in my veins. I launched myself over the low fence that was half buried in the bushes lining the property and left the cacophony of shrill barking behind. My back screamed, but I did not lessen my pace until I had arrived at my car, heart boxing the walls of my chest. Sucking wind, frantic that I couldn't get enough air into my lungs, the panic rose up in my chest and made my head swim. I ducked behind the wheel, focused on taking measured breaths, trying to quell the rising panic attack.

Letting my head rest against the steering wheel, I shuddered in the shadows as the adrenaline began to drain out of my veins and the coldness set in. I shoved my hands in my coat pockets, trying to stop the trembling. In my rear-view mirror, flashing lights rapidly approached and I slunk down further in my seat. The police car rushed past me, sirens switched off for stealth. Straightening up, I jammed the keys in the ignition, started the engine, and hit the accelerator. Wrenching the steering wheel to a hard left, I zoomed off in the opposite direction.

It wasn't until I was several streets away that I noticed the throbbing pain in my hands, and the growing chill that penetrated my clothes. The car reeked of earth, mud, and foliage. The rental agency was not going to be impressed when I returned the car the next morning.

Outside my window, the blur of city lights gave way to the growing darkness of the countryside. Into a blackness cut by two small headlights, I wound my way home.

I drove for three-quarters of an hour, nerves jangling, the clock blinking two a.m. on the dashboard. It was the first time I had noticed the time since leaving my house. What the bloody hell was I doing?

I was mad to break into Walker's house in an attempt to find scratch marks from a century ago. I had very nearly been caught, too.

So why didn't I give up—concede to academic failure and go down for the count? I paused a minute in thought, before the answer came to me, flashing across my heart in a single pulse—the pursuit of Henri gave a passionate imperative to my life, such that I had not felt since childhood, digging in the field, knowing I'd find my father's watch if I just dug deep enough, fought hard enough, and searched in the right places. And—*sod it!*—I was going to do the same with Henri. I wouldn't stop until I had proven his existence. And if I discovered that he was a complete fabrication, then that would be that. I'd walk away from my farce of a career and give Clara the attentive father she had always wanted and deserved. But, in the meantime, I had to find out the truth of what happened to Henri in that basement, and the journal, I felt sure, held the key.

Chapter Eighteen

Henri is fading back into his former state—the very condition in which I first discovered him in the Haitian village. His eyes have dulled, glazed over, and sunk back in his head. The boy requires sustenance and I have been made to understand that it is not the food of the civilized that sustains him—he feasts on the living.

It is necessary that I keep Henri in an animated state so that I may continue in my scientific study of the boy. There is so much yet to comprehend in regard to the physical, intellectual, and emotional characteristics of this boy; I must conduct careful, controlled testing to measure the scope of his capabilities—to say nothing of a more complicated inquiry into his taste for live organs. It seemed clear that consuming the polecat's heart had re-engaged Henri's energies, activating his molecules, and now, deprived of that sustenance, his molecules are returning to a compact state. Perhaps any cure is only temporary, or perhaps I haven't gone far enough to cure the boy.

It is necessary that Henri remain animated so that I may continue to study his responses, and therefore I must discover a way to furnish him with small prey. Where might I find a constant supply of such needful things? It would be too difficult and time consuming for me to trap his food myself. I must find a supplier. London is full of rats, but they are such filthy creatures, populating outhouses and rubbish heaps, carrying fleas, and capable of delivering a punishing bite, and I will not risk infesting my household, should any escape.

Aviculture, I understand, has become a popular pastime with many enthusiasts keeping parrots, finches, and lovebirds. I will ask James to procure several breeding pairs of parakeets and cages for me. The birds' existence must be concealed from Betsy for had she knowledge of them, she would insist on being involved in their breeding, and then how would I explain their sudden disappearance? While birds are indubitably noisy creatures, the brick walls are impenetrable to sound, and the adjacent windowless room will serve as the perfect place to house them. Now, I have only to sneak the birds into the house, while Betsy ventures out on some outing or another.

I shall leave off now, and pen a note to James, requesting that he procure birdcages, pertinent literature on parakeet breeding, as well as several male and female parakeets from the nearest emporium in readiness for my arrival later this afternoon.

Wednesday, July 26, 1865

After delivering the note to Mr. Turner, I returned to my study—with a quick glance to Henri to ensure he showed no signs of waking—opened a small trunk, and pulled out a book, a fine example of anthropodermic bibliopegy, the art of covering a book in tanned human skin.

The pages within contained the illicit poetry of Mrs. Abigail Emerson, revealing the intimate nature of her affair with Jack Murdock. Abigail's husband, Richard Emerson, discovered the poetry and murdered Murdock in a jealous rage. A trial ensued in which the poems were admitted as evidence in the case, remaining in the courthouse after Richard Emerson's execution. Gerald Monette, the surgeon who conducted a public dissection of Emerson's corpse in London in 1824, had a section of the skin tanned. He acquired the poetry and had it bound with the skin of her husband as a gift for the doubly grieving Mrs. Emerson. Unfortunately, it seemed the book was too much for her to bear and she did away with herself shortly after receiving it. I had acquired it at her estate sale.

I wrapped it carefully in brown paper. James would be delighted, and the proceeds would keep me in birds and cages for quite some time.

I bent over Henri, slumped in the chair, and assessed his condition. His pulse labored at thirty-five beats per minute; it had returned to the feeble cadence of Henri's pre-waking state.

I unfastened the boy's bonds and laid him on the floor, swaddled in a blanket. I determined, too, that I would obtain a proper mattress upon which he could sleep.

After ensuring the window was secured, I left the room, locking the door behind me. If by chance Henri did wake again, he would be quite captive within this room.

While at luncheon with Betsy, I took the opportunity to declare that she looked ghastly pale.

"Do I?" she asked with concern.

"Yes, quite! You need some color, my dear, quite desperately. You simply must get out today."

"Oh, do come with me, then," she insisted, grabbing at my sleeve. "Let us take a lovely carriage ride down by the pond. It has been so long, Edward. I do so love it there."

"Alas, my darling, I simply cannot today." I proceeded to explain that I was utterly swamped with work.

"Oh, Edward! I shall refuse to go without you," Betsy pouted.

"Come now, you shan't argue with me. I insist you take care of yourself. The nurse is quite capable of caring for the baby, and you mustn't ruin your health for the sake of my schedule. I won't allow it."

"All right, Edward, if you think it best," Betsy agreed, with an air of resignation. Rising from the table, I kissed her cheek and give her hand a squeeze. "Good girl. I'll call for the carriage to be ready for you within the half hour."

Soon thereafter, Betsy appeared at the bottom of the staircase, looking the prize in her walking-out dress of striped taffeta with a fitted jacket, her silky hair parted in the middle, her curls flowing from underneath her bonnet.

"Take a good long trip now won't you, darling?" I smiled. "I want you to come back all rosy-cheeked and ruby-lipped."

"Yes, I shall. I will make an afternoon of it."

I helped her into the carriage, stepped away, and she was off.

Shortly after Betsy's departure, the groom readied the second carriage for me and I drove myself into the city.

As I neared The Curiosity Shoppe, the reckless nature of my undertaking began to worry me anew. What kind of child would eat live animals? It was utter madness and I was advancing the lunacy by providing him with such gruesome sustenance.

Yet, what choice did I have if I desired to truly understand Henri and his dark compulsion? If I failed to provide Henri with live organs, I would be unable to continue with my studies, and would have nothing to present to the world but the unfortunate circumstance of a poisoned child. I would quite likely suffer overwhelming rebuke for not seeking conventional medical care for the boy, perhaps for even considering such a controversial endeavor. I had, after all, promised Emmanuel that I would make every attempt to save his brother.

I had to put aside fears that might constrain me, and successfully complete my studies—for the sake of science, for the sake of my own promises to the boy's family, and, indeed, for my own advancement, a devotion to which I owed my own growing family. I must pour all my energies into this experiment and see it through irrespective of the distasteful way in which Henri's life is to be so sustained.

At last arriving at The Curiosity Shoppe, I entered and met James at the counter.

"Edward," he said, shaking my hand. "Wonderful to see you again. Here are your birds, just arrived moments ago from the Pantheon Bazaar."

Three iron birdcages sat upon the counter; one contained ten jade-colored parakeets that leapt, in lively fashion, from perch to bars and back again; the second was empty, and the third contained two more parakeets.

Indicating the third cage, James said, "This is an established breeding pair which should settle in quickly. When you get them home, you must provide them with a small breeding box. The bird with the blue band over its nose is male, the other, with the pink band, is female. The rest of the birds have not paired yet, so you will have to watch for signs. When you see a pair start to favor each other, you must remove them into the third cage. They will never breed amongst the others—they need isolation. This guide will provide you more information."

"Splendid," I said. "And feed?"

"Certainly." James produced a brown paper bag.

I presented James with the skin-bound book of poetry and explained its history. We thus settled our accounts and James helped me load the goods into my carriage. Our transaction completed, I departed with haste for home, stopping briefly at a clothing shop to purchase a few child-sized blue-and-white striped shirts and a pair of trousers.

Upon arriving home, I saw that Betsy's carriage had not returned, so availed myself of the opportunity to rapidly transfer the birdcages into the basement storeroom—making room amid Christmas decorations and cast-off furniture, among which I discovered a small mattress that would be ideal for Henri.

With the aid of a stepladder, I screwed hooks into the ceiling joist, and lifted the cages one by one, slipping their iron loops through the hooks. The excited chirps of the parakeets filled the small room as they bounced and fluttered, causing their cages to sway.

Would I be able to breed the birds at a rate adequate to keep up with Henri's demands? The boy had devoured a polecat the previous night and was already passing from vitality into his former comatose state. The aviculture instruction manual revealed that the incubation period lasted twenty days, with an additional twenty-eight to thirty-five days until the chicks fledged. At five to eight eggs per brood, I calculate that I will need several breeding pairs as well as a constant supply of feeder birds to establish a bustling system. More cages will be required. What a lot of bother. Rats would have been more practical—but I cannot abide the filthy creatures, so this seems my unrivaled option.

I moved two males and two females into the third cage, in the hopes they would sort themselves into breeding pairs. The other cage—containing the remaining six birds—I will use as feeders for Henri. Finding a small discarded saltbox among the storage items, I filled it with straw, then placed the saltbox in the cage for a breeding box. I have my start, but I need more cages for subsequent pairs in order to create an efficient breeding system to keep Henri well satiated. But until I can establish such a system, I will have to ration his meals.

After bringing the mattress into my study, I redressed the comatose Henri in the clean clothes, hoping this would aid in mitigating the stench that emits from him. I took a strip of linen and tied it around his neck for a bib, then laid him on the mattress and tucked his blanket around him, all the while trying to avoid his chilling gaze which fixed straight ahead.

Returning to the bird room, I succeeded in capturing two male birds and placed them within a jewelry casket. I would give Henri the first bird and assess his response before providing the second. I returned to my study, with the birds flapping and chirping inside the box. Sliding a hand beneath the casket lid, I grasped the darting body of a bird, and pulled it from the box, slamming the lid shut. Kneeling on the edge of the mattress, I brought the quivering bird up to Henri's face, passing it under his nose. In the dim light, Henri's muscles begin to twitch like those of a cat poised to leap. He was awakening out of his trance-like state.

The boy inhaled deeply of the air—something I had never before seen him do—then Henri sprang upon my hands and snatched the bird from me. What I witnessed next was something that shocked me beyond measure, turning my stomach and dampening my forehead in a sudden sweat. The boy, his bony fists wrapped tightly around the small bird, twisted its head until its tiny vertebrae snapped. Then he closed his grip around the bird until it burst apart. Raising the mess to his mouth, and with the most abhorrent slurping sounds, he gorged himself on the dead thing. When he had completed his feast, he tossed the drained carcass to the floor, before looking about, hungry for more.

It was a few moments before I could regain my composure. Henri's eyes had now flicked open, regaining the consciousness that only moments before had been veiled behind that ghastly fixed stare. He was regarding the casket in my hand, and, for a moment, I feared he would lunge at it. Reaching within the box, I suffered a hard peck on my thumb and jerked my hand away in startled surprise. In an instant, the bird had flown from the box, and whirled, fluttering and squawking, about the room. Henri pounced, and flew over my desk to bat at the bird, knocking it from mid-flight. Before I could again catch my breath, he had shoved the bird's body between his jaws, tore its head asunder with a single bite, and spat it out onto the floor. I watched in tremulous horror as he sucked the blood from the bird's throat, as one would suck the water from a coconut. Henri's eyes darted from the now empty casket to my face, the body of the hapless bird dangling in one bony fist.

"No more," I said in Creole, shaking my head.

Henri's eyes narrowed at me and I wondered if he comprehended my words. I took a step toward him. "Do you understand me?"

The boy brought the carcass to his mouth once more and drained the last drops of blood and entrails before dropping it carelessly to the floor. Bringing a hand to his mouth, Henri licked his fingers one by one, lapping every particle of blood that remained. He raised his eyes to me, watching for my next move.

"You enjoyed the birds, did you?"

Henri glanced at the empty casket and uttered a discontented grunt.

I retrieved the box and held it up for him to see. "There will be no more today. But if you are a good boy, I shall bring you more tomorrow."

The boy emitted a low growl, and slapped the box from my hand, sending it tumbling to the floor.

"No, Henri!"

The boy never blinked but only narrowed his eyes at me again. "You must wait until later. Later. Do you understand me? *Es'ke ou konpran sa mwen di'w?*" The boy turned away, and I felt sure he had understood, but was clearly displeased that no more birds would be forthcoming.

This feeding had succeeded without measurable disorder. The boy appeared calmer, more lucid, than when I had discovered him yesterday after killing the polecat. I believe the *bokor*'s poisons are dissipating as a result of my bloodletting and calomel treatments.

I placated the boy with soothing, comforting tones. I would do well to gain his trust and respect; after all, he had only just returned from unconsciousness and has been incontestably fearful and distrustful.

This dependency on live food presents a new complexity to the *zonbi* phenomenon, and one I could have not anticipated. It will require me to run various tests and observe the outcomes in order to understand the intricacies that prompt such behavior. Is this penchant for live food a temporary state, from which I can transition him to a diet of properly prepared cooked food? Undoubtedly, careful study and experimentation will tell in due course.

I sat by Henri's side for several hours, continuing in my consolatory intonations. He was like a nervous cat ready to flee at the least provocation, but I gave him no cause to, and he appeared to become more accustomed to my presence. Dare I conclude that Henri is beginning to view me as a trusted parental figure, or am I merely a temporary provider to whom he is largely indifferent? He never removes his gaze from me—the way it bores into my soul is unsettling—and monitors my every move, as though *he* were studying *me* for some scientific purpose known only to himself.

I spent the remainder of the afternoon educating Henri on his condition, explaining—in a haphazard mixture of English and Creole—that he was my ward now, and that it was my duty to take care of him. He should view me as his father, I informed him, and he must try hard to be good and I would see after his needs. If he misbehaved, he would only harm himself and I did not want that to happen. Henri appeared to listen to all that I said, but, given his impassive demeanor, I had no understanding as to how my words truly affected him. I felt, however, that I was making great strides in establishing a trusted connection with this beleaguered child— he showed no inclination to fits or terrors, and I saw little need to restrain him. Neither did Henri demonstrate any intention to flee as I approached, seating myself by his side.

It became evident that Henri's linens required changing. The consumption of the polecat heart and the parakeet entrails had revived his digestive system. Despite the advances made this afternoon, I felt that Henri would still shy away from my touch. True enough, as I slowly reached for him, he drew back, emitting a low warning growl. I advanced slowly but the boy leapt away from me, screaming.

"Easy there. I'm not trying to hurt you," I whispered. Nevertheless, the boy was wary of me, and if I persisted, I feared it would break what little trust I had thus far established.

The only recourse, I now conclude, is to cease feeding him, allowing him to fall back into a state of lethargy. It will not take long; perhaps by tomorrow afternoon he will be sufficiently complacent to allow me to change his linens.

By this time, the day was growing late and my thoughts began to turn to my family above stairs. After inspecting the window and locking the door behind me, I left Henri and proceeded upstairs to dinner. I felt myself to be in good humor, having made significant progress that would ensure the successful conclusion of my study before the committee of the British Association for Scientific Advancement convened. So satisfied was I in my efforts that I fairly skipped into the company of my adoring wife and handsome child.

Chapter Nineteen

Walker's account of Henri's regression into a comatose state when deprived of live food was puzzling. I had been lounging in bed for the previous hour, alternating between reading the journal and *Passage of Darkness*, but had not discovered any reference to this strange phenomenon in zombie folklore. Considering that Henri's taste for live food might be suggestive of some kind of feral child, I leafed through my Victorian reference books to find any mention of feral children. I found reference to a twelve-year-old boy named Victor who had been found living in the woods in eighteenth-century France. The local commissioner, Constans-Saint-Esteve, observed that there was "something extraordinary in his behavior, which makes him seem close to the state of wild animals." There was puzzling mention of an "unusual diet," but no specific example. Certainly, it seemed possible that a feral child might resort to eating small animals for survival; indeed, I knew of incidents where adults stranded and desperate to survive had resorted to cannibalism. Could Henri's desire for flesh stem from some similar circumstances? Walker's notes, however, contained no suggestion of a feral child. Before Walker had brought him to London, Henri had been living in a hut with his family. Perhaps, too, there was a medical explanation for the boy's recurring relapse into a trance-like state. My brain twisted around the subject, trying to make sense of it, to gain some kind of foothold on the truth, but there were too many questions, all cumulating in the fact that nothing could be solved without tangible proof.

It was now past eleven and I was not the least bit hungry. I had returned exhausted from my botched burglary at three in the morning, climbed into bed and had promptly fallen asleep. It suddenly occurred to me, however, that I had to return the rental car by noon. Pulling on clean clothes, I headed outside and drove the rental car back to the agency.

Within my own car again, my thoughts continued to churn on Walker and the boy as I navigated through the Great Dunmow streets toward home. Pursuing the door scratches was a dead end—whether they existed or not, I was unable to determine. I *was* determined, however, to find out if the boy had lived, or if his basement incarceration was a fictional story Walker had invented to promote his business. What avenues of proof could I possibly pursue 125 years later? Nothing immediately came to mind.

As I passed the library on White Street, it occurred to me that there might be some kind of public record that would shed light on the situation. A census report might reveal if Walker had claimed the child as a dependent or a servant. If Henri had died in Walker's care, the parish records might still contain his death certificate. The National Archives were the logical place to start, although they would probably be closed for the holiday season. I bit at the jagged end of my thumbnail as my gut began to churn.

Bloody hell. The first week of my holiday had come and gone, and I had not rested or taken it easy, as had been suggested. I grinned—I'd become embroiled in the story of Henri, the *zonbi* child. Not exactly what the university had recommended. But unraveling this puzzle felt good! In one week I had gone from a washed-up old codger facing the demise of his academic career, to a man with something interesting to pursue, something to remind him that his fascination in things long buried had not left him. The university had been wrong. The key to my revival was not in resting, but in relentlessly pursuing the journal until I discovered the truth about Henri. As unlikely as the storyline was—a *zonbi* child eating live animals seemed the

142

stuff of gothic fiction—I fervently hoped that some aspect of the journal would be of academic significance. I did not want to dwell on the probability that Henri was entirely a fabrication of Walker's devious scheming; this eventuality—if determined with certainty—would likely send me spiraling back into despondency, with all hopes of returning to work refreshed and renewed lost. Regardless, I had to find the truth; I had to know what really happened in that dark basement 125 years ago.

Without warning, I swerved the Volvo into the turning lane on Stortford Road, cutting off the driver behind me and earning me a prolonged honk, but I didn't care—I had to get to The National Archives in London, immediately.

As luck would have it, I found The National Archives open. Hunching over the viewer, my neck tensed and knotted, I scrolled through the microfiche containing the 1871 census until I found the district of Lewisham, and the address I was looking for. Penned in century-old handwriting were the names of Betsy Pamela Walker, Charles Bernard Walker, and a record of the various names of the servants who had lived on the estate, but no record of Henri. The census report showed Betsy to be a widow, proving that Edward Walker had died prior to 1871. Walker's journals had suggested the *zonbi* boy was twelve or so in 1865, which would make him eighteen at the time of the census. Perhaps he had since returned to Haiti, or maybe he had died.

Rising from my seat, I returned the microfiche to the shelf, and approached the woman at the help desk.

"Excuse me, can you tell me where I should look to research a death?"

"Oh, you'd want to have a look at a register of deaths," the middle-aged desk clerk told me, peering over unattractive glasses.

I nodded.

"We don't keep them here. You would have to go to the registrar's office in the township of the person or persons you are looking for. Do you know where that might be?"

"Yes, Lewisham."

"Okay, let me look up the address for you." Thumbing through a nearby directory, she jotted down the address on a piece of paper: *Laurence House, 1 Catford Road.*

"Yes, I can find that." Thanking her, I left.

An hour later, I arrived at Laurence House. The gentleman in the admissions office was a young lad in his late twenties. He had a dull look about him, as though just waiting for something to do or something to happen.

"How can I help you, sir?" he asked, brightening.

"Yes, I was sent over by The National Archives. They said you have death records here?

"We do. What year are you looking for?"

"I'm not sure exactly, but after 1865. Well, anytime in the sixty years after 1865, I would say."

"Well, there will be quite a number of records to go through for that timeframe. Infant mortality, you know…one moment." He left me standing at the desk while he ambled off toward the rear of the building. Moments later he returned with a copy register and handed it to me.

"If we have the death record that you are looking for, it would be recorded in here. It goes by year so just start at the beginning of— what did you say? 1860?"

"1865," I corrected.

"Right. Return the book to me when you're done, and if you want a copy of any death certificates just let me know the registration number and I can fetch those for you. There will be a small fee."

"Brilliant. Thank you." I took a seat at a nearby table.

I began my search of each death entry starting in 1865. Edward's death record showed up almost immediately. He had died on October 16, 1865, only three months after bringing the Haitian boy home with him. The cause of death was marked *dyscrasy,* a term that sounded familiar to me, but I couldn't recall what it meant. Perhaps this was the tropical disease Ruth spoke of?

I browsed through the census dates, leafing through 1866, 1867, and on. The penmanship varied over the years, sometimes cramped and difficult to decipher and, on other occasions, a neat and legible script. My eyes scanned for either the first name of Henri or the last name of Walker, as I was unsure how it might have been recorded.

Flipping through subsequent pages, I made my way into the 1940s and 1950s, still finding nothing. It seemed unlikely that Henri had lived to the age of 100, so I returned to 1865 and checked the names again. Going more slowly, I compared the birth and death dates. Many of the recorded dead were infants and young children. Sprinkled among the entries were women who had died in childbirth, and men who had died in their forties or fifties as a result of accidents at work or bouts of pneumonia or tuberculosis. I paid particular attention to entries for boys of Henri's age, reasoning that Henri's name may have been altered for the death certificate, but to no avail.

There was, it seemed, no record of his residence with the Walkers in 1871, and no record of his death. I was not yet ready to give up, to conclude what was starting to seem obvious—that the boy had, in fact, never existed at all. There had to be another way to go about this, I pondered. What had transpired in the three months that Walker had the boy in his care? It was possible that Henri had recovered from his ailment, and Walker, finding nothing of scientific interest, had sent him home to Haiti. The other possibility was that after Walker's death, the boy had been discovered and turned over to an orphanage or a workhouse or turned out on the street by a vengeful Betsy. Perhaps he had been sent to an asylum. The Victorians had a generous definition of insanity, which resulted in crowded institutions where patients were treated like animals— starved, neglected, mistreated, and drugged. Had this been Henri's fate?

Passing over the dates in the 1900s, I came across a death I hadn't noticed before—Betsy's. She had died in 1915 at the age of seventy. Skipping forward through the years to 1930, I discovered the entry for Charles' death. It struck me that one's lifetime could be summed up in a single line in a book full of deaths; that I, too, would one day be just a name and a date, forgotten amidst a sea of countless entries. My life, my strivings, my concerns, would dwindle into nothingness, meaninglessness—faded words on a musty page.

I made note of the registration numbers, took the book up to the desk, and requested a copy of the death certificates. Producing my wallet, I paid the fee. After several minutes, the clerk brought me the death certificates of Edward, Betsy, and Charles.

"Can you tell where these people were buried?" I asked the young man.

"Yes, I have that information here as well. Let's have a look. Ah, okay...they are over in the Brockley Cemetery, just north of here at the corner of Brockley and Ivy Road."

I thanked him and left. Even though I couldn't find a death record for Henri, I was keen to visit the family burial plot. Perhaps something would come to me—some unexpected morsel of information.

I was growing weary by the time I arrived at Brockley Cemetery, but my excitement at finding Edward Walker's grave, the burial place of the very man whose intimate confidences I had been privy to, gave me the needed energy.

The woman in the cemetery office was bent over a book when I arrived, and a curtain of black locks hung about her face. She wore a nametag, which read, *Katie*. Wide blue eyes expanded like saucers when she looked up at me. She was a stunning woman, in her early thirties.

"Oh, hello. May I help you?" Katie smiled politely, displaying even teeth.

I leaned on the counter and smiled. "I'm looking for the grave of someone."

"Which someone?" she inquired.

"His name was Edward Walker. He died on the sixteenth of October, in 1865. I've managed to track him here."

"Right. Let me go and look up the burial records."

I took a seat on the wooden bench while Katie disappeared into a back room. When she returned, she handed me a map.

"Found him," she almost sang. "His plot is located in section *F*."

"Where's that?"

"It should be just out that door and down the path to your right."

"I'm horrible with directions." I smiled, sheepishly.

"Poor dear," Katie chuckled. "Okay, I'll take you there." She gathered up a large piece of paper and a stick of charcoal and motioned me to follow her with a bright, "Come on, then."

Katie explained as she went that the art supplies were for taking imprints of the headstones; most visitors liked to do this as a way to take part of the history home with them, she told me.

"I see," I said. "Yes, I should very much like to do that."

I followed her out into the English weather, which had turned surprisingly sunny. The graveyard was confined within a low stone wall topped in moss. Together, we strode along a winding pathway fringed by decaying leaves, through a cemetery crammed with headstones.

"Now, I don't know what condition the headstone will be in, or if there will even be one.

They tend to deteriorate, you know…and there were a few bombs during the blitz."

"Right."

"It was 'Walker,' was it?" she asked, her breath escaping in hazy trails.

"Yes, Edward Walker."

"And may I ask your name?" Katie asked.

"I'm Duncan, Duncan Clarke." I extended my hand, which she gripped firmly.

"Nice to meet you, Duncan. I'm Katie."

"Yes, I know…the name tag." I pointed to her shirt.

"Oh, right." She blushed. A few meters further on, Katie stopped.

"It should be somewhere around here. Some of these are hard to read. Check over there behind you, no, to the left. Yes, that's right, up this way, toward me."

"These are from the early 1840s," I said, then—"Oh wait, here, we have it right here."

The headstone was intricately carved, with eroded scrollwork on the edges. Dulled marble cherubs perched on the capstone and a deeply-grooved script spelled out the name *Edward Philip Walker*, his birth date, and the date of his death. Beneath was the epitaph, *Beloved husband and father.*

Katie joined me. "Was he a relative of yours?" she asked, sweeping aside the leaves from Walker's headstone.

"Well, not really, no," I replied absently, feeling a shivery chill. I was standing before the century-old grave of the man whose notes I had studied, whose script I had run my fingers over, whose possessions I owned and whose secrets—or lies?—I kept. This was as close as I could come to a personal meeting with Walker—no, Edward. For in that moment he was as real to me as any intimate friend could be.

"Just a type of fascination, then." It was a statement, not a question.

"Yes. You put that very well. A type of fascination…peculiar thing, really." An odd feeling came over me, as if I were out of place somehow, a stranger in my own time. A life like Edward's would have suited me better, I acknowledged; a life far away from the demands of academia; a life of ease and pleasure spent travelling the globe in pursuit of exotic antiquities and scientific anomalies. I closed my eyes, feeling the intensity of my desire to be part of Edward's world, to live a life like his. And I could come close, oh, so close, if *only* I could discover some kind of proof that the boy had existed. If *only* I could see into the past with clarity. I rested my hand on Edward Walker's headstone. *Edward, please tell me the truth*, I pleaded, silently. *Please give me something to go on.*

Katie handed me the charcoal. "Here," she said, "I'll hold the paper up and you capture the impression." She held the paper flat against the stone, and I rubbed the charcoal stick over the paper, creating an imprint of the tombstone pattern and words. We worked our way down the design until the task was completed. It was quite a stunning little art piece. The intricacies of the stone had transferred beautifully, creating a lacework pattern. I would have to find a safe place to put it, away from the mice.

Glancing at Betsy's headstone—situated next to Edward's—I discovered it was dated more than forty-five years after Edward's death. It struck me as sad that Edward had died so young, before seeing his son grown or his grandchildren born. At Charles's grave, I felt a pang of empathy—like him, I too had lacked a father's guidance.

While I had not expected to see any grave markers announcing Henri's burial place, a quick scan of the area confirmed my suspicions.

"Did you want to do a rubbing of the other family stones, too?"

"No, I'm most interested in Edward's, I think."

Katie nodded, and silently we walked back through the graveyard and into the office.

"Thanks, then. For this," I said, holding up the imprint, which I had carefully rolled up.

"No worries," she said. "Hey, you're all right, aren't you?"

"Yes, why?"

"Back there at the grave, you sort of spaced out. I just wanted to make sure you were okay to drive."

"Oh, yes. Quite fine, thank you."

CHAPTER TWENTY

While driving home, I decided that the back seat of my car was the safest place to keep the rubbing, away from the destructive habits of the mice. My thoughts wandered to the sketch of Henri that Edward had drawn, and a new thought gripped me—if the drawing of Henri was fake, how was it Edward could have created such an accurate rendition of a boy tied to a chair? The rudimentary nature of other drawings within the journal, made it clear that Edward would likely have needed the aid of a model to sketch from. The Old Masters had used live models, and while Edward was no master painter, the proportions of his drawing had been perfectly rendered. The Old Masters had used a camera obscura, a device which contained a lens that projected the inverted image of the live subject into a box. The artist could then trace the image onto a piece of paper. *Trace.* It had struck me as odd at the time that Edward had used this word in his description of drawing Henri. Had Walker used a camera obscura to so expertly draw the image of Henri?

An art history professor I once knew told me that Victorian artists often disguised their camera obscuras as books they brought along on sketching sessions—books usually ascribed with some sort of nature theme, such as reference manuals for studying flowers or insects, or— butterflies! Could it be? I gripped the steering wheel tighter and punched the accelerator, biting my lip as I hurtled toward home.

I burst through the front door, ran to my study and flicked on a lamp. From the top of the typewriter box, a shadow launched itself across my desk and disappeared behind Walker's crates. The inked sketch of Henri in its wood frame clattered to the floor, breaking the glass.

"You goddammed vermin! Tampering with my evidence, are you? Well, not today!" I exploded in rage. Pouncing on the crates, I dragged them across the floor, and the mouse, now exposed, bolted to the other side of the room. I clambered over the crates, grabbing at the rodent, which shot from my fist, ricocheted up my sleeve, and launched itself off my shoulder. I tried to smash it under my shoe, but it was too fast, fleeing behind my desk. Gripping the corner, I wrenched the desk away from the wall as the tip of the mouse's tail disappeared into a tiny hole in the baseboard. Dropping to my stomach, I peered at the hole, which was no bigger than the pad of my index finger. Amazing what a mouse could fit through. With a snarl, I realized my mistake: I'd been seeking larger crevices.

Retrieving a hammer from the garage, I returned to my study and knocked out the wall around the hole that had swallowed my little friend. An odd sensation of glee crept across my heart, and I imagined a legion of tiny furry dead bodies and an end to the sleepless nights and constant squeaking and rustling irritations.

Crawling along the floor, I bashed holes in the base of the wall at various intervals. There would be no more hiding—I'd lay bare every access point, every hideaway, and then fill the walls with snap traps.

I went from room to room, smashing holes in the wall, discovering mouse shit, torn paper, food piles, and urine-soaked wood. Racing upstairs to my room, I pulled all the furniture from the walls and got down on my knees, hammering holes to expose all of their secret places. In Clara's old bedroom, I pulled out the bed, dresser, and night tables, smashing above the baseboards until my hands wrung with the tension and sweat dripped from my brow. "You're dead, you sodding bastards!" I whooped. Mice scurried behind the disintegrating wall, fleeing in all directions, dodging my flailing hammer.

At last, with heartbeat thundering in my chest and not a mouse in sight, I dropped the hammer. Now that the framing was exposed, my house smelled strongly of mice and their filth. Storming to the kitchen, I grabbed a jar of peanut butter and a spoon. I baited the spring-loaded traps and thrust them into the holes I had created. My sweat-soaked hair tumbled across my brow.

The sharp chime of the doorbell broke my concentration. *Bugger!* What was it now? Maybe if I didn't answer it, they would go away. The bell rang again. Reluctantly, I opened the door to find Diane on the threshold, all dimpled and red-cheeked and smelling like Chanel.

My stomach flopped at the unexpected site of her.

Her fixed smile dropped into bewilderment when she saw me.

"Duncan. I came round to see if I could get my clock." Her eyes focused on my forehead, eyebrows knitted together. "What on earth is that on your head?"

I brought a hand to my head and felt the greasy smear of peanut butter, suddenly aware of how terrible I must look, and her with her red lipstick and coiffed hair. I stepped back into the hall and muttered, "Come in."

Diane followed and shut the door behind her. "Duncan, I—good God, what's gone on here?" her eyes widened at the sight of the lounge: the destruction, the mess, the smell.

"The exterminators. They make a wreck of things, but at least they are thorough."

"This is dreadful!" Diane exclaimed. "Now, I don't know much about exterminators, but I would think that—"

"No reason to think, Diane, I've done all that."

"So I see. Look, Duncan, Clara is worried about you. She says she's been calling and leaving messages, but you haven't returned them. She's told me you aren't doing very well. I needed my clock, so I thought I'd come round and see for myself. Are you okay?"

Her concern disarmed me, and my heart darkened with the sting of cynicism that this beautifully put-together woman, whom

153

I had loved and lost due to my own ineptitude, would show me any compassion now. "I'm fine. Why does everyone ask me that?"

Diane's eyes softened into pity.

"Stop looking at me like that. Have a seat and I'll find your clock."

"Duncan, wait." She grabbed my sleeve. "I'm sorry things ended as they did, but I've come to realize that we are just two different people and I think the pain of that, the pain of not being able to be what the other needed, caused us to be at odds. Maybe we aren't half as mad at each other as we are at ourselves for making the wrong choices."

Her eyes glistened with emotion, and I felt my heart soften toward her. Maybe she was right. We had tried so long and so hard to make things work, that it had become another duty, like doing the dishes or paying the mortgage. It was a relief really, this realization.

I smiled against the tug of my aching heart. "I think that's the most brilliant thing I've ever heard you say."

Diane smiled back. "The truth shall set you free." She let her arm drop from my sleeve, and I felt like I could hug her then—kiss her forehead, smooth her cheek. But she wasn't mine anymore and hadn't been for a very long time, just as I hadn't been hers.

"I'll go get that clock." I stepped away from her and returned with the clock from my study mantel.

"I suppose I should put it in a box for you, but I don't know…" I looked around, searching both the room and my memory for where one might be.

"Oh, that's okay. I keep a basket in my car, to keep the groceries from rolling round."

"Right, then." I stood there, not knowing what to do next. It didn't quite seem appropriate to ask her if she'd like a cup of tea or a stiff drink, but it also didn't seem right to excuse myself by saying I had work to do.

"Duncan, do you need any help?"

I was taken aback by the question. "No. I'm—I'm doing great. Never mind what you've heard. Truly, I'm wonderful, chipper. You watch, Diane, something amazing is going to happen to me; I can feel it in my bones."

"I'm glad to hear it. You deserve good things, Duncan." Diane hugged the clock to herself and then turned and pulled open the door. "Goodbye," she said over her shoulder. I closed the door and stood inhaling the cloud of her fading perfume.

Then I remembered why I'd raced home—the camera obscura! I bolted over to the typewriter box and rummaged inside for the book on butterfly collecting. Placing it on my desk, I carefully opened it, and watched in amazement as a cardboard telescope with a lens fixed into it rose up like a phoenix.

I traced a finger over the base of the device where the paper would be inserted and felt shallow grooves. Grabbing a pencil from my desk drawer I began lightly scribbling over the base of the camera obscura until an image emerged. It was unmistakable—a boy, tied to a chair! His tormented eyes stared right through me.

Good God! Was this the evidence I needed to prove Henri's existence? The indents in the camera obscura had shown, beyond a doubt, that Edward *had* drawn the boy from life. I had something here—something that strongly suggested Edward had had the boy, exactly as he said.

My body trembled with excitement and I grinned as the potential implications struck me—perhaps, just perhaps, I'd found something quite extraordinary, with evidence convincing enough not only to alter the university's opinion of me as a washed-up professor, but to launch me into the realm of academic prominence and renown—the likes of which I had dreamed all my life. But, I cautioned myself, every piece of evidence must be perfectly assembled, my argument infallible before I made my case. I would be required to prove my theory, to defend it before a group of peers, to debate contrary interpretations. The camera obscura evidence, although compelling, could be readily criticized and discredited. While there was the image of *a* boy, tied to a chair in the camera obscura, there was no evidence to prove that this image was Edward's *zonbi* child. Critics would claim that Edward had obtained some London street urchin and paid him a fee to pose tied in a chair. I would need to build a better argument, amass more facts. I wasn't done with Edward's journal yet.

Chapter Twenty-One

Thursday, July 27, 1865

This morning I awoke in Betsy's arms. We had spent the previous evening together eating and relaxing while the nurse put Charles to bed. Betsy's complexion did look much improved after her outing and she had chattered about every detail of her carriage ride through the countryside. She raved about the Japanese and Asiatic lilies, the orchids, and all the other exotic flowers. I quite enjoyed how she carried on—it was good for my soul to hear of her happiness. We had tumbled into bed as though two chance strangers, new at love. Her excitement had infected me and moved me to a passion I had not known for some time. I quite successfully banished all thoughts of Henri from my mind and enjoyed a temporary respite from my troubles.

Our passion spilled over into the morning hours and we emerged from the bedroom rosy-cheeked and invigorated.

I was confident that it would be an easier schedule today, with an afternoon visit to change Henri's linen and another in the evening to feed him.

We breakfasted in the gazebo in the garden as the birds swooped around us and butterflies flitted about the flowers. The bees were also out in droves and congregated on the jam pot. I used my newspaper to sweep them aside. Betsy admonished me, "Oh Edward, leave them be. I do not wish to get stung. You are only succeeding in agitating them." I laughed and continued to swing at them, trusting that the only agitated one I saw before me was Betsy herself.

After breakfast, we took a stroll through the garden. Betsy

imparted her ideas on how to restructure the landscaping, displaying much knowledge and enthusiasm. I agreed, of course. I had little gardening experience, a fact she always chose to overlook, so I would often just smile, nod, and feign interest, seeking only to ensure her happiness.

We spent the afternoon in playful abandon with our child. How he delighted when we shook his rattles for him, creating a feast of bright colors and engaging sounds. My son's eyes captivate me; they are rife with intelligence and wonder. I could not help but compare them with the empty hollowed-out eyes of the disturbed child I hide in secret. The very notion of the disordered boy in my basement clawed at my stomach and prompted a ghastly unease.

Nevertheless, despite the occasional troubled thoughts of Henri, Betsy and I enjoyed a lavish lunch in the solarium with Charles content in his pram. The quail and potatoes were excellently prepared, and the dessert was quite extraordinary. How blessed I am to have one of the best cooks in London at my disposal. We filled the remainder of the afternoon engaged in comfortable talk, discussing politics, art and the latest social news. When I prepared to take my leave, making reference to pressing business matters that required my attention, Betsy protested charmingly. Since I was so enjoying her company, I readily complied—having little wish myself at that moment to exchange the sunny garden room with its delightful aromas for the dim basement study filled with a most wretched stench; or to leave the company of my delightful wife for that of a vacant-eyed *zonbi* child. Henri, in his comatose state, would continue in a state of quietude. I could afford the time.

&

It was past supper by the time I returned to my study. Lighting a lamp, I could discern Henri's form, unmoving upon his mattress. As I drew closer, I could see that his eyes had assumed their usual deserted appearance. I brushed his arm, but he did not startle nor stir—he was again entranced.

I began the unpleasant task of changing his linens and cleaning his face and hands from the dried blood, feathers, and entrails that yet remained on his skin. His wounds had not improved, but remained inflamed, oozing pus. I changed the bandage, musing upon how much longer I could stand to be his maidservant. Such circumstances would, naturally, be beneath my dignity—a man of my standing and prestige in society waiting on a boy such as this. My reward for self-abasement in the service of science will, however, be considerable, and in due time my studies, undertaken with meticulous attention, will reap untold riches.

During the changing of Henri's nappy, I took note of the color and appearance of his feces. The sample was the size of a small stone, about an inch across, and equally as hard and dry. The color I noted as a dark brown. I found a glass jar, deposited the sample inside, and sealed the lid. I disposed of his soiled nappy in the upstairs laundry basket among the baby's used linens. Upon checking the birds, I observed that the one breeding pair had produced five eggs. Although I was ecstatic at this successful breeding, I realized that I would still require additional birds and cages in which to house them.

Reflecting on the outcome of Henri's last feeding and his relative calm after the small meal, I thought to test his state of agitation were he to eat three birds instead of two. Seizing three female parakeets, I managed, amidst much flying feathers and squawking protest, to confine them within the casket. Upon returning to my study, I released the birds, and almost instantaneously, Henri came to life, sprang from the mattress and sailed over my chair, snatching the birds from the air and choking down their lifeblood. He regarded me with famished eyes, his tongue sliding out the corner of his mouth to catch a stray drop of blood. His eyes darted to the empty casket, his muscles twitching and tensing, as though readying himself to lunge. I explained, with stalled and anxious breath, that I had no more birds, but Henri growled, shook his head, and in one swift movement, upset my desk, crashing all to the floor.

I noted the rise in agitation, presuming the increase in food had roused the boy to renewed peaks of aggression.

"No more. Gone." I showed him the empty box.

Henri shrieked.

I seized Henri's arm in an attempt to restrain him; he flailed, screaming and striking out with his feet, struggling to free himself. I embraced him in a bear hug and pushed him toward the chair. Henri's only defense, his gnashing teeth, came within inches of my face, and I ducked my head to the side to avoid them. The boy shrieked and groaned as I used my full weight to pin him down. He tried to squirm and twist away from me, but, with great effort, I was able to reach around and tie first one wrist and then the other, before quickly moving down to his ankles, and securing them, too, to the chair.

Tying the gag over his mouth, I collapsed by the side of his chair, exhausted. It occurs to me now that when Henri eats, he gains an extraordinary strength and an insatiability that I have never witnessed before. It is as though the food prompts and stimulates his hunger rather than satisfying it; this is another aspect of his physiology that I cannot explain. His behavior seems analogous to an alcoholic who craves more liquor once they have begun. It would be best to limit the boy to two birds per meal.

I stayed with Henri through the night, again trying to calm him with my voice as hours passed, hours in which he struggled and moaned, until at last wearied, he fell into silence. I shall leave him in this state and retire to bed.

Friday, July 28, 1865

My waking thoughts fixated on the fact that I had but one male parakeet left. I urgently needed to procure more. The considerable quantity of birdlife necessary to keep Henri nourished was far more than James alone could supply; a more ambitious plan was now required.

After a modest breakfast of boiled eggs, sourdough bread and tea, I slipped out of the house before Betsy had roused herself. The carriage ride into London was conducted in the rain, the short streak of hot weather having exhausted itself in a torrent of tepid showers. The drumming of rain on the leather roof quieted my thoughts enough for me to formulate a plan to keep Henri regularly supplied with food. The Bazaar on Great Marlborough Street accommodated a high-volume bird trade and would well suit my needs. At two birds a day, Henri would require sixty birds a month. With a breeding pair producing an average of seven birds every eight weeks, I would require twenty breeding pairs to maintain Henri in a sufficiently animated state to enable ongoing study. Such a number of clamorous birds were certain to attract Betsy's attention, irrespective of the fuss and expense. If Henri's ration could be reduced to one bird daily, or if he were fed on odd days only.... A general aviary would be required to house the feeder birds, and additional breeding cages. A comprehensive system such as this would take time to establish.

Upon arriving at the bustling market, I stopped to procure the lumber and wire netting required for aviary construction, in addition to padlocks for the structure and for the storage room door. I then sought out the bird vendor and requested his entire inventory, which amounted to twenty-five parakeets, in relatively equal mix of males and females. In addition, I purchased the ten cages he currently possessed, and ordered seven more, to be ready in a fortnight.

"There you are, sir, twenty-five birds and ten cages with the remaining seven to be ready two weeks hence. I have included a complimentary bag of seed. Thank you for your patronage." The vendor beamed at me.

"Do you expect to have more birds available when I come for the cages?"

"Oh, yes. I expect so, sir," he replied, smiling and nodding.

The vendor's assistants carried the birds to my carriage, wrapping blankets around their cages to quieten their squawks. "Keep the birds snug and away from drafts," one young man told me, "and they'll be with you a long time. They are hearty, so keep them that way."

I nodded, climbed into the driver's seat and departed for home.

Upon my return to the manor, I unloaded the cages of birds and building supplies into the basement storage room. Had Betsy discovered me in the process, I had an excuse at the ready: these were rare types of parakeets and a client had asked me to care for them until his return to London six months hence. My objective was to wean Henri from live food within a six-month period, and instill within him an appetite for refined, civilized food. I set to work building a makeshift aviary and within two hours had completed the task. Placing two males in the jewelry casket, I let the others loose in the aviary and padlocked the door. The birds would have to choose their own mates before I set them up in the new breeding cages.

Within the study, Henri sat slumped in the chair, as I had left him. Taking a moment to assess his condition, I observed that the flesh on his bones had filled in considerably over previous days; his color, no longer ashen, has taken on the rich appearance customary to a darker complexion. Intending to weigh the boy, I removed his restraints and set him on the platform scale. He has gained five pounds in four days, bringing him to an even fifty pounds. I can scarcely account for this astonishing weight gain. Perhaps, I mused, the boy's agitated state has so altered the motion that keeps his molecules at their natural distance, resulting in a weight gain that appears unnaturally robust.

I laid Henri down on the mattress and picked up the casket, which held two birds. The boy's eyes flashed at the sound of the birds' frantic chirping, and I was struck anew by the fiercely ravenous hunger in his eyes as he fixed his gaze on the box. Henri's tongue, coated in some kind of white secreted matter, snaked out to lick the corners of his mouth. I released the two parakeets into the room, noting that as the boy leapt for the birds, his agility was improved, his reflexes tighter. In rapid pursuit of the birds, he scaled bookcases leaping from one shelf to another with the surety of a leopard cornering its prey. Then, he seized the parakeets, ripping them from the air with remarkable precision—it was as if he knew where they would fly, before they themselves had so decided. Henri's ability to heal to such a remarkable degree, in such a short span of time is indeed phenomenal, and I have every hope that he is capable of similar advancements in mental comprehension, ability, and intelligence. It is clear, however, that Henri must first master self-restraint and impulse control.

The annual meeting of the British Association for the Advancement of Science is a mere month away; I have only a short time in which to gain control over the boy, for I would certainly be obliged to exhibit the boy in his animated state during the course of my presentation. Thus, it is critical that Henri learn to obey my commands. I cannot have him running wild in the auditorium, streaking after birds, climbing over seats, and disrupting my audience of fellow academics. I would be dismissed as some kind of charlatan—a laughing stock that sought to disrupt the sober proceedings of an esteemed scientific institute with the antics of an ungoverned child. It was imperative that Henri responded promptly and obediently to my every command.

The boy might be trained as one would a puppy. With the help of a leash, I could teach him to heel, to not advance on the birds until I give him leave. Thus Henri could be instructed in self-control. Subsequent to mastering this, I could train him to respond to voice commands, facilitating the eventual elimination of the leash.

I am assailed by a momentary qualm—might it be considered immoral to affix a leash to a child? After wrestling with this matter for some time, I have come to the conclusion that Henri, with his vacuous insensibility and his inclination for live organs has surpassed all consideration as a child, instead appearing, by all accounts, as a unique example of some previously undiscovered dark subhuman condition and thus a specimen fit for scientific study. I must proceed, dedicated to the discovery of the affliction that plagues the boy, the causes of it, and the means by which it might be resolved. To this purpose, I summon all my courage, dispense with caution, and forge ahead.

Thursday, August 10, 1865

For the past two weeks, I have been working with Henri, using the aforementioned method of impulse training.

I regret to report that progress has been limited and painstaking. Despite my tight leash method, whenever I release a bird, the boy tugs and strains so violently against the tether that it is frequently torn from my grasp. On the rare occasions when I have been able to secure hold of the leash, my wrist has been brutally wrenched causing me much discomfort. When Betsy asked as to the cause of my pain, I told her that whilst driving the carriage the previous afternoon, the mare bolted—spooked by a dog in the street—requiring me to yank sharply on the reins, thereby straining my wrist. Betsy pursed her lips in disapproval, remarking that we employed Master White for the express purpose of driving the carriage and that I should let him do so. I nodded in silent acquiescence.

It is becoming more difficult for me to overpower Henri physically, grown as he has in brute strength over recent weeks. I have secured a hook into the stone wall on which to affix Henri's leash. With bird cupped in hand, I have attempted to approach him, all the while commanding him to resist leaping for the bird until I allow him to do so. In all instances, verbal commands have proven futile.

Henri is obstinate, impulsive, and persistently anti-social. He exhibits no awareness of his environment and lacks any apparent understanding of action and consequence. He seems governed, after all, entirely by instinct—an instinct to feed.

I am, I fear, failing miserably in all attempts to instruct the boy in self-regulation and can succeed only in meeting his basic needs of food, shelter, and hygiene—and even in that, I feel my stamina greatly diminished and fear that I cannot endure this arduous routine much longer. I must begin to consider alternative options: place him in the care of an asylum or return him to Haiti. This endless loop of trial and error, without discernible progress, taxes my mind and fatigues my body. I do not know for how much longer I can endeavor to proceed before I must relinquish the task and admit defeat. Until such a time, however, I shall sharpen my mind, rouse all my wits, and strive mightily to discover the answer to the puzzle that is Henri. For the prize—a successfully reclaimed *zonbi* specimen with untold applications to scientific advancement, and fame and fortune showered upon the house of Walker!—warrants one last desperate attempt.

Friday, August 11, 1865

Henri determinedly resists all my efforts to establish trust between us two; his black eyes radiate a ravenous hunger and an abiding—and, I fear, a growing—hatred. His gaze is dark and terrifying, and penetrates to my soul, instilling such an emptiness there that I am chilled from the effect of it. I have become concerned at the prospect of surrendering to an asylum what I am certain is an unrealized, inwardly lurking evil.

Every day I begin with a strict application of the leash method and, at the day's end, allow Henri his sustenance. I have raised one brood of parakeets from my original breeding pair, and three other breeding pairs have produced clutches, but they will not be mature enough to feed to Henri for another week. My supply of feeder parakeets is growing low, although I have once returned to the bazaar to fetch additional birds and breeding cages.

On alternate days, I have reduced Henri's daily diet to a single bird. Henri, as a result, has become more agitated, straining at the end of the leash, growling and lunging at my hands in search of additional food. He has, however, in the regular application of reduced consumption, become slightly less agitated and tends more to his previously languid state. The difficulty, however, is that I require his animation in order to fully assess his reactions and responses for my scientific study. When my breeding system is at full strength, and mature birds are readily available, such conservation will be unnecessary. I anticipate, at that point, I will be able to test the limits of Henri's fully animated state.

The boy continues to exude the most repulsive, reeking stench and no amount of washing or linen changing ameliorates it. This pungently distasteful odor has steadily worsened since Henri has come into my care, and I am at a loss to explain it.

The tremendous effort required to maintain this scientific enquiry has become a daily burden, and the myriad deceits and deceptions required to keep Betsy's questioning at bay, is increasingly exhausting.

My wife besieges me daily with endless questions as to what my work entails and why I insist upon traveling to London with such frequency. She complains that we have been entirely absent from polite society since my return. As such, she has informed me that the Halliwells have invited us to the country for the weekend, and that she has accepted the invitation without first consulting me! Betsy has now declared a temporary ban on my work, asserting that I may well withdraw from society, but she has no intention of losing her own friends and acquaintances. Betsy has set her mind firmly upon the prospect of a country weekend and will accept neither protests nor contradictory arguments. And in truth, I am not entirely displeased with her; for I am myself brightened at the thought of fresh country air and the restoration of health and good humor. Henri, alone and without sustenance for three days, will slip back into his comatose state, to be restored to animation upon my return.

Henri is a specimen substantially stronger than that which first stepped upon English soil. It is hard to comprehend that this boy—who has since gained a robustness to his musculature and an alertness to his gaze—is the same limp bundle of bone wrapped in skin that I first brought to my study.

Despite these improvements in his physical appearance, all attempts to control Henri have been wholly ineffective. I find myself in need of a new stratagem, a revised methodology. A weekend away will provide me the opportunity for reflection in this regard.

I have not fed Henri since yesterday, to allow for the changing of his linens before I leave for the weekend. As expected, his vacant gaze, complete with a languid inactivity, has returned, and, as the past portends the future, he will not wake until I again bring him a live morsel. I will fill the seed and water dishes in my storeroom aviary to ensure the birds will continue to thrive in my absence.

I take my leave, with a profound relief at the respite offered, and embrace the company of my family and friends for the weekend. Over the course of my stay, I shall deliberate upon a revised method by which I might yet discover the secrets behind Henri's ailments.

Sunday, August 13, 1865

The weekend excursion has proven to be an exceptional delight. Joining us at the Halliwells' summer home were several other couples, all of whom were rightly enchanted with our little Charles, who cooed and gurgled in delight at their attentions. Our hosts have treated us to many a sumptuous feast—this night we dined on asparagus soup, spiced veal, escalloped tomatoes, and French biscuits, and for dessert, a delicious coconut cake. After which, the men retired, as is our habit, to the smoking room to talk of politics and business, and the women were left to themselves.

The weather has been miraculous, the heat insistent. Saturday afternoon was spent swimming at the seashore; and, in the evening, we gathered on the patio, well entertained by much laughter, conversation, and drinking. The Halliwells have been entirely gracious, our accommodations superb, our mattress of goose down eminently comfortable. It has been a delightful retreat, and I have been grateful for the opportunity to rest both my mind and body.

I have not, I admit with a measure of guilt, spared a thought for how I am to deal with Henri henceforth. The children present have provided a welcome distraction, and I have delighted in their shouts of joy and their childish games. Henri's life consists of nothing but darkness and dread. He does not laugh at a silly game or know a world of young friends. I have seen nothing that suggests even the possibility of a return to any normal state of childhood—if indeed Henri had ever truly enjoyed one. It seems likely, after all, that the *bokor*'s poison has produced lasting effects. The thought that rehabilitation was impossible, that I would be doomed to care for this flesh-eating creature for the rest of his days, fills me with an unmitigated horror.

A carefree weekend at the Halliwells' summer home has anchored within me an understanding that this is the life of my desires. These recent weeks spent locked away in a dark basement feeding a half-crazed child an abominable diet of live food while denying myself the pleasures of this world, is indeed no life at all—rather a kind of death.

It has become clear to me now that I cannot rehabilitate this boy, that his sickness bespeaks of something more profound even than a *bokor*'s poisoning. This child is deeply disturbed, and I am, I must admit, neither a physician nor a Doctor of Psychology. Further, I must certainly lack a scientific mind, for I cannot determine the roots of the boy's behavior, let alone concoct a likely remedy. I cannot help but feel that I have been a right fool to have adopted this course, but I console myself with the fact that it is not too late to make amends, that an idyllic life with my wife and child is still within reach. For, I have now discovered, my strong desire is for nothing more than to be a loving father to Charles, and not to care for this demonic child of insatiable appetite. Upon my return, I shall make immediate plans to surrender the boy to The Surrey County Pauper Lunatic Asylum. My journey with this boy has come to a final, regrettable end.

CHAPTER TWENTY-TWO

I had finished the first journal. The lack of a death record for Henri in the parish of Lewisham now made perfect sense—if Edward had placed him in an asylum in Tooting, the hospital admissions books would contain a record of Henri's admission and subsequent death. My gut fluttered in nervous excitement—the hunt was on! And, I admitted to myself with gleeful relish, I thrilled in the chase, in the feeling that I was getting ever closer to the truth of the matter, and to obtaining proof that Henri had indeed existed. I would have to make some phone calls—do some additional digging, but I felt— almost as if I were following a breadcrumb trail that Edward had left for me—that soon enough I would have answers to all the questions that currently beset me.

I was perplexed that Edward had given up on the boy so soon after acquiring him, after having taken such pains to bring him to England. Given his dedication to research and the extent to which he had already gone to feed and keep the boy, would he then so quickly abandon the enterprise? Simply wash his hands of the boy and resume his life as before with the luckless Henri consigned to an asylum?

I felt a restless dissatisfaction; I needed to learn more. Perhaps an asylum doctor picked up the examination where Edward had left off? Asylum records might document the outcome of this boy's life and answer the questions that Edward now could not. Regardless, if the records existed, I would finally have official proof of Henri's existence. And, of course, there was the second journal.

With hands shaking slightly, I opened the typewriter box and exchanged the first journal for the second. The leather journal was dilapidated and worn, with several pages already loosed from their binding. I felt the excitement pulse in my veins as I carefully opened it to the first page.

Chapter Twenty-Three

I have failed so miserably. Dear God, how could I have been so wrong? Should anyone discover my writings, I beg they will not judge me too harshly. What could have possessed me to leave Henri alone for the weekend? I would give my very life to go back, to give my regrets, my excuses to the Halliwells; perhaps then, my soul might have been preserved, for surely, now I will go to hell for eternity! What follows is my confession. I shall lay bare my soul and if anyone should find this journal and turn it over to the local constabulary, then I shall take my punishment, but I cannot deny what has happened and it is here I must confess it.

On the late afternoon of Sunday, August 13, 1865, I approached the door to my study—as I have done for the last three weeks—with the best of intentions to care for the child.

I was confident that I would again find Henri in the comatose state that he had typically assumed after being deprived of sustenance. With two live parakeets in his feed casket, I opened the door, expecting to see the boy reclining on his mattress on the floor, but instead, I was astounded to find Henri perched atop my bookcase, lips pulled back in a horrifying display of gnashing teeth. He seemed to be waiting for his meal, every muscle strung to pounce. Without hesitation, the boy launched himself down upon me, knocking me to the ground as he tore at me, seeking to free the birds contained within the casket I held in my hands. When I refused to let go—as my main thought was to thwart his will with mine—he bit at my arms like a vicious dog, without hesitation or self-control. Dropping the casket to defend myself against the boy's attack, I scrambled to my feet, my forearms throbbing with pain and bleeding profusely through teeth-punctured skin. The casket broke open upon impact, and the birds flew out the open door behind me, with Henri bolting after them.

Heart pounding with fear, I raced after the boy, up the stairs and into the kitchen, but he was gone out the open kitchen door.

I cried out in despair, realizing that even if I were to give chase, I would never be able to catch him, and could only watch helplessly as he disappeared among the trees.

Running to the stable, I pulled the mare from her stall, saddled and mounted her, then raced off in the direction I supposed my ward had taken.

I searched the streets of Lewisham, venturing down myriad back alleys, thrashing through the underbrush, and peering along forgotten paths—everywhere I could think of that the boy might hide. I galloped to the busy market place, inspecting where the pigeons flocked, hoping to catch Henri feasting there, but to no avail. All the while, I fretted about the grievous consequences of this boy being loose on the streets, aware as I was of his demented state, and aware that unrestrained feeding would only lead to a violent increase in appetite.

I hunted frantically for many hours, until the late afternoon had faded into evening. The mare finally slowed her pace, her head hung in weariness, flanks drenched in sweat. I, too, was exhausted in every way a man in my circumstance could be. Betsy would wonder what had become of me, as I had missed tea and dinner as well—although worrying after Henri had caused me to lose my appetite. I turned back for home, intending to restore myself with some small refreshment, and then redouble my efforts with a fresh horse.

Panic crept over me as I worried, with the time I was losing in returning home to exchange my horse, what kind of mayhem Henri would inflict, unfettered, on the streets of London. What if he attacked some larger prey, like a street dog, or worse, what might happen if a person attempted to prevent Henri from feasting? He would, I knew, savage any person who happened to stand between him and his next grisly meal. I nudged the tired mare, but she refused to pick up the pace. The sweat trickled down my back. I was at the mercy of fate.

I looked to my hands and arms—bloody bite marks ran the length of them beneath my torn shirt. My face stung—most assuredly also gouged by that dreadful creature.

I was desperate with worry. With free rein to feast at will, to what heights might Henri's aggression rise? I had never allowed him to eat until his heart's content, though he had forever demanded more and more; and this attack on my person, it bespoke of a quick rise to violence to obtain that which he desired. I knew he would stop at nothing now to get his fill. In what state would I find Henri, if indeed I found him at all?

It was eight p.m. by the time I had stabled the mare and returned wearily to the house, pulling my shirt collar up to hide my scratched face. Betsy met me in the foyer, seething with indignation and demanding to know where I had been. Turning away from her, I retorted that I had been called out on business and was in no mood to appease her insistences with apologies or supplications.

Betsy persisted, demanding to know how I could have worried her so by disappearing for hours. I kept my back to her, eager to hide my wounds, and returned her questions with a stony silence. I hastened to the kitchen, instructing Cook to serve me some small morsel as Betsy trailed behind. She continued pestering me with dozens of senseless questions, until at last, pushed beyond all endurance, I snarled at her to leave me alone. In a huff, Betsy stormed from the room. I felt a momentary regret but would repair the damage later, once Henri was safely back in my study under lock and key.

After a hasty meal, I retrieved a bottle of ether from my study, the quilt from Henri's bed, and a rope. Venturing out into the evening, I hitched a sprightly gelding to the carriage, for I realized it would be quite difficult to transport the crazed creature on horseback. Lighting the carriage lanterns did little to dispel the gathering fog that had begun to roll in. I started out, scanning vigilantly for any shadow or human form resembling the escaped child.

I traveled the suburbs and boroughs, advancing upon London as I combed every side street in search of Henri. I frequently mistook a thin street urchin or grimy chimneysweep for the boy, stopping the carriage and hastening out, only to realize my error. At times I called his name, although I was sure that would not attract him, but it appeased my conscience somehow, as if reminding God that I was here searching so he would not punish me too severely for my failings in allowing this monster to escape my control.

Women of ill repute propositioned me at every turn, and I offered them instead sixpence for news of an escaped boy, but they only mocked me: "Aye, I saw him, he gave me a shilling for his own fun, he did." Vile, useless whores.

Alas, after hours of fervent searching, my efforts had yielded nothing, and I had no choice but to turn again toward home. Heavy with fatigue and worry, I fell into bed fully clothed.

After an all-too-brief slumber, I awoke in pain from my wounds. The whole of my forearm was inflamed, with redness extending from wrist to elbow. In the bathroom mirror, my countenance glared back at me; I looked ghastly, with bloody scratch marks travelling up the length of my throat. Betsy might have inquired after these, too, but it appeared she had slept in the nursery with Charles, in a fit of pique to punish me. I covered myself as best I might, but the marks were evident. After forcing down a little breakfast, I set out as daylight was breaking. One final section of the city remained to be explored and if I did not discover Henri there, I would have to retrace my steps and again comb over every blessed inch of the city.

Master White, the coachman, met me in the stable and inquired if I would be in need of his services. I dismissed him, citing that I preferred to do my own bidding that day. I adorned the carriage with freshly filled lanterns and checked within for the blanket and rope. The bottle of ether, along with a rag, I kept safe inside my pocket. At the last minute, I added to my goods a sharp pocketknife. I chose the Arabian gelding from the stable, as he was of younger, stronger stock than the Morgan I had brought the night before. He would be better suited to extended travel than the older horse. With my carriage readied, I started again for London.

In the early morning hours, the streets were already bustling and I had little notion as to how the boy would respond to the crowded, noisy London streets. The shopkeepers were sweeping their stoops, and setting out their wares along the walkways, anticipating their first customers and I imagined their horror, should they discover the bloodied corpse of some poor alley cat that Henri might have feasted on in the night. Worse yet, what if some fishmonger or muffin man happened upon Henri in the act? A constable would be summoned, and what would happen should Henri be cornered?

Recalling Henri's aversion to light and noise, I reasoned that he must have retreated into a shadowed alleyway, and so henceforth, I concentrated on the dank underground, checking beneath viaducts and bridges, within tunnels and coach houses, in dark stables and gloomy storehouses, and all other secluded areas into which a boy could tuck himself.

With each new possibility, there followed the instant when my hopes were shattered, as I found the place empty, and empty, and yet empty again. The situation was driving me to madness, but I had to press on. I could not abandon my search until I found the fiend.

It would be easy for any reasonable man to walk away at this point, to claim no responsibility. Regardless of what Henri did, it would be quite impossible to trace the boy's history back to me. Henri could not speak and therefore could not point to the man who had let him loose in the streets. There was nothing to hold me accountable, and therefore I could not be blamed.

Undoubtedly, someone would eventually report him to the authorities and he would be rounded up for the institution. What would it matter, really, if I turned back for home and forgot all about this dreadful child? Yet how could I leave Henri to do untold damage? To attack any beast at will. I recalled the manner in which he had eyed me when I stood between him and his food, eyes hungry and craving, and felt in that moment that he could, that he would—

Well, I dared not think it. But, I had to forge ahead until the creature was again safely confined. My conscience forbade me to turn away.

Again, I had spent another long day in pursuit of my escapee. This time, unwilling to return home to change my horse, I opted to take breaks, twice relinquishing the horse to a livery stable where he could rest and be watered. During these times, I continued my search on foot, weaving amongst back gardens and narrow passageways, where horses could not go. This search, too, yielded nothing as to the whereabouts of my sinister ward.

It was well after twilight when, conscious of my own need for refreshment, I searched for a respectable tavern. Entering the dimly lit, crowded establishment, I found a seat against the back wall and ordered a plate of oysters with my ale. As I waited for my meal, I desperately sought some solution, some forgotten facet of research that would provide some clue to lead me to the fiendish boy. Weary with exhaustion and overwrought with worry and guilt, I lacked an appetite, but choked down the oysters regardless, deeming it a necessity if I were to have the strength to continue the search.

Sometime later, a snippet of conversation from a nearby table pulled me from my thoughts. My heart jolted with what I heard, and I leaned in to listen.

"Yes, I say, he darted in front of my carriage. I near about trampled him. This boy had no knowledge of the ways of street traffic, bolting in and out of the path of carriages like a scared rabbit, as though he'd never seen them before. And when I shouted a warning at him, he did not even look up, nor jump back. It seemed he had no understanding of the English language. It was the queerest thing."

"He deserved to get crushed, the little street rat!" the speaker's rotund friend chortled.

"Aye, he gave me quite a start, he did, what with his dark skin, sunken eyes, and bloodied mouth—looked like someone punched the piss out o' him; he was a right outcast!"

Bloodied mouth? It was as I feared, then. My gut lurched, and the oysters threatened to rise again. Swallowing hard, I turned to the man, and said, "Look here, my good man, I need to find this boy you speak of, and there is something in it for you if you can give me more precise information as to his probable whereabouts."

Eyeing me with some suspicion, the man replied, "Sir, I've no idea where'd he'd be now. It was last evening when I encountered him, around eight o'clock, as I was coming home to the missus."

"Another ale," I called to the barmaid, and motioned for her to place it on the table in front of the man. He raised the glass to me and emptied half of the golden liquid down his gullet in several long gulps. "Tell me, then, where did you encounter the lad?"

"Why, it was down on St. Katherine Docks," he said. "But don't tell the missus I was there," and he and the men laughed uproariously and smacked each other on the back.

I foraged in my pocket and placed a few pence on the table. "Here's for another," and I turned back to my table, threw down more coins for the barmaid and, swilling the last of my ale, made haste for the door.

St. Katherine Docks was several miles away—a notoriously sordid area, positively overrun with streetwalkers and ne'er-do-wells. The docks would be pullulating with filthy rats, enough to satisfy even Henri's insatiable appetite. Whipping the gelding into a gallop, I hastened through the dark fog-choked streets, my thudding heartbeat matching the cadence of the horse's hooves.

Turning into the borough where the tavern goer had indicated he had last seen Henri, I slowed my carriage to a stop, climbed out, and unhooked the lantern from the front. It was plain to me that he whom I sought would not be along the roadway, but deep in the shadows of the dock or lurking among the surrounding buildings, hidden under the veil of fog.

The area was deserted; the longshoreman, I presumed, had long since returned home, the sailors chosen their companions for the evening—hustling them into the cheap rooming houses that lined the boardwalk down the way.

For the next hour, I trespassed where I ought not, peeping through the slats of the storage houses along the docks. Doors were bolted with locks and chains, and I worried that Henri had found his way within during the day only to find himself trapped come nighttime.

All was quiet except for the periodic clang of a chain striking the mooring at a wave's rush, or the anguish of wooden pillars groaning together. I began to conclude that my quest had been in vain, and, with dashed hopes and a despairing heart, I turned back to my carriage. Then out from the blackness, close by, came the thud of something hitting the dock's wooden slats, followed by a woman's scream, cut short.

I dashed across the dock, chasing the utterance down a ramp that led to the river. A dreadful gargling sound drew my attention—that of a throat filled with fluid—and I faltered as a cold chill ran through my veins. I was gripped by an overwhelming urge to bolt back to my carriage, but steeling myself, I pushed on. As I neared the scene, my eyes strained to reach beyond the halo of my glowing lantern. A sudden breeze parted the fog, enough for me to discern the once billowy cheap satin skirts of a streetwalker now deflated on the ground; two black boots twisted and thrashed from within. Hunched over the woman, was a small dark figure, a tattered blue-and-white-striped shirt on his back.

Henri anchored himself to the woman's chest, legs straddling her ribs and digging into her sides to prevent her from arising. She writhed, trying to curl away from him, but he held her pinned. A voice within urged me to hurry, to tear Henri from the poor woman's chest, but before I could react, something in Henri's hand glinted as he bowed over her, propelling his arms at a fantastic rate, shredding her chest like a sickle through wheat. I was transfixed with terror, unable to move, unable to react. Then Henri buried his face in her bloodied chest and feasted.

Choking back the bile that rose in my throat, my mind refused to comprehend the savagery of which this small child was capable. Weak with shock and dread, I gripped the mooring to prevent myself from losing consciousness. I trembled deep inside, afraid of his rage, afraid of his strength, and most of all, afraid of his appetite and what he had grown to become. I was routed by the realization that I had harbored this predatory monster within my very sanctuary, sheltered him in close company with my wife and helpless child. I had brought this scourge into my own house! Into my own country!

And now it had killed—not just a few birds or even a polecat, but it had taken a human life! What had I done? Dear God, please forgive me. Dear Lord, I beg of you to be kind to me on judgment day, for I knew not what this boy was.

At last, my sensibility awakened, I extinguished my lantern and recoiled into the shadows, baiting my breath and praying that Henri would not take note of me. If he did, would he remember the days of deprivation in my basement? Would he remember the leash? And would he come at me next, exacting some sort of retribution for how I had treated him, how I had deprived him of that for which he truly hungered?

Under the veil of darkness, lit only by the gaslights that lined the storehouses, the fog swirling underneath, I stole back to my carriage to fetch the rope and blanket before returning to the scene under the pier where Henri, in a fixated trance, still feasted on the now lifeless unfortunate. Creeping toward the boy, I shuddered as the loathsome sounds of the boy's unholy feast filled my ears. The woman's blood surged in torrents over his hands, glimmering black in the moonlight. As I was almost upon him, Henri turned to me, his teeth tugging at the woman's heart, tearing the still-beating organ from her chest, before I smothered him in the blanket.

My arms locked around his shoulders, but his strength was far greater than I had anticipated. Henri—in a rage of thrashing, shrieking, and gnashing teeth—tried to lunge at me. Slipping in the woman's blood that puddled around her body, I lost my footing and we almost went over the ramp into the Thames, but still I held him fast. Henri struck at me with the metal shard he had used to carve up the woman's chest, but I succeeded somehow in pulling my torso back while tightening my hold on the boy, causing him to drop his weapon to the ground. I kicked it into the inky current. The boy emitted a piercing scream so ghastly it disarmed me for a moment, and his head connected with my chin. My vision exploded in stars, but I dared not let go. He was a flesh-eating aberration now and I fought for my life. I knew if I lost my grip, he would tear me apart.

Henri would not surrender to me, and so I hung blindly on, unable to reach the rope to tie him or the ether to knock him out. With a surprising surge of strength born of desperation and fear, I propelled Henri's body skyward, smashing his head against the pier's beam. He continued unabated in his ferocious fight, so I rammed it again, managing to stun Henri momentarily.

Seizing the ether from my pocket, I doused the blanket and yanked it tight over his nose and mouth until Henri's body went limp. Then, with trembling hands and the greatest of haste, I strung the rope around the blanket, tying the boy within using a multitude of knots.

Depositing the blanket-wrapped creature on the ramp, I turned to the ghastly scene of the desecrated woman behind me. Her eyes haunt me still, transfixed as they were in a horrible expression of terror. I turned away from the sight of them, acting fast to make scarce the evidence and get on my way before the creature woke again. With his increase in strength, I feared that given another chance, I would not be able to subdue him again. Dragging the body of the woman by her wrists, I rolled her into the murky swirl below, and held her until she sank like a plundered ship, the curtain of darkness closing over her as at the conclusion of some awful play.

The planks were slick with blood and the stringy remnants of flesh, intestines, and the dark lump that was her heart. I searched frantically for a bucket with which to wash the offal away—just as I wished I could wash away the remembrance of it all from my mind—but found nothing and so I had to leave it all. Although the mess would be evidence of some sort of foul play, without a witness there was nothing to link the crime back to my vicious ward and me. No doubt, many unfortunates have met a dark end on the London docks in the course of a night, with many such cases remaining unsolved. This would be yet another—barely notable.

I hoisted the dead-weighted boy over my shoulder and hurried to my waiting carriage. Maneuvering Henri inside, I climbed into the driver's seat and whipped the gelding into a frenzy. As we galloped toward home, the carriage twisted and swung so wildly that I feared it might wrench itself apart altogether, but I dared not slow down, lest the monster wake again.

With troubled mind, I pondered what I was now to do with the bloody beast that lay insensible within the carriage. I could not surrender him to an asylum, for how would I warn them of what he was capable? How could I describe the savage murder of a streetwalker without arousing a full investigation of the case, implicating myself in the process? The police would certainly charge me with the heinous murder—I, who retained guardianship of the boy, and knew of his evil nature, but yet fed his hunger for live animals.

Clearly, I had wrought this terror on London. And if I should neglect to tell the authorities of Henri's taste for live food, how then would I explain a twelve-year-old child bringing down a full adult and so desecrating her? They would indeed think that I was the one who had committed this brutal horror and was using the child as a scapegoat. How could the police perceive the situation in any other light? Heaven only knew what would become of me should they discover that I had kept the boy confined in a basement, away from light and air, in a cloud of noxious stench and vapors, hungry and leashed. Would they incarcerate me, where I, too, would be confined in deplorable conditions and half starved, or would they simply hang me?

I would have to be deranged to draw attention to the debacle that had just unfolded before me. Yet what on God's earth was I to do with the thing now? It was as I had feared—his incessant feeding had transformed him into an irrepressible fiend.

I whipped the horse on, weaving through the darkened London streets, thundering through fog and swirling shadows, my heart a hammering machine, driven to the brink of capacity. My mind whirled with thoughts, with plans, on what I was to do with the abomination that lay behind me, subdued for the moment in an ether haze, a haze that would all too soon wear off, and then—oh, horrors of horrors!—it would struggle to wrench the bonds that held it, to come after me!

At last, I had come to know the true meaning of the word that Vincent had whispered back in the village—*zonbi*. The word throbbed in my brain, as the sweat of my brow near blinded me, my arms straining to direct the power of the galloping horse. And I knew in that moment that I had no other choice but to destroy it.

CHAPTER TWENTY-FOUR

Good God! Henri had become—what? Some sort of demonic beast that lived on organs and blood, and needed no other nourishment—lying lethargic until the next feeding? Not recognizing or responding to even basic forms of human interaction? But not just that—could it be believed that this boy was some kind of inhuman monster, that possessed the strength to take down a full-grown woman and butcher her in such a grotesque manner? It seemed highly probable that this was a deliberate fiction, intended to flesh out some kind of moneymaking scheme. What a fool I had been, chasing Edward Walker all over the English countryside; surely, he was chuckling in his grave. While the journals themselves were of slight academic interest, it was the interaction with Haitian *zonbi* folklore that made Walker's entries of profound interest, and if the boy was a hoax, then all the rest would be called into question, and I—I would be back where I started. I returned the journal to the typewriter box.

It was very late, but I wasn't tired. My brain had kicked into overdrive and refused to be redirected or contained. Science did not have all the answers—this I'd learned in my thirty-year career as an anthropologist. There were at least as many unanswered questions as answered ones. I'd learned to always seek out the possibilities, to cross-examine, to cross-reference and to avoid becoming close-minded. And while I was fairly convinced that Edward's story was a fabricated tale in the popular theme of the Victorian gothic, I felt that my investigation was, perhaps, not quite complete. While the image on the camera obscura did not constitute verifiable evidence, a London murder in 1865 would be another story entirely. Crimes of that kind went on public record. The public library opened at nine the next morning and would have a repository of old newspapers from 1865. If the streetwalker had met the end that Edward had described, there would be mention of it somewhere.

Early the next morning, after a restless night's sleep, I drove to the British Library Newspaper Collections division in Colindale, North London. Approaching the help desk, I registered for a reader pass, and pulled up a listing of newspapers in circulation in 1865. Starting with the *London Standard,* the *London Daily News,* and the *Kentish Gazette,* I threaded the spool of microfilm into the machine and started reading. I scrolled through the months of the year until I found the paper dated August thirteenth, the day on which, according to Edward's journal, Henri had escaped into the London streets. I passed over the usual news of the time—reports of petty crime, social updates, political commentary—until my gaze landed on a shocking headline from the August fourteenth morning edition that stopped me cold.

SISTERS BRUTALLY MURDERED IN WAPPING

Upon the evening of Sunday, August 13, the horrifically mutilated bodies of two sisters, Martha (aged 31) and Margaret O'Neil (aged 33) were discovered by their cab driver, John Cooper, in the area of Wapping, at the corner of High Street and Scandret Street. The poor unfortunate victims of this brutal attack were returning home to Southwark after a day of shopping in the city, when an impulsive decision caused the permanent tides of fate to turn against them. Upon a whim, they asked Cooper to wait in the carriage as they intended to purchase oysters from a nearby fishmonger. When some half hour had passed, and the sisters had not

186

returned, Cooper, whose fare was yet unpaid, sought them in the street. He discovered the two women sprawled in an alley in a pool of blood, with the chest cavity of each ripped open and both their hearts stolen.

"I never heard them scream," Cooper told the *London Daily News*. "There was a hurly burly band playing just outside the alley. Had I heard, I would have been able to save them." At the time of this writing, the murderer is still at large. Police advise all women and children to travel in the company of their husbands, fathers, or another adult male family member until the suspect is apprehended.

In the August fourteenth evening edition, I came across another gruesome headline.

London Mutilator Strikes Again: Murder of Whitechapel Woman

The eviscerated body of a young woman was discovered around six o'clock in the morning of Monday, August 14, behind a rubbish heap at the north end of Clegg Street, throwing the residents of Whitechapel into a renewed state of terror and panic. The victim has been identified as twenty-four-year-old Laura Fiennes, a shop girl from Inverness. This murder, the second in the East End in as many days, is being investigated by authorities for a possible connection with the Sunday night murder of the O'Neil sisters who had been mutilated in a similar fashion. The poor Miss Fiennes had been returning home Sunday evening after socializing with friends when she encountered the barbarous villain in the open street. One can only imagine her horrific last moments as she fought for her life. However, her efforts to defend herself were no match for the strength of her attacker, who subdued the pitiable woman. As with the O'Neil sisters, Miss Fiennes was cut open with her innards and heart removed. A street vendor, who has desired to remain anonymous, found Fiennes' ravaged body and summoned the police. Police are currently seeking witnesses to the crime. Please contact Officer Robert Hooley at The Metropolitan Police Service, 4 Whitehall Place, if you have any information regarding this incident.

I sat in silent shock for a few moments. The murders had taken place during the time that Henri had been loose on the streets. Assuming that these women were indeed Henri's victims, he had then been responsible for four killings—if one included the St. Katherine Dock's woman whose death Edward had witnessed. While I had seen no report of a female body being fished from the Thames, the details of the other three murders, and the timing in which they occurred, were highly suggestive that one individual had murdered them all. The newspaper descriptions of the shredded victims and the removal of the entrails and heart corresponded with the murder of the streetwalker that Edward had recorded in his journal. But the question persisted—could this really have been the work of a *zonbi* child? It was possible that Edward, having read the accounts in the newspaper of a serial killer at large, was then inspired to fabricate the story of the *zonbi* child terrorizing London.

Another newspaper had reported that the Metropolitan Police had disclosed a link between the three murders: each had taken place less than fifteen minutes apart, within a few blocks of each other.

The evening headlines of August the fourteenth continued the run of horrifying reports and I could only imagine the panic generated amongst the residences of Wapping.

Mayhem in Wapping as Butchery Continues

An additional murder victim has been discovered in a dockside warehouse, and the residents of the East End of Wapping are in a great state of despair. On Monday morning, police found the mutilated body of Joseph Bakowski, a sixteen-year-old longshoreman. As with the other victims, his chest had been ripped open and his heart removed. Police have determined that the attack also occurred on Sunday, August 13, as Bakowski was locking the warehouse at the end of his day's work when he was overtaken by the murderous villain as he prepared to leave for the night.

The police are raising the level of their advisory to include young men, and those who may be of a weaker constitution, to keep alert, stay off the streets at night, and travel in pairs. Citizens are reminded to report any and all suspicious activity to Officer Robert Hooley at The Metropolitan Police Service.

The August fifteenth evening edition reported that the police had retrieved the unidentified body of a woman from the Thames. Her chest cavity was cut apart and her heart removed.

I paused and rubbed my tired eyes. If Edward had plagiarized these actual London murders—attributing them to the beastly activity of a fictional *zonbi* child—would he not potentially implicate himself in the process? If the journal was intended to make the public believe that Edward Walker had harbored a demonic *zonbi*, then the account would have damned him by association, complicit in the cover-up of the St. Katherine Dock's murder. It seemed a terrible risk, if it were an elaborate hoax.

Returning to scan the microfilm, I found no reference after mid-August to any further murders, but only brief reports reminding citizens that the murderer had yet to be apprehended and to maintain vigilance in nighttime outings. By the end of the year, even these reports ceased, overtaken by mundane articles about stock markets, business, society, entertainment, and the other usual fodder of newspaper buzz. With the assistance of the desk clerk, I printed out all the newspaper articles pertaining to the murders, including the ones urging citizens to vigilance, and left.

On the drive home, despite the persistent skepticism of my rational mind, I couldn't help wondering if Edward's account was true. Was it physically possible for a boy to progress from a comatose state to that of a murdering lunatic? Henri could have possessed an alarming tendency to violence before the witch doctor poisoned him; perhaps the *bokor*'s curse was the village's punishment for unacceptable behavior. Or the poison might have altered his brain chemistry, transforming in him a tendency to antisocial behavior, normal in recalcitrant boys, to a full-blown psychopathy.

I wondered, too, about the effect of high doses of tetrodotoxin and calomel—it seemed that such a chemical cocktail would have profound effects in an adult, let alone how it might affect the physiognomy of a small child; although, Edward had only given Henri a small dose, could mercury have affected his brain so rapidly? The rest of the journal would doubtless reveal how Edward disposed of the child. I pressed my foot to the accelerator and sped for home.

As I started up the pathway to my house, I heard a muffled ringing and, after scrambling to find the right key, I burst through the door and sprinted down the hall to seize the phone.

"Hello?" I gasped, struggling for breath.

"Dad, there you are! I've been calling and calling. Are you all right?"

"Clara." I felt immediately irritable at her insistence on treating me like a child. "Yes, of course I'm all right. Why wouldn't I be?

"Well, don't act so glad to hear from me. Look, Mum says she was there and your house was ripped apart and you were acting odd. She's concerned about you, and so am I. What have you been up to? It feels like you are avoiding me."

"Look, I am *busy,* Clara. Do you understand? Busy."

"What do you mean, *busy?* You're supposed to be resting. Have you decided about the therapist yet, and the leave of absence? Mum thinks you really should see one."

"No, I haven't thought about it. Actually, I feel great, the best I've felt in a long time."

"Really? What changed?"

"Well, I remembered my love for my work."

"Your work? Surely you are not talking about those horrible dead babies?" I could hear the agitation in her voice.

"Yes, that, but it is so much more than that. Something I can't tell you about just yet. Look, I have to get off the phone now. I have something very important to look into."

"Dad, wait! Please tell me what is going on. Things are finally better between us, and now you are slipping away again—" Her tone was insistent, strident. I had had enough.

"Look, I have to go. I am sorry Clara, but I am very busy right now and these matters simply won't wait." I hung up and went to retrieve the journal.

Chapter Twenty-Five

It was three o'clock in the morning when I at last returned to the manor. Increasingly anxious about the *zonbi* regaining consciousness, I stopped the carriage several times on the way home to douse the blanket anew with ether.

I left the *zonbi*—for I can no longer refer to it by any human name—in the carriage inside the coach house while I settled the Arabian in his stall. I then carried the fiend into the house, stealing down to the basement for what I had sworn would be the last time.

I dropped the bundle that was the *zonbi* in the desk chair and released the ropes that bound the blanket around it. Its body slumped, eyes closed, head lolling to one side as I tied down one wrist and both ankles. Rummaging through my desk, I found my medicinal supply of arsenic raided from an old field-medical kit from the Napoleonic war. After filling the syringe with the poison, I withdrew a handkerchief from my pocket and cinched it tightly around the *zonbi's* upper arm until the vein became discernable. I injected the arsenic into its arm, draining the syringe down to the last. I felt its pulse slow, growing weaker until it faded away. Holding my hand close to its mouth and nose, I felt no expulsion of air. I placed my head to its chest; the heart was silent.

There, it was done. After all those months of attempting to keep the thing alive, I had dispatched it. A wave of palpable relief overcame me. I would at last be free of the monster and the city would be saved from any further rampage. I dropped to my knees and begged the Lord to have mercy on me on the day of judgment, and to remember that while I had been responsible for bringing this evil fiend to London, it was also I who had now rid the world of this abomination. In that moment, I made a promise to God that I would never acquire another curiosity. After the disposal of the *zonbi*, I would pen a letter to James, offering my entire collection for sale. At last, relieved of all fear and vexation, I could now feel the full horror of the *zonbi*'s dark deeds. I collapsed against my desk, overwhelmed by grief and despair.

After some minutes, I endeavored to regain my composure. My next task, before I could rest, would be the disposal of the *zonbi* corpse. It must be buried where none would ever discover it, but where? Would I to bring it to some pauper's gravesite, it might still be removed by grave robbers, seeking to sell corpses to the medical community. If I thought to bury it in some overgrown section of a park, it would surely be discovered come autumn, when the trees and shrubs lost their leaves. Were I to throw it on some burning garbage heap in the city, there might be a chance that the bones would remain, laid bare by the light of day. Given my own culpability in these atrocities, I must now maintain a stern and vigilant watch over its foul remains. I had little choice but to bury it upon my very property. But where? I thought to unearth the polecat—where the soil was already loose and the digging easy—and toss the remains of the *zonbi* down the pit, together with the weasel. It was half past three in the morning. I had an hour or two before the glow of morning light would illuminate my deed.

Retrieving a shovel from the shed, I crept to the patch of earth where the polecat lay buried. The soil yielded to my spade with ease, and before long, I had unearthed the blanket that contained the carcass. Hauling the bundle out of the ground, I proceeded to expand the pit by length and depth to make room for the corpse of the *zonbi*. The sweat poured from my forehead and my clothes were sodden by the time I concluded my work. The site was ready; now it was only a matter of depositing the creature within it.

Returning to the basement, I entered the room, bathed in the glowing lantern light, and jumped back in horrified fright to see the *zonbi*, bolt upright in the chair, eyes wide and alert, staring into my soul with an icy, evil hatred.

My heart beat wildly and my body was seized by a fit of trembling. By all that was unholy the *zonbi* lived! How could it be immune to arsenic? The fiend began to thrash at its restraints and wail at the sight of me, loud enough to wake the dead. Galvanized by horror and a renewed determination to end this nightmare once and for all, I sprang upon it with such force that the chair tipped back and crashed to the floor. I seized the *zonbi*'s throat with both hands and wrung its neck with a strength that sprang from the depths of my soul—born from both terror and survival. The *zonbi* gagged and spat and I felt its trachea collapse in my hands as I crushed its windpipe with a sickening crunch of bone and cartilage. As a man possessed, I could not let go until long after the *zonbi* had died under my hands. Trembling still, I noted its lack of vital signs; its dark face, contorted and still, had assumed a bluish tinge, its neck retained the scarlet impressions of my handprints. It was gruesome to look upon and waves of nausea overwhelmed me.

I bent over the rubbish bin and vomited. When I lifted my head again, terror had me scrambling back to the corner of the room. The *zonbi*'s eyes flickered open and it glared at the ceiling from its supine position on the floor. Dear God, this hellish demon was immortal!

I fumbled in my pocket for my knife, and in a rush of strength and bravery, fell upon the anathema, dragging the blade across its throat. Its skin parted like wet tissue paper. I waited for the blood to gush forth, but it did not. Its eyes held my gaze in the dim glow of the lantern, refusing to give themselves over to death. The devil child was indestructible.

The fiend's lips curled back to reveal blood-stained teeth. With its free hand, it reached for me, gouging its sharp nails into my skin. I felt pain rip through me, and I yanked back but its grip was too strong, and it held me fast. Its head lunged forward in a quick movement, and it bit at me, snapping its jaws like a hungry dog. I reeled backwards, dragging the chair, along with the devil-beast, across the floor in a desperate effort to free myself. With the knife, I stabbed at its hand until it released me. The *zonbi* thrashed in his chair in an attempt to jerk it across the floor to get at me, to tear me apart, to devour my heart.

The ether! Lunging for the bottle I had left on the desk, I snatched up a linen strip, killed the lamp, and frantically attempted to remove the stopper from the bottle, hands trembling and slippery with sweat. Succeeding, I then doused the cloth. With the blood pounding in my ears, I gingerly approached the flailing *zonbi*, who swiped at me, rocking the chair with fury and rage. Sidestepping the wildly swinging arm, I pivoted to come behind the fiend and thrust the cloth over its snapping mouth. Its hand came up to attack my arm in an attempt to thwart my effort to subdue him, its mouth biting down on my hand, trapping my cloth-wrapped fingers between his teeth. I cried out in pain but held on, pushing the ether-soaked cloth into its nostrils, until the *zonbi* again collapsed, sedated. Grabbing its arm, I retied it and checked the other knots. Then, I fashioned a gag, lest it wake again and start up the wailing. My breath was coming hard, and a wave of dizziness overtook me. I bent over my desk, gasping, trying to reclaim my equilibrium and steel myself for whatever would come next.

When I was certain that the fiend was out cold, I locked it in my study and ran behind the shed where I had left the yawning grave exposed. The sky had lightened in my absence and I had to work quickly to fill in the dirt.

Back in my study, I administered more sedation to the bound *zonbi*.

Now, I sit here trying to make sense of what has happened and determine what I am to do next. The devil has come to visit me, and the devil protects his own. The *zonbi* is my curse. It is truly my ward, beyond the temporary bonds of earth. It cannot be killed; it is a scourge on the earth that cannot be expelled. I fear that I will never be rid of this fiend; the best I can manage is to ensure that it never eats again, and this deprivation might, in the end, prove its ultimate demise. My last and only recourse is to starve it until I can conceive of a way to discard it forever.

CHAPTER TWENTY-SIX

Shocked, I closed the journal. My head was swimming and my eyes burned with the effort of deciphering Edward's erratic scrawl. Whatever this boy was, whatever mental condition he suffered from, he was a medical miracle! How could he survive the poisoning, starvation, strangulation, and stabbing and still live? It was impossible.

I still could not put my finger on Edward's motivation, however, in penning such a tale. Why would a serious businessman, who was already successful in the curiosity trade, invent such a narrative—clearly lifted from the deeds of a serial killer who had wrought havoc in London at the time? The publication of such a story (if that was indeed its purpose) would arouse the suspicions of authorities seeking the Wapping murderer. Or, at the very least, such a publication would make him, and his family, a subject of ridicule. Edward was smarter than that. And what of the ragged penmanship in the second journal, the blots and scratches, the way the nib dug forcefully into the page? If Edward were seeking to fool a crowd for personal gain, he would want to ensure that the *piece de résistance*, the height of the narrative, was clearly legible. It also seemed baffling that a man who went to great lengths to hire a street urchin for his camera obscura drawing would then copy a highly sensationalized news story of the day—a story which would have been well-known to all his potential readers. Nothing made sense.

Temporarily out of ideas, I reached for my copy of *Passage of Darkness* and flipped to where I had left off, scanning discussions of actual zombie cases. I read of a young girl who, after rejecting the advancements of a *houngan* (a powerful *Vodou* priest), had fallen ill and died. At the funeral, someone had dropped a lit cigarette onto the deceased girl, resulting in a burn mark on her foot. Months later, people reported that they had seen the girl in the presence of *houngan*, but the sighting wasn't widely believed until the *houngan*, growing nervous at the exposure, released his zombies. When the girl, suffering from madness, returned home, she was recognized not only by her appearance but also by the burn mark on her foot. Then I remembered the account of the feral boy with his unusual diet and how—*fuck*, that goddamned phone never stopped ringing!

I snatched up the receiver. "What?" I snapped.

"Dunny, how are you?" my brother answered in his annoying drawl. "Say, I've just had a phone call from your daughter—Clara, isn't it? Hadn't heard from her in years, and now out of the blue… she wants me to check up on you. What's up?"

I felt the blood heating my veins. *Goddammit, Clara!*—enlisting my brother who has been absent for years? A brother who didn't give a damn about how I spent my life?

"I'm just *fine*. I don't know what the bloody hell Clara is on about! I'm doing a bit of private research on a project. I'm onto something important, and she wants to harass me with questions about how I'm feeling all the sodding time. I tell you, Joe, I've never felt better in my life. I've never felt more vital, more relevant, more alive." *Ugh, did I really just say that to my brother?* My cheeks burned in humiliation. We'd never discussed feelings before. I was losing myself.

"Glad to hear it. These women, they worry about the daftest rubbish. Mine is always telling me to cut back on the booze and to take my vitamins. They just don't understand men. We work hard, we need our vices," Joe commiserated.

"Yes, yes, you're right!" I laughed—a childish chortle. I was finding my own vice. After years of repression and dead ends, I had finally found what I'd been searching for my whole life. I had found the gold watch. *This shall be yours after I die. Would you like that, Dunny? Would you like that, eh?*

"I've got to go now. I've got something important to take care of." I hung up the phone without waiting for Joe's reply. Returning to *Passage of Darkness*, I tried to pick up on the thought I had been pursuing when I'd been interrupted by the phone. *Ah yes, coming back from the dead, insanity, strange diet...* Reading on, I came to a paragraph that detailed the means by which a zombie might be woken. A jolt ran through me when my gaze fell on the word—*salt!* Flipping rapidly through the pages of the first journal, I found the account of July 25, the morning before Edward went to The Curiosity Shoppe to get the screen for Betsy. Bacon! Edward had attempted to feed the *zonbi* salty bacon, had inserted it in his mouth and held his jaw closed— long enough for particles of salt to dissolve on Henri's tongue, to seep into his bloodstream.

Turning the pages, I eagerly read again the account of how Edward had found Henri later that same afternoon: alive, enraged, feral, ravenous. Edward had unwittingly brought Henri to life, to rage, to his hunger for killing, and his insatiable thirst for blood. *My God!* My heart raced, my hands trembled with a growing shock. Increasingly, the pieces of Edward's story were falling into place. Edward, clearly, had no understanding of the role of salt in *zonbi* lore, and his use of bacon to rouse the child was entirely unwitting. Was this not proof, then, that all had happened as Edward Walker had stated? While I sought to retain an intellectual skepticism, I felt evermore certain that the *zonbi* child had existed. Given this preponderance of evidence from a multitude of sources, how could I not be convinced? And my mind began to whirl with the thrilling implications, and what this might mean for—

The phone screamed, shrill and long. I calmly rose from my desk and ripped the fucking thing out of the wall.

CHAPTER TWENTY-SEVEN

Wednesday, August 17, 1865

Sleep eludes me, and nightmares fill my head that only worsen by the light of day. I have withdrawn from Betsy and my child. I dare not face even myself, so how can I face them? I, who have brought this evil upon my city and bear the responsibility for the grisly death of innocents. I spend the full length of days and nights in my study, watching over the *zonbi*, keeping it under continuous sedation as it has been disinclined to return to the comatose state it previously assumed when deprived of food—so filled up with the life essence of the hearts on which it has feasted. Mr. Turner has several times renewed my supply of ether, and twenty gleaming amber bottles line my cupboard shelf.

I have read the dailies since the thing's return. They report four deaths by evisceration with hearts removed—hallmarks of the *zonbi's* terrible work. Five, including the dockside woman. My shame and despair continue to build, expand and compound. It is my fault! I beat my chest, tear at my hair, and cry piteously, praying that God above understands that I had no notion, no idea of what this thing was capable. I continue wracking my brain for some sort of notion as to how I might dispose of this damnable creature. Should I bury it alive, it would only claw its way out of the grave. Should I throw it down a well, it would wail and screech until someone recovered it. I racked my exhausted brain for other ways in which the beast might be killed, but I knew—had seen it with my own eyes—that *nothing* I could do would kill it.

I know not how to remedy the situation, so I keep the *zonbi* sedated, weak, and immobile, until such time that a solution presents itself. It is most difficult to keep up my own nourishment under such circumstances. And, having little opportunity to eat, I grow weak and weary, overwhelmed with fatigue at this Sisyphean task.

I have taken pains to fortify my study, ensuring that the room is impenetrable to all garden pests, rodents, even insects—for I am wary that even the most seemingly innocuous spider or fly would be sufficient to strengthen the beast. Twice a day, I allow the sedation to wear off so that I may check the fiend's state, only to find that it is still alert from previous feedings.

Oh God! How much longer must I endure? How much more time must pass for the life to recede in its blood, before I will be relieved from this dreadful duty? I am beset by the constant fear that it will escape, that the presence of my dearest wife and child will awaken the *zonbi's* need to feast. And these horrible thoughts strengthen my resolve to nevermore leave it unattended.

I resign myself to the eternal fate of unrelenting confinement to my study in company with this hateful, putrid creature. This journal is my only release. I am doomed to conceal this nightmare and keep it unto myself for I have none with whom I might share this horror, none who might advise me. I fervently, desperately desire a final solution but remain at a loss as to how I might proceed. I am adrift and lost in perpetual torment.

In my seclusion, I have become intimate with these walls, these stones, and the dismal darkness. I recognize the rhythm of the fiend's breath, like a perpetual traveler knows the grooves in the road, or the rattle of the carriage. I have not taken a comb to my hair nor changed my clothes in many days; I am filthy beyond compare, but I care not. I am concerned only with discovering a way to rid the world of this *zonbi*, so that I might, someday, hope to resume a natural life.

On the one rare occasion when I felt it safe to escape for a moment, I stole to my aviary, transferred the parakeets to portable cages, and released them to the midnight skies. Upon my life, I swear that that abomination shall never eat again!

Wednesday, August 23, 1865

A week has now elapsed since the *zonbi* murdered those poor people and devoured their hearts. It continues to respire in low rumbles, slumped forward, tied ever-tightly to my desk chair. And I am still without plan or strategy by which I might be rid of it. Betsy is desperate to obtain my attention and affections. During the few times that I pass through the house—for a meal or to use the privy—she pesters me ceaselessly, begging me to explain my reclusive despondency. She tries to make me hold our son. But I will not risk the baby's smell upon me, lest the *zonbi* sniff it out and wake again to feed. Betsy tries to pull me into her caress, but I turn away. I am not the same man she married. I am changed. I am stuck in purgatory, living a prolonged nightmare of which there appears to be no visible end.

Thursday, August 25, 1865

Glory be to God; the hour of my deliverance is finally nigh! I wept, as I scanned the dailies for further developments in the case of the five murdered London citizens and spied an article announcing the relocation of The Consolidated Bank, from its current location on Broadwick Street to its future location on Threadneedle Street. The building that had previously housed the bank will now become a haberdashery and The Consolidated Bank vault, designed and installed by the Chubb Vault Company before the erection of the bank walls, shall be boarded up behind the wall of the new shop, too large and ponderous, as it is, to relocate.

It came to me in a flash—if I could smuggle the *zonbi* into the vault at precisely the right time, I could forever entomb him within! The vault would be buried to the world, lost and forgotten, as would the abomination locked inside. If I could but muster the strength for this well-timed venture, it would secure my freedom and ensure the safety of London. However, how was I to learn the combination to the vault? I was determined to somehow gain this knowledge; there was, quite simply, no other option.

Something bloomed in my mind—a hint of an idea. And to execute it, I needed to venture out. Alas, what was I to do with the *zonbi* while I fulfilled my plan? Even with the door locked, I was loath to leave him unattended with my wife and child only feet away. I needed to think of a secure way to contain him in my absence. Then the notion of the aviary occurred to me. Throwing the blanket over the fiend's head and roping it around him, as I had done for the carriage trip home, I cautiously opened my study door, checking the hallway was empty, and then dragged the chair containing the *zonbi* into the storeroom. Dousing the blanket covering its mouth with ether, I pushed the sedated *zonbi* into the empty aviary and locked the cage door. Securing the padlock to the storeroom door, I felt the agony of anxiety, praying that these impediments would sufficiently contain him.

Hastening to the bedroom, I removed my filthy clothes. Mr. Turner had drawn a bath for me and I took much satisfaction in scrubbing every inch of my body until all trace of *zonbi* stench had been removed. The wounds on my arms were beginning to heal and, with my spirits high, I entertained near giddy thoughts of my imminent freedom—provided I was careful and calculated everything perfectly. After dressing in my most elegant and professional attire, I opened my wall vault and withdrew one hundred quid, tucking the notes into my wallet. Then I proceeded to the carriage waiting outside and instructed Master White to make haste to The Consolidated Bank without delay.

This area of Soho was an odd mixture of once-palatial houses—

now in various stages of decline—a few shops of seedy description, some grease-boiling houses, cowsheds and slaughterhouses. A decade previous, cholera had raged through these streets, and the neighborhood's economic recovery had faltered in the years following. The bank had good reason to depart from its current premises. My good grooming, in contrast to the surrounding riff raff, was sure to get me what I so desired.

Checking my reflection in the bank window, I slicked down my moustache, removed my hat, and smoothed down my hair. I must free myself from the devil that plagued me, and this was my one remaining hope. I gathered my courage and stepped, with jaunty confidence, through the doorway.

Inside, the bank was modestly trimmed with simple Greek pillars and gleaming granite floors; iron caging encased the teller wickets. Men waited in line for the next available teller. I paused to fill out a bank slip at the counter, penning in the name "Winston Walton" as I sized up the tellers. I had to select the right one—a teller who was young and inexperienced, one I could successfully deceive and dupe.

Sallying up to the counter, I greeted a young gentleman of about nineteen years with hearty salutations. While he appeared confident at his station, I suspected his age belied his experience and he would become easily flustered if my request deviated from the usual deposit, withdrawal, or note payment. Sliding the bank slip toward him, along with the notes I had pulled from my wallet, I explained in pompous tones that I was departing for France and wished to convert my twenty quid into francs. I then asked, in the impatient tones befitting an important man with little time to spare, how many francs would that provide me. Confused, the teller informed me that he would have to consult with his superior. After a few moments, he returned and conveyed the information I had requested. I then bid him convert a certain portion of the money into drachmas, liras, guilders, and rupees, for my extended voyage, and would he please calculate the amounts for each, to the closest equivalency of twenty quid.

The bank clerk flushed, cleared his throat, and excused himself again with an apologetic smile. He returned shortly thereafter with a ledger containing the sums of each denomination and currency with the signature of the bank manager at the bottom. As he busied himself procuring individual currencies from his cash drawer under the counter, I noticed a drop of sweat forming at his brow, and his hands quivering as he haltingly counted out the money. Now was the time to proceed with my inquiry as to the vault.

The young man's attentions were clearly on his math rather than his mouth, which was exactly as I had hoped. In the course of idle conversation, he provided information as to the timeline of the vault decommissioning, the closing of the bank, and the boarding up of the vault. By the time he had finished counting and distributing the currencies to me, there was only one question left to ask.

"It must be that the bank manager—who has had to diligently remember the combination to the vault all these long years—will now be able to forget it. Won't that be something?"

"Oh heavens, no," the youngster replied, "not Mr. Miller, he has a mind like a sieve. Just between you and me, sir, he keeps the combination at hand to consult every day."

"Fancy that!" I replied with a broad smile. "A bank manager without a head for figures!" I leaned in closer and added, "Perhaps the only figures he is noted to pay mind to are those of the female persuasion?" I winked at the young lad and delighted in the crimson color that flooded his countenance.

Thanking the teller for his assistance, I walked away from the counter, before pausing and turning back—

"Say, that reminds me," I continued with a smile, "I would like to meet with the manager—Mr. Miller, is it? I have reason to take out a substantial loan for an expedition that promises to be very lucrative. May I secure an appointment?"

The teller disappeared into the back and then reappeared several moments later.

"Mr. Miller will be pleased to see you in ten minutes. Please take a seat over there, and I will call you when he is available."

Tipping my hat to the young man, I settled into an upholstered chair, one of many that lined the perimeter. Customers came and went, the lines lengthened then dwindled, and every minute that passed seemed an hour. Everything depended upon my ability to get Mr. Miller out of his office long enough to probe his desk and commit to memory the combination of the vault. Unlike the bank manager, I had a faultless memory.

At last, the teller summoned me to the manager's office. After shaking hands, I took my seat at the receiving end of Mr. Miller's mahogany desk. I rested my hands on my lap, consumed by the thought that beneath the polished surface of the desk lay information that would save me—if only I could gain access to it.

"Well, what can I do for you today, Mr. Walton?"

I proceeded to explain that I sought a loan to fund my next excursion, a year-long trip to the Orient. The manager took notes in a ledger as I expounded upon the treasures the Orient had to offer, and how I planned to conduct the trip.

"Very good, sir. May I inquire as to the size of the loan you seek and the duration you anticipate for repayment?"

I revealed an impossibly vast sum and Mr. Miller's eyebrows shot up in surprise. I then proceeded to request that the loan repayment be extended over a thirty-year period, propelling it, as I well knew, into a high-risk category.

"I see, I see," Mr. Miller replied. "Would you have statements,

Mr. Walton, that show your banking and business history? A list of pertinent assets, for example?"

"Why, my good sir, did you not pull my file? I have been conducting my banking here for the past three years. You can see for yourself the history of my transactions and I assure you, sir, they will provide you with more than adequate proof of financial stature."

Mr. Miller, confused, began to apologize for his lack of preparedness, and, rising from his chair, begged to excuse himself while he retrieved my bank records.

The moment the door closed, I dove across the desk and started desperately ransacking the drawers. I searched through one and then another until I had exhausted all but one, a slim drawer at the center of the desk. I tugged at it but its lock held fast. Heart thumping wildly in my chest, I threw myself under the desk in an attempt to wrench the drawer open and it was then that I saw it!—glinting from the underside of the desk, strapped to the bottom of the drawer, the key gleamed like a beacon in the fog.

Ripping it from its fastenings, I jammed it into the lock and opened the drawer. Inside, on a folded piece of paper, lay the combination to the vault. Rapidly committing it to memory—let my memory not fail me now!— I made quick associations to the numbers: the first, the year my grandmother had immigrated to England; the second, the age I am now; the third, the year in which my beloved Betsy was born.

I closed the drawer and locked it and, with fumbling hands, returned the key to its leather strap under the desk just as footsteps approached the door. They stopped and then the knob turned. Bolting upright, I feigned interest in a watercolor on the wall behind Mr. Miller's desk.

"Not as limber as I used to be and sitting tends to cause my muscles to seize. That's a lovely watercolor, did you paint it?"

"My niece. Isn't she talented? Three years under the tutelage of a private art teacher. I daresay she is well on her way."

"Indeed, she is. Such extraordinary talent," I acknowledged, resuming my seat with a feeling of profound relief.

"It seems," Mr. Miller cleared his throat, "that we have no record of a Mr. Winston Walton on file. You bank with us quite often you say?"

"I do. Perhaps you should consult with your tellers. They have established a rapport with me over the last few years. Indeed, I know them by name."

"If that's the case, then I do beg your pardon, Mr. Walton."

"Are you suggesting that you have mislaid my file? One of your most influential patrons and you do not even know who I am?" I raised my voice in feigned vexation. "Well, sir, I have the most serious concerns as to how you run your institution, and I feel compelled therefore to take my business elsewhere. I bid you good day, sir." I exited his office with haste. So abrupt was my departure that the man barely had time to protest. I heard him call out "Mr. Walton!" as I exited his office and marched across the granite floor to the heavy glass door.

At last, I had what I needed to rid myself of the *zonbi* who has been my life's curse.

Chapter Twenty-Eight

Wednesday, August 30, 1865

I awoke on this morning—the day of my freedom!—with great angst for my impending task. The knot in my stomach would not abate and I managed to keep myself from sinking into the depths of fear and despair only by clinging to the thinnest thread of hope— that I could be rid of this hell-sent creature forever.

The bank would be decommissioned; its interior due to be dismantled at six o'clock this evening, after closing on its final day of business. A construction crew would wall up the vault the following morning, in order to have the haberdashery ready for its September fifteenth opening. I planned to arrive after nightfall, when I would break into the bank, unlock the vault, and seal the *zonbi* inside, all before the construction workers clocked in at dawn.

I awaited the twilight hour in my study, attempting to diffuse my nervous tension by busying myself preparing for the exploit. I packed a small travelling bag with the lock-picking tools I would require, a collapsible pocket lantern, and my hunting knife. Casting a glance around the room for anything else I might need, my eyes settled on the woodcarving that Emmanuel had given me on that fateful day back in Haiti. Its eyes seemed to mock me from where it stood on my shelf. I shoved it into the pocket of my coat. Anxious to be rid of anything that would remind me of my horrific ordeal, this, too, was destined for the safe. As the hour drew close, I wrapped the sedated *zonbi* in a blanket and carried it out to the stable. Preparing an ether-soaked cloth, I tied it over the fiend's mouth to ensure it would remain sedated during my journey, afraid as I was that it would reawaken at the scent of a bird or rat. I had calculated that

I must administer an ether dose every fifteen minutes, with a final dose being supplied just prior to the break-in. After which, I would discard the empty bottle in the street so there was nothing linking me to the sedated creature, should I be caught exiting the bank.

Lifting the *zonbi* into the carriage, the blanket dropped away from its hideous visage. Its eyes, now closed, had sunken into their sockets; its cheeks were sallow and its countenance, a veiny tissue-paper mask. I shuddered, and my stomach lurched in fearful anxiety, as I pulled the blanket back up over its head.

After tucking it into the carriage, I climbed to my seat, terrified that somehow the carefully orchestrated plan might unravel itself.

The Arabian's hooves clattered against the stone driveway and he whinnied as we passed under my bedroom window. Looking up, I could see my beloved Betsy's hand part the curtains. I no longer cared that she saw me. I had but one thing on my mind—the successful completion of my mission to rid myself of this terrible *Vodou* curse, this immortal evil that has so haunted my life, my future and that of anyone else cursed enough to encounter it.

The journey into London was long and I was obliged to make frequent stops to etherize the *zonbi*. Fortunately, it was a dark night, the moon hidden behind a thick veil of fog, and I had taken the precaution of drawing the heavy curtains closed, as one might for a sleeping passenger. My passenger was indeed sleeping, but it was sleep of a most insidious nature.

At last, I arrived at Broadwick Street and, rounding the corner, I regarded with consternation the many wagons and workers still engaged in the task of disassembling the bank's property. Men grunted under the gaslights, dismantling shelving and loading heavy furniture onto wagons. I assessed their progress as I slowed my carriage to pass the congested work site. My body grew cold with fear at what I estimated to be hours of work yet ahead.

I had little choice but to drive on, past the bank, circling the streets of London, filling the clock with pointless wandering, as the gelding's hooves beat against the stone streets, and the occasional late night reveler distracted my thoughts from the horror inside the carriage behind me. The late summer night air was beginning to yield to the coolness of autumn, and I pulled my coat tighter around myself and prayed for the speedy conclusion of the workers in their task—that they might work diligently with the expectation of returning home to their families. In my heart, it was all I dared hope for—that I, too, might return to a life that awaited me like the promise of heaven to a body in the throes of its final death rattle.

I could only drive on through the night and return with repetitions as widely-spaced as I dared. Somehow, amidst my rising agitation, I diligently marked the intervals in which to administer the ether. With each stop, the bottle grew lighter in my hand, and the weight in my heart grew heavier.

On my fourth circuit past the bank, I saw that the workers had removed many structures from within the bank. Broken bits of metal grating, formerly separating teller from customer, lay in the street. Desks and chairs were stacked on the sidewalk, waiting to be loaded onto wagons and fewer men bustled in the street. Through the bank window, I could see the vault—liberator of my soul!—standing in the corner.

Continuing reluctantly on, my thoughts were always attentive to the *zonbi's* raspy breathing behind me, and I stopped more often to check on my dreadful burden. Little ether now remained. I had estimated that the fiend would remain sedated long enough for me to break into the bank, and subsequently the vault, but this delay could prove fatal to my plans! The prospect that I would not have sufficient ether to ensure the *zonbi's* continued unconscious state worried at my mind as I rattled through the streets.

Finally, I could wander the city no more, and hung in the shadows of Wardour Street, listening for the whistle of the workers and the diminishing noises that would signal their departure. Drawing my collar up around my neck, concealing the lower half of my face, I slumped in my seat and turned my eyes to the ground. On an occasion when a thick roil of fog cloaked the carriage, I stole to the passenger seat to check the *zonbi's* breathing. It continued slow, deep, and raspy in the manner to which I had become accustomed. Should it lighten and begin to quicken it would indicate the monster was about to wake. Oh, if only the workers would hurry about their business! I doubted that I had more than a single dosage of ether left and could scarcely wait any longer. They simply *must* finish directly!

A hansom passed by. My heart seized at the sight of a rat scurrying across the cobblestones to duck under my carriage. Panic seized me, and I sprinkled the last of the ether on the cloth. My hands burned, alive with blisters from my repeated handling of the solvent. While the *zonbi* still seemed deeply sedated, the weight of the knowledge that it could all change in an instant pressed down upon me, filling me with fear. The rustle and scent of rats that even now scuttled beneath the very wheels of the carriage might be sufficient to rouse the demon. I knew now that I could not hold it, its strength like none I had ever seen. Were I to perish at the *zonbi's* hands, it would then be free to rule the night and there would be no end to its rampage. I shuddered, screaming in my heart for the workers to cease and desist, to clear out and let God's will be done!

Finally, I could afford to wait no longer. Seizing my bag, I crept from my carriage and, clinging to the shadows, approached the building. The workers were exchanging weary farewells; they were in the process of dispersing into the night, taking the vestiges of the bank with them. I peered through the bank's window, alive with fear at the prospect of the treacherous task that lay before me.

Breathing deeply to steel myself, I pulled my tools from my bag and went to work at the door, tugging at the tumblers until I had coaxed them loose and they fell away. The door yielded to my touch, swinging into the dark interior of the bank.

Racing back to the carriage, I tore the fiend from the back. Had I heard a slight change in breathing as I lifted him? I couldn't be sure. Cold sweat trickled down my brow, wrought by the terror of carrying against my breast the accursed *zonbi*, who threatened to wake at any time.

Rushing it into the building, I almost lost my balance on the slick granite floor under my hastening feet. The light from the streets was dim, obscuring all but the largest of shapes from my eyes. Laying the limp body of the *zonbi* on the floor beside me, I felt through the gloom to find the cool, protruding bars of the vault's lock. I grasped the handle and squinted at the lock—there was not enough light to illuminate the dial and discern the numbers. There were neither blinds nor drapes on the window to conceal the light of my lantern, but I had no choice but to light it.

Rummaging in my bag, I felt the smooth metal of the lantern and pulled it free, just as I heard the sound of footsteps on the walkway outside the bank. My eyes darted past the window to the street beyond. By the light of a streetlamp, I caught sight of the unmistakable blue cape of a bobby. Heart in mouth, I ducked down, crouching mere inches from the *zonbi*. The blanket lay askew, revealing its ghastly face—sunken eyes seemingly fixed on me in the punishing gloom. It was then that with surety I heard the change in the cadence of its breathing. It grew lighter and its pace increased. I was transfixed with fear, the blood pounding in my ears. I prayed that the bobby would keep on his course and leave me be. His footsteps stopped mere yards from the door—the door, I now realized, that I had left ajar! *Go on then, go!* my mind cried out in utter torment, as I begged the God that had abandoned me to return and grant me this one last request. The constable paused, and I held my breath, waiting for him to enter and discover me, but it was not he that entered through the open the door, but the smell of pipe tobacco. I breathed a relieved sigh as the sound of his footfalls disappeared into the night air.

Regaining myself with no small effort, I opened the collapsible lantern and lit it, turning the dial down to its lowest setting. Holding it up to the vault lock, I caught a glimpse of the *zonbi's* face and noticed the slightest tremor as an eyeball rolled under its half-closed lid.

Then, before I could lay a hand on the dial, there came out of the darkness the low rumbling growl of a mutt, from the direction of the bank door, and out of the darkness, the gleam of two eyes advanced slowly towards me. The stray's lips pulled back to reveal its glistening incisors.

Gasping, I shrunk back into the darkness, shading the lamp with my palm. Before I could speak a word, the *zonbi* sprang at the mutt, sending him barreling into the shadows. The air crackled with the dreadful dance of snapping jaws, snarls, and animal screams. I leapt to open the vault, falling upon the dial with one hand while I held up the pocket lantern with the other. Hand trembling, I spun to the first number, then to the second. At the last spin of the lock, I heard the piercing yips of the dog in agonizing death throes. I knew that any moment now, the *zonbi* would come for me. Yanking down on the handle, I released the vault lock, and jerked the door open.

The *zonbi* knocked me sideways with such incredible force that I slammed against the wall. The lantern skidded across the floor, extinguishing itself.

The loathsome beast emitted an ungodly yowl that filled me with terror. I felt the weight of the thing bounce up my thighs, claw its way across my midsection to land on my chest with a force strong enough to knock the air from my lungs. I struggled to breathe as I fought for my life in the dark, frantically tucking and twisting away from where I sensed it was, only to have it reappear, pinning the other side of me. I grabbed for its throat, but my hands slipped through the air, returning nothing. As we wrestled on the cool granite floor, I could only grope for a limb, a body, a presence, as the light I so desperately needed to subdue the beast lay tauntingly out of my reach.

A jagged, searing pain ripped at my side, as some kind of blade slid across the surface of my skin. And I realized that it had somehow obtained my hunting knife and was using it against me. The fiend hissed and screeched as it worked on me, tearing to get at my heart, evading my grasp as he worked, twisting and ducking under my swinging arms. At last, my fist closed around a handful of sticky curls, soaked as they were, with my own blood. With every ounce of the strength I had left within me, I wrenched the *zonbi's* head backwards; its neck snapped back, twisting its body away from me. I held it fast at arm's length as I jerked my legs out and scrambled to find my footing. The monster screamed, scratching and clubbing at the arm that held it. It was all I could do to hold the fiend, my arm a fiery paroxysm of pain.

I fought to position myself at exactly the proper angle and swung the vault door with force, smashing the *zonbi's* skull into the solid steel. As the creature fell limp in my hand, I hurled it into the open vault. Then, thrusting my hand in my pocket, I pulled out the carving and threw that in the vault, and slammed the door closed, spinning the lock. I had, at long last, cast the demon into the abyss.

The searing pain from my injuries then seized me, and I dropped to my knees, clutching at my chest as blood seeped through my fingers. I tried to close my coat around myself but it hung in shreds from my shoulders. Locating the blanket in which I had wrapped the *zonbi* beast, I pressed it to my wounds in an attempt to staunch the

215

flow of blood. Seizing my bag, I staggered toward the bank door, pushed my way through, and stumbled toward my carriage.

Then, I stopped with a lurch. I could not leave the ravaged dog inside the bank for the workers to discover. That was sure to bring the police and prompt the discovery of the horror in the vault. Grimacing at the thought and almost swooning from the pain of my wounds, I returned to the bank.

Retrieving my pocket lantern, which had been discarded in the fight, I set it upright and lit it. The dog, sopped with its own gore, must have weighed more than four stone. Rolling it onto the blanket, I folded the ends around the carcass and dug my hands beneath it, securing my grip. I cried out with the effort of lifting the dog corpse; an agonizing white-hot heat lanced up my body. I stumbled over the lantern and it skidded across the floor and went out again. Staggering out of the bank, I wrestled the stray into the passenger seat and closed the door, breathing heavily, hands pressed to the wounds in my side. What of the blood and gore that splattered across the bank floor? I would never be able to clean it in my current state—I could barely stand as it was. I had to vacate the premises, now, lest I was discovered.

Scrambling to the driver's seat, I whipped the gelding into action, fleeing Broadwick Street with a bolt and rumble, until I was like any other late-night London traveler.

Despite the torment of my piercing wounds, I felt triumphant, having succeeded in my impossible task. Oh, I had come very close to failing but I had persevered and now was free. God had spared me the horrifying fate of being forever chained to that ruinous demon *zonbi*. Now, if only it should remain undiscovered until after the workers had sealed the vault behind a wall. I worried, though, that the blood left on the bank floor might arouse suspicion. As the carriage lurched and jolted through the London streets, I fretted as to whether the morning workers erecting the wall might hear the *zonbi*'s screams from inside the vault. Was the vault wall thick enough to muffle its cries? If anyone should find and release the *zonbi* in the hour of his waking hunger, then the city of London would be at its mercy.

With growing dismay, I realized that I must return, before early morning's light, to wipe the blood from the scene. My heart thudded in my chest as the carriage hurtled down the cobblestoned streets at a breakneck pace. Would I have sufficient time to return home to obtain the necessary cleaning supplies, change my clothes, and dress my wounds? I could sleep the sleep of the dead come the morrow—and for the rest of my days—but the evidence of the night's violence must be removed. As I hastened toward home, my thoughts circled back to the fiend. Perhaps at this very moment it was rousing from its stupor. I imagined it erupting in a rampage, fighting to free itself from its steel tomb, eventually exhausting itself in frustrated torment. The monstrosity that I had shut up in the vault had once been an innocent boy and, while I felt a momentary yearning loss for his fate, I knew that the beast he had become was a horrifying scourge on society, a merciless killer of innocents, and an insatiable consumer of hearts. I felt wracked by guilt that I had risked the life of my dear wife, my own child, and of countless members of society by bringing this creature, this *zonbi*, this demonic child—whom God himself had abandoned—to England. And it may be that the blood I had shed in ridding the menace from society was enough to atone for my sins. I prayed that it was so.

Stopping the carriage on Westminster Bridge, I lifted the bundled dog carcass from the passenger seat and dropped it over the railing into the oily Thames, joining the other carrion and rubbish that the great roiling City of London would sooner forget.

Thursday, August 31, 1865

The cool grey of daybreak was at my back as I stopped the carriage a few yards from the bank, where the *zonbi* lay entombed in the dark belly of the steel vault. While early street vendors were starting to emerge, my sedate progression through the streets was unremarkable and largely, I hoped, unnoticed. Parking in the still-dark alley on the eastern side of the bank, I lurched for the bank door, wincing at the sharp pain of my wounds. In the early light, I saw the smeared pool of blood and gore staining the granite floor. Crouching painfully, I sopped up the blood, cocking an ear to listen for any cries from the direction of the vault. There was nothing, and I breathed a sigh of relief. When the mess of the previous night had been mostly remedied, the stain now a larger smear of pale brown—that could, indeed, be any manner of dirt—I hobbled through the bank door and made my way to my carriage, tossing the soiled rags into the passenger seat.

I had survived; I had bested the *zonbi* and now the future belonged to me. I had bought it with my terror and with my strength. I had paid for it with my dedication to righting the terrible wrong committed against God—the restoring of the dead to life. Oh, how I would now embrace my freedom! I made a vow as I began on my journey homeward, that I would never again think upon this gruesome chapter of my life. I would return home and embrace my wife and my child. As I drew away from the bank, a cart loaded down with boards stopped behind me, and a merry shout rang through the street, "Right, then, let's get started, boys!"

With a bob of his head, the Arabian broke into a hearty trot. I will forget you, Henri, demon child, boy *zonbi*. You will not hold dominion over my heart and mind, nor will you ever kill again. I have conquered you, and now I banish you. For evermore. Amen.

Chapter Twenty-Nine

Closing the journal, the sound of my own heartbeat loud in my chest, I struggled to grasp what I had just read—Edward had succeeded in disposing of the boy in the bank vault. Did the vault actually exist somewhere and, if so, could it really be true that this *zonbi* child had been locked in it for 125 years, right under the nose of the bustling city? Once the vault had been walled up, only the renovation of the building, or its subsequent demolition, would have revealed its existence; even then, after it had been sealed and its combination forgotten, only a blasting would open it again. It was all too possible that here, in the city of London, where buildings remain intact for centuries, that the vault still lay undetected and undisturbed. A thrilled excitement lurched from my gut and raced through my veins. My God, if they were truly there, if Edward Walker had recorded *actual* events, I could find the remains of a *zonbi* child! My mind racing, I concluded that the constant temperature and desiccation within the vault could have preserved the bones sufficiently so that I could perform DNA tests; examinations might reveal what kind of disease or anomaly had afflicted the boy, or the elusive formula of the *bokor* poison that had induced his comatose state. There had to be some scientific explanation for Henri's behavior, for his ability to stave off death, if only temporarily. For now, I had to find the bank's location.

Wracking my brain, I tried to establish some means by which I could determine the exact address of the bank, something that Edward had neglected to mention in his account. All I knew was that it was somewhere on Broadwick Street. Then I remembered Edward's mention of a newspaper account he had read regarding the decommissioning of the bank. I had possibly read that same newspaper and possessed, even now, the printout. Retrieving the copy of the paper from my desk drawer, I was elated to discover the article about the bank's relocation and—delight!—the address: 10 Broadwick Street. Examining a street map, I found the block where the former bank was located—a Soho neighborhood filled with cafes, art galleries, and bookshops. If Edward's journal recounted actual events and, assuming the vault still lay undisturbed, then I was potentially sitting upon the find of a lifetime—a hair's breadth away from my greatest desire!

First, however, I would need to gather particular information, such as, was the building still in existence, and would I be able to access the vault? I had worked out the second and third numbers of the vault combination from viewing Edward's and Betsy's ages on the census. Edward's age had been thirty-five at the time of the writing, and Betsy's year of birth was forty-five but the first number, the date Edward's grandmother had immigrated, eluded me still. I also worried that I was on a fool's errand. After all this trouble and effort, and assuming Edward's story to be true, would Henri's bones still be intact, or would they have long ago turned to dust? I would, I determined, reconnoiter the Broadwick location first thing the following morning.

I slept fitfully that night, plagued by fragments of dark dreams that left me sweaty and restless, but rejoiced as morning approached, eager to start my mission. Grabbing a piece of toast to eat in the car, I set out for Soho. Braving the London traffic on a Saturday was something that I had never looked forward to, but this morning I found it downright unbearable. Honking my horn and cursing at snail-slow drivers, I balanced the map book in my lap, referring to it as I narrowed in on Broadwick Street. Slowing to peruse the street addresses, I spotted number ten, a tired looking bookshop on the corner sporting the name Next Chapter.

Parking several streets up, I walked to the bookstore; as I approached, I studied the brick façade for any remaining tells that suggested its past life as a bank. Little of its former state remained, only two Doric columns on either side of the front door. Glimpsing the window posters that announced an after-Christmas sale, I pushed the door open, and a sharp bell announced my arrival.

I was at once in a cramped space divided by tight aisles that led to an open seating area in the back of the shop. There was only one other customer present: a woman wearing a vintage-style hat who was bent over a book, with four or five more tucked under her arm. The reading nook in the rear was a pleasant spot, with two armchairs and a small coffee table; one side of the wall, decorated with brightly painted chairs and a flower throw rug, was designated for children. The back wall, comprised of heavy floor-to-ceiling bookcases, was filled with children's books and toys. I was approached by an enthusiastic salesman who asked me what I was seeking, and I, being quick-minded with my own brand of enthusiasm, the roots of which he could not have imagined, replied that I was looking for some books for my five-year-old grandson.

"Bit of a drag having a birthday so close to Christmas, poor chap," I acknowledged ruefully.

The salesman smiled, pulling several books from the shelves and placing them in my hands: books about magicians, dragons, elves, fairies, and zoo animals. After the salesman had withdrawn to let me examine the books, I studied the construction of the back wall of the shop. The bookcase was an open shelving unit; I could see the same patterned wallpaper between the shelves that decorated the other walls of the shop. Reaching through the shelf, I tapped on the back wall and a sound reverberated—indicating a hollow cavity behind, I was certain of it. The clerk raised his head at the noise, looking down the aisle in my direction; I smiled and raised a hand in a tentative wave, picking a book up from the table. He smiled in reply, turning to the female customer as she approached with a question.

The bookcase was solid, screwed to the wall. In order to access the room beyond the wall, I would need to empty the bookshelf and move it. Casting my gaze around the bookstore, I saw no sign of an alarm system and an unobtrusive door along the side wall— an emergency exit—had a simple keyhole lock, one that I could probably pick.

Paying for several books I had chosen, I gave a last glance to the far wall before exiting the shop, confident that the walled-up vault lay behind it. Before heading back to my car, I ducked down the side lane beside the bookshop and examined the emergency door. It appeared to be a lock that I could pick, with practice. First, however, I must complete the sequence of the vault combination.

Driving back home through the London streets, I was slightly distracted by my thoughts as to how I was going to obtain that one missing number. It was going to be a significant task to unload and dismantle the loaded bookshelf in front of the false wall, and then to break through it; I could not afford additional time to play at vault cracking. The first number in the combination corresponded to the date that Edward's grandmother had immigrated to England. There were eighty or so possibilities, depending on the age of the woman at her death. Did Edward refer to his maternal or paternal grandmother? Edward had been born in 1830, a citizen of England, which meant that his parents must have resided here at the time of his birth. As for either of *their* mothers, their immigration could have happened in any year preceding or superseding Edward's parents' birth. All the way home, I tried to think of a strategy that would narrow down these available dates. There must be some clue that I had missed, some additional strand that I had not yet followed up on.

The more I thought about the multitude of possible dates, and odds against finding that first number, the more dismayed I got. By the time I pulled into my driveway, I was so anxious, so clouded in thought, that I didn't noticed Clara's car parked in the street. When I opened my door, she was standing in the hallway, her face tight with shock, her back rigid, and her hands clamped down on Tommy's shoulders preventing him from coming to greet me. The boy's eyes were wide in a chalk-white face, as he looked at me with fear. Why had she come here? Why had she brought my grandson? This was no place for either of them right now. If only she had given me space as I had asked.

"Dad! What is going on? What is the meaning of all *this*?"

Gaping holes marred the walls, revealing the jagged edges of drywall and the struts within. Gyproc dust powdered the floor like snow where I had tracked it from room to room. Carpet, which I'd pulled away from the walls, was frayed and shredded from the mice. A pile of chewed, soiled newspapers stacked by the door slid into disorder. Dirty dishes formed crusty china towers on the surfaces of desks, mantels, and side tables. And the mice...some were caught in traps—I had not yet had the time to dispose of them. Others, I could hear scuttling in the walls. The place had looked better, but Clara didn't *understand* how meaningless this was in view of what I was about to uncover.

"Who invited you in here?" I grumbled, brushing past her, as I retrieved the framed drawing of the bound Henri and slipped it into a desk drawer. I didn't want the boy to see it; didn't want Clara to see it.

"Dad, what is going on? I haven't seen you in...how long? I call, and you are rude to me, then you don't answer your phone at all, and the machine doesn't even come on. Now, I come here and see *this*? You've destroyed your home, Dad. Why? I want to help you."

"Oh no, you will *not* look at me like that! I'm busy here, trying to save my job. Don't you understand? No, you wouldn't. You're just a silly little housewife. You wouldn't understand about such things!" My anger spilled out, despite myself. "And you've brought the boy with you—for what purpose, Clara? Look how terrified he is. Look at how he looks at me, how you both look at me!"

"It's the mice, Dad. He's afraid of them. He's here because he misses you. He doesn't understand why you won't see him, see us. Dad, I—" Clara let go of Thomas, whose eyes had filled with tears, to take a step toward me.

"Clara, I have no time for this. *No* time!" I stormed to the door and whisked it open. Rattled with anger, I glared at her, the litany running through my mind: *Get out! Get out!* Thomas was wailing now. The noise hurt my head, making me feel nauseated. Eyes downcast, Clara steered Thomas past me and I heard her choke back a sob, soft and low, in the breath-pause between the boy's howls.

When they were clear of the door, I slammed it behind them. Something inside me twisted and a cough of emotion rose in my throat. I was too busy now for explanations, for managing confrontations. When I was lauded for my discovery, when my academic peers recognized my value, *then* I would make it up to Clara. She was my daughter, after all, and it was her job to forgive me. I couldn't be the father she needed right now. I couldn't be the grandfather I wanted to be. But when all this was done, I would be someone they could both be proud of.

I turned my attention back to the first number of the vault combination. I had not come across any information about Edward's family or extended family in his journals. *Sodding hell!*

Shuffling through the death certificates, I tried to gather my thoughts. How was I ever to find out the year that Edward's grandmother had immigrated to England? I paced the house, running my hands through my hair, closing my fists around the strands, feeling the tension pulling at my scalp until, at last, an idea came to me. Plugging the phone back into the wall, I dialed the number of The Brockley Cemetery. A female voice answered pleasantly, "Hello?"

"Hello—is that Katie, then?"

"Yes, this is she."

I could hear the smile in her voice.

"Katie! Glad I reached you. This is Duncan Clarke. I was there the other day, searching for a grave. You assisted me with a rubbing?

"Right, Duncan, how are you?" she asked warmly.

"I've been just fine, thanks. Listen, I'm still working on this genealogy project, and I've got a couple of questions, I wondered if you could help me with. How would one go about finding out the precise year someone had immigrated to England? Sometime either in the late 1700s or early 1800s, I am thinking."

"That can be very difficult to determine. Do you know where the person emigrated from?"

"No, I'm afraid I don't. I actually don't have much information at all. Just that I really need this one date. It's hard to explain, but what are my options?"

"Well," Katie began thoughtfully, "you'll need to know several things about the person: their family name, where they emigrated from, where they immigrated to. Unfortunately, the first census wasn't completed until 1835. Is this someone related to the family that you were looking into the other day?"

"Yes, it is the grandmother of the man actually."

"Paternal or maternal?"

"I am not sure."

"Oh dear, that does make it quite difficult. You see, you'll have to locate the maiden names and married names of both the chap's grandmothers, since either one of them could have immigrated either as a married woman or a child."

"Of course. With marriage records and birth certificates and the like?" I asked, feeling, despite myself, increasingly despondent at the time required to obtain these documents.

"Yes, then from there you'd have to try to find ships' records, assuming such records still exist."

"Shit," I muttered under my breath.

"Well, there is one other thing I can think of," Katie mused after a moment. "Do you have any of his possessions? Any papers or mementos or anything of that nature?"

"Yes, a journal, some papers," I replied cautiously.

"If you have a family Bible, for example, sometimes important family dates were recorded there, like marriages, births, and deaths. If the woman in question immigrated for the purpose of marriage, as was sometimes the case, there might be a trail to follow."

Thanking her and bidding goodbye, I hung up the phone.

With a renewed sense of urgency, I returned to the crates that still stood in the corner of the study, amid the growing debris that had accumulated around them. I *knew* there was no Bible within, but I had to look again; I was desperate. Removing all the jars from within the crate, I ran my hands along the inside, searching perhaps for some secret pocket that escaped my notice before. No family Bible. *Dammit!*

Dialing the Walker's number, I swallowed hard as Ruth answered.

"Hello, Ruth, it's Dr. Clarke—"

"Oh, Dr. Clarke, what can I do for you?" Her tone was direct, if a bit reserved.

"Well, I have something of an odd request. I wondered if there was a family Bible among Edward's things that didn't make it into the crates? Maybe you were keeping it as a family heirloom?"

"No, there was no Bible, I am quite certain. I believe we gave you everything of his estate that we had."

"Are you quite sure? Perhaps one of your relatives hung on to it?"

"Dr. Clarke, there is nothing else here. I hope you had a happy Christmas and I wish you all the best for the New Year, but please, don't call here again. Goodbye."

"Wait, please—" the click interrupted my words.

"God damn you!" I threw the phone at the wall, and mice scattered in a cloud of gyprock dust. It was all slipping away from me! I was so close, so palpably close! I felt my throat close up and found it increasingly hard to breathe; a pounding pain throbbed behind my eyes. With fists clenched in my hair, I squeezed my skull in damnable frustration. There *had* to be another way. I could go public with my research, but it was too soon. After all, I didn't know yet what I was dealing with—the remnants of an honest to God *zonbi* or those of a poisoned, mentally disturbed boy? This was a journey Edward Walker and I had taken together; the Victorian curiosity trader had reached out across the intervening years to impart this knowledge, this understanding, to me alone. It was now a matter of trust between two gentlemen. I had three days before my meeting with Human Resources. Time was running out and the only place left to look was the place where I had first begun: the journals.

CHAPTER THIRTY

Sunday, September 10, 1865

For the last two weeks, I have endeavored to put the whole horrifying incident out of my mind, but I cannot. The *zonbi* haunts me still. I had hoped that the joy of life would again embrace me, and I strive desperately to find delight in my wife and my son, but I cannot now be happy. I am lost, adrift somewhere between the hither and the eternal—detached from my earthly existence.

When I look into the eyes of my child, I see only the dark, lifeless eyes of that *zonbi* child. Then, my mind's eye flashes to the vacant eyes of that poor unfortunate on the dock, ropes of wet hair framing her dead face, lips twisted into a ghastly grimace of fear—and the guilt rushes in like a tidal wave. She is dead because of *me*, because of my insistence upon bringing this aberration to London.

In my desk drawer, I keep the newspaper clippings with the illustrations of those victims whose only error was the chance encounter of meeting the *zonbi* on the street, whose only want was to return safely home, but who instead met their demise on a dark London street in the most horrific way imaginable. I long to make amends to their families, their loved ones. Once, I went so far as to obtain the address of the parents of the O'Neil sisters, with the intent to visit them in the hour of their grief and offer them some type of recompense beyond the usual platitudes that such an occasion warrants. But to do so would be to implicate myself in these crimes and so I do not, as much as the restraint now pains me. Then more guilt storms in, so dark and foreboding that it causes me to wish not only that I had never laid eyes on the maleficent creature, but that I, myself, had never been born. For how dare I now enjoy this life, when my fateful decision has caused so much destruction, so much loss of life?

Betsy continues to reach out to me, but I find no comfort in her embrace. She deserves so much more than I can now offer her. I am unworthy of her love and affection. I am a treacherous soul and cannot forgive or forget my own dark deeds.

From one unconscious moment to the next, as I lie sleeping, I am tumbling and trembling in a state of purgatory. With every dream, I am intimately reacquainted with my crimes. I relive them again and again. I am the demon feeding the devil. I am entangled in a loop of horror and inescapable sin. At times, the *zonbi* is I, and I am twisting in hunger and alive in my sinful desire for blood. I stalk my own kin, feasting on Betsy's tender throat. I wrench my child from her breast and do my worst, ruin his flesh with my teeth, feast on his blood, as I had witnessed the *zonbi* inflict upon countless animals and, in turn, the poor woman under the pier. My eyes cannot forget what they have seen. My heart cannot forget what it has learnt under the tutelage of my evil soul. I am doomed to repeat it all every night as I dream.

By day, my nightmares weave themselves into the waking fabric of my life. When I look upon Betsy's face, I see what horrors I have inflicted upon her in the darkness of my subconscious imaginings. When my son's laugh falls upon my ears, I hear instead his screams rising from the depths of my terrifying dreams. My study has become a place of refuge. Here, I am able to escape the pain in my heart that my family's presence evokes. I dwell in darkness, and this darkness is my garrison. It covers me as armor to my heart and a bastion to my soul. I have removed all reflective surfaces, having caught a glimpse of myself on one particular occasion—I recognized in my own eye, that same tortured look I had once witnessed in the *zonbi's*. It seems that the horror of what has happened, the dreadful knowledge of what inexplicable evil exists out there, has left its dark fingerprints on my soul and I cannot escape its hold.

I have removed everything from my study that reminded me of the demon *zonbi*. I have taken away all possessions of the curiosity trade, dismantled the aviary, and disposed of the materials. Upon further reflection, I have concluded that to sell the remainder of my collection to James would be to encourage another to follow in my path, to perhaps also stray into a dreadful course by a dangerous fascination with the macabre. Thus, I have packed into two crates the bottles of mutated creatures, medical kits, and journals, which had so engaged me in previous days. The mere sight of them only serves to drag me deeper into the ocean of despondency, where I struggle against the tides that threaten daily to drown me.

I do not know if I shall be heaved about by these violent waters, to have my soul beaten bloody against the rocks until I die, or if I shall rise from the swell, cling to a piece of driftwood until I can be pulled from the wreck by the hand of love, the hand of human goodness and kindness. Thus far, those hands only appear to me as bloody talons which cause me to recoil and dip beneath the waters anew.

Wednesday, September 20, 1865

It is now twenty days since I have abandoned the *zonbi* to its steel tomb, and my nightmares become increasingly severe. Every night it is the same—I am inside the bank and I hold in my hand a torch, so ablaze with roaring flame that it is like to consume the Tower of London itself. Then, the walls around me burst into flame, and I struggle at the vault while the bank burns. Next, in a moment of horror, I realize that the *zonbi* demon stirs on the ground beside me! I fumble at the lock, fingers slick with sweat and trembling with fear—I have forgotten the combination! As the *zonbi* rises to its feet, teeth glistening red in the firelight, I reach out with my torch and set it ablaze. Its skin blisters then boils, in such detail that I wonder what diseased portion of my mind could so perfectly and horrifically create this scene in such vivid recounting. Each evening in my dreams, I am doomed to relive the burning of the fiend. Each night, instead of dissolving into ash, the searing corpse of the *zonbi* pounces upon me, and, unable to free myself of him, we both die together in a shrieking fiery paroxysm of pain. I wake to the sounds of my own screaming.

Betsy has called the physician on several occasions, and hovers anxiously in the doorway while he subjects me to his examinations; he has naught to prescribe but bed rest—oh, what a farce this is! Little does he understand how the bed provides no rest for me! In an effort, no doubt, to earn his fee, he has also prescribed various pills and elixirs to calm my nerves. He has tested me for all number of tropical diseases and has shoved a depressor down my throat more times than I care to recall. In addition, the physician has subjected me to intrusive regimens involving the bowels, which have had no positive effect upon my state. He suspects that I have contracted some unknown tropical disease from my travels, and that I will either purge it from my system or it will consume me; which, we can only wait and see.

At this newest diagnosis of my condition, Betsy has arranged for my own bedroom, far from her and my baby. I lie in quarantine, drifting from a waking hell into slumber plagued by fiery nightmares. Upon occasion, I hear Betsy's prayers, soft and solemn on the breeze that blows from her room to mine; these holy incantations do nothing to protect me or comfort me.

I have entrusted Mr. Turner with the key to my study and have instructed him to bring to my room my crates and my typewriter box. These contain all the possessions that whisper of the evils of this past year: the scarificator, the medical journal, the mutated fetuses and the last two stuffed animals in my collection. I keep these close to me, fearing that if they fall into the wrong hands, they will be used against me.

Thursday, September 28, (I believe) 1865

I feel confident now that my decision to lock the *zonbi* in the vault was entirely ill-conceived. How greatly vexed am I that I did not burn the *zonbi's* bones as I should have done. For disguised in my ghastly dreams lie a message from some divine source. I feel a certain conviction, at last, that flames and fire are the *only* elements that would annihilate the *zonbi* and remove it forever from this earthly realm. If only I could heal my now-frail body, overcome this persistent malady and rise up out of bed, I could set alight that creature which yet remains alive in the vault.

But I have not the strength to do so. My body is no longer my own. I wish to raise my arm but I cannot. I wish to move my head but my will is broken. Sleep calls to me more and more, and my writings require tremendous effort and, after, I must rest for a good many days.

New Entry (date unknown)

My nurse informs me that a whole fortnight has passed since I last roused myself enough to enquire. I have spent this time entirely consumed in my dream-state. My illness has manifested to such a great extent that I have barely the strength now to hold this pen. I fear that I shall not rise again with the strength needed to complete my task of burning the bones, which lie unknown to anyone else in this world.

I have not seen Betsy or my son for many days but have ridden on the ribbon of their laughter emanating from down the hall, and, at times, from just outside my door. Time passes in an anguished blur, and I know not when my wife last attended my sick bed or know if my cries of terror are heard beyond my bedroom door. I need to rest again, but the place where I must go to rest is a perpetual state of hell. Yet still I go—for there is no escape from it.

New entry

I rise again, and if there is a reader, my hope is that you are still with me. I cannot write much more. Only please, know what you must do. I have given my life for you to follow in my wake. Take up the torch. Burn the thing that haunts my dreams and has stolen my life from me. Burn it! I shall prepare the way for you. With all my strength, I shall. It will be the last thing I do. Be I bound for hell, or forgiven through this, my final action, and my heavenly home awaits, I shall not go forth until I have prepared the way for you, dear reader, my redeemer, my savior.

New entry

The frost now covers the ground. I have managed to rest enough to restore my strength for my final journey; I must crawl from my bed and across the floor to where my crates are stacked. Someone had placed them there, long ago, when I was moved from the tranquility of the room I shared with Betsy and my child to this room of loneliness and purgatory. It was assumed that I would rise again and return to my old pleasures. Alas, but one task remains for me now—to hide away these journals for you, my dear reader, after which I shall depart from this world forever. If you have been a good and careful reader, you will know where to find the combination to the vault among my possessions, for I dare not write it down here for casual eyes to discover but would rather entrust it to you who have journeyed with me in spirit and soul. If not, then tear through all that remains. It is only by destruction that you may find that which will deliver you, me, and all of humankind from this curse. Preserve nothing until you find it. Then go and burn the immortal flesh of the *zonbi*, who was once a boy called Henri. Fear nothing—not even your own death—in the destruction of that insatiable evil. I go now, to make my final journey before I die. Heed my words. The last breath to leave my lips shall be a prayer for you.

Chapter Thirty-One

The almost indecipherable scrawl of Edward's last entry had me leaping up from my chair to return to the crates. But I had been through them innumerable times; there was *no* clue there to the vault's combination. Somehow the answer was right before my eyes, if I only knew where to look. What was it Edward had said in his final entry? *It is only by destruction that you may find that which will deliver you.*

I dragged the crate with the bottled fetuses—jars sloshing inside—into the back garden. I took each jar from the crate in turn and hurled them to the stone patio where they exploded into shards of glass and human tissue. Poring over the ruined contents, I hunted desperately for some clue to the combination of the lock, but to no avail.

Upturning the second crate onto the study floor, I shredded the mummy hand and the shrunken head, and ripped apart the stitching that held the stuffed rat and kitten together, pulling out the stuffing compressed within. Coming up empty, I seized the trepanning kit and then the scarificator, dumping them out on the floor. But despite the destruction lying in pieces about me, I found nothing. *Nothing!*

Think, Dunny, *think!* Where else was there to look? And then my gaze came to rest on the discarded box that had contained the scarificator. Jerking the box out of the rubble, I tore away the threadbare velvet lining and there, tucked inside, was a neatly folded piece of yellowed paper. Unfolding it, I breathed a sigh of relief—scratched in India ink were a sequence of numbers: 79 35 45—the combination to the vault.

235

Chapter Thirty-Two

It was New Year's Eve, and London would be alive with music, fireworks, and drunks—a perfect night to break the *zonbi* out of the vault. With all the commotion, none would notice a boring old codger in black, slipping in and out of the shadows with his cello case, perhaps on his way to a New Year's Eve gig. I'd removed the cello, a survivor from my college days, and lined the case with a plastic sheet and bed linens. I gathered an electric torch, my break-in tools, a mallet, and some lubricant for the lock, and shoved them all in my rucksack.

The noise associated with demolishing the bookshop wall would be covered by the deafening explosion of fireworks. The bookstore would be closed the following day, and the burglary would remain undiscovered until the second of January. The window posters would make it difficult for anyone to see anything that went on within. I would need most of the night to complete my task—I had an entire bookshelf to empty and tear down, a wall to break through, an old combination lock to liberate, and a century-old vault to pry open. I would enter the shop through the alley door, after first jimmying the lock.

Edward had been fiercely adamant that the remains of the *zonbi* should be burnt. In those last days, however, he had been sick with fever, almost certainly delirious. Regardless, I had come too far to destroy the remains of the *zonbi*. This was my one chance to seize my opportunity at true scientific stardom. I was not prepared to lightly relinquish this opportunity by recklessly burning a corpse of tremendous historical interest because of the rantings of a madman.

Donning the same dark outfit I had worn on my previous illegal excursion, I worried about being caught in the act. I had had no luck breaking into a quiet residence secluded among the undergrowth, how would I fare in the middle of a busy city, surrounded by lights and people?

As the time to depart drew near, I began to feel nauseated. My body developed an all-over tremor and I broke out in a sweat. *Come on, Dunny*, I muttered to myself. This was the gold watch I'd been looking for my whole life! My father's gift. *Edward's gift.*

I had estimated that I would need two hours to unload the bookshelf, break through the wall, open the vault, and retrieve Henri's remains—or verify that they did in fact not exist, an outcome I could not bear to consider. Driving into the city, I timed my departure to arrive at the back-alley door by ten. Soho was a mad house, and I drove around in rising agitation for almost thirty minutes, looking for a parking spot. Finally, I found one. Jesus, I wanted to vomit. The internal shaking had only intensified, and I tried to focus on taking deep and regular breaths. Grabbing my cello case and rucksack, I slid from the driver's seat into the cool night air.

Shuffling down the London streets, I kept my gaze low, sidestepping the merry makers keen to get to their evening parties. Finally arriving at the back door of the bookshop, I glanced round. No one paid me any attention. I worked in the shadows, wriggling the slender pick tools in the lock until, with an audible click, it yielded, and the door swung open. Footsteps and voices approached, so I stepped inside and closed the door behind me. I waited for an emergency alarm to sound and readied myself to run if it should. One second, then two passed, and nothing happened. All was silent.

Muted street light streamed between the window posters, casting the tops of the towering bookcases in a golden yellow glow. Edging my way down the back wall, I approached the seating area at the rear, and the false wall that hid the vault. Setting my equipment down on the floor beside me, I wasted no time, quickly removing books from the shelves and placing them in the aisles. Trip after trip, and piles of thin picture books lay in stacks on the floor behind me, like miniature skyscrapers in a doomed city.

Next, I unloaded the thicker books, youth versions of *The Adventures of Huckleberry Finn* and *Moby Dick*, along with the full-length novels, heavy in my arms. Each time I heard a voice my heart would stop, and I'd duck down in the shadows, heart pounding with the certainty that I was about to be apprehended, that the revolving lights of police cars would appear through the postered window, that I would be handcuffed and locked away, and that I would never know the truth. But each time, the voices faded away and I grew more confident that these were just pedestrians going about their own business, and that no one was truly interested in what might be going on behind the posters in the window.

As I worked into the night, the piles of books became disheveled and scattered, taking over the aisles, and filling the floor until, finally, the bookshelf was empty.

Shining my torch beam on the bookcase, I discovered it was joined in sections that stretched across the entire back wall. I had no notion as to how large the bank vault was behind the wall and how closely the wall had been erected to the front of the vault. I decided there was nothing to be done but to dismantle a random section of the bookcase and investigate the particular portion of wall that lay behind it.

Pulling a battery-powered drill from the rucksack, I climbed on a chair and began to loosen the screws that held the shelf units together.

Successfully dismantling the top level of the bookcase, I stacked the sections on the floor behind me, sweating profusely from the effort of maneuvering the heavy pieces of wood, from the anxiety that gripped me every time I heard outside laughter or saw the shadowed forms of people passing. I tried to work more quickly, fumbling and realigning my tool time and again, my ears ringing at the squeal of the drill bit as it bounced out across the top of the screw. I imagined the sedate clerk who worked here in daylight hours, and almost laughed at the imagined expression on his face should he find me here now. How insane I would appear to him, or to anyone opening that door. Dismantling a bookshop on New Year's Eve in a bizarre act of inexplicable vandalism by a university academic! Finally, I had removed the top section, and began working on the middle and the bottom of the cubby system. At last, the wall stood free and clear before me.

Drunken whoops of laughter came from the street and I glanced at my watch: two minutes to midnight. Londoners had gathered on the sidewalks, reveling while they waited for the countdown of the New Year and the ensuing fireworks. Hunching down, I wondered if a late-night carouser taking a piss in the alley might notice the damaged lock on the bookshop door and notify the police who were, no doubt, out in full force this night. The sweat trickled down my face, but I dared not wipe it away. In two minutes, Big Ben would chime, and the sky would be filled with the clamor of fireworks.

Hastily rummaging through the rucksack, I retrieved the mallet just as the revelers began their countdown. Some must have gathered not far from the front doors of the bookshop and I could hear them as I myself numbered among them.

10—I took in a breath.

9—I steeled myself.

8—I ran my hand over the wall, and found the place I would aim my strike.

7—I arranged my hands on the handle.

6—I took another deep breath.

5—I lifted the sledgehammer.

4—I took a practice swing, slow, calculated.

3—I wound my arms back into position.

2—I tensed my muscles.

1—I swung.

Fireworks exploded in the night sky accompanied by the strike of Big Ben amid the drunken whoops and cries of "Happy New Year!" Colored light bounced off the bookshop walls as my mallet blow sailed right through the wall with a chalky thud and then rang against metal. *Bullseye!*

Seizing my torch, I shone it into the fresh hole. A dull metallic surface, dusted in the powder of broken drywall, met my gaze. *The vault!* I struck the wall repeatedly in concordance with the detonation of fireworks and street shouts, all of which combined to produce a deafening roar. Rivulets of sweat soaked my shirt and caused my hands to slip on the handle of the mallet; my hair hung like a wet curtain in front of my eyes.

I flung the broken chunks of plaster into the debris behind me in a mishmash of fallen books and cubby pieces. I didn't give a damn about the bookshop. I had to complete the task, retrieve the remains, and get out before someone discovered this lone vandalizer in the dark bookshop and called the police.

I had now revealed the length of the vault. Forgetting entirely about the risk of discovery, I stood poised in the space between hope and glory, the way a child's aspiration of happiness lies between his imagination and a thin layer of wrapping paper on Christmas morning. My torchlight illuminated the combination dial, a black circle the size of my fist with numbers etched upon its outside circumference. My hand curling around the cool steel, I tried to turn the dial but it would not budge. Removing the lubricant from the rucksack, I sprayed the lock, and the cool liquid ran over my fingers and dripped onto the floor. The sting of the fish oil burned in my nasal membranes as I maneuvered the dial again, forcing it one way and then the other. When it still refused to give, I gave it a whack with the mallet, until I managed to work the mechanism back to life; millimeter by millimeter it began to loosen and turn. Finally, the dial swirled in a full turn and I was ready to try the combination.

Returning the combination to zero, I stopped first at seventy-nine, then around in the opposite direction to thirty-five. Then, holding my breath, I turned it again, stopping at forty-five. Breathing hard in nervous tension, my body streaming sweat, I turned the stiff handle and yanked the door outward until it came reluctantly away. Heart beating wildly, I took a gulp of air and ventured inside.

CHAPTER THIRTY-THREE

A deafening boom of fireworks assaulted my ears as from within the gloom of that age-old time capsule a shape rushed me before I had time to strike, sending me reeling backward through the hole and onto my back on the bookshop floor. Something hooked my trouser leg, the weight of it pressing against my leg.

"Bloody hell!" I yelled in fright, heart thudding against my chest. Kicking it off me, I scrambled to my feet, feeling for my torch that had bounced out of my hand.

Shaking, I guided the beam of light to the object at my feet. A dark and shining corpse was all that was left of the *zonbi* child. It must have been leaning up against the door of the vault and had fallen on me when I had opened it. Shining the beam down the length of the shape, I saw Henri for the first time. He was all sharp bone, dried skin leather, and mummified flesh, similar in appearance to the Egyptian hand that had been among Edward's possessions. Moving cautiously toward it, I directed the light onto the skull, where two ominous eye sockets, dark and deep, revealed themselves. There were no signs of life there. Henri was long dead.

"Hello, Henri. Delighted to make your acquaintance," I whispered in the darkness, feeling a surge of triumphant satisfaction.

This was it: *habeas corpus*. I had the body: the subject of the camera obscura, the actual remnant of a Victorian-era tale of horror and mayhem. Now that I had the corpse, I could run the DNA tests I so longed to do, to authenticate Edward's claims. I would at last know if his body held the key to discovering the secrets of the *bokor* poison, of the odd states of comatose vacancy and insatiable appetite as described in the journals. Once I discovered what substances still remained in his cells, I could start to determine the truth of the journals, which would earn me the kind of accolades I richly deserved. Stuff North Roads. This discovery would allow me to write my ticket worldwide.

The fireworks had ended, and it was time to go. Moving quickly in the darkness, I pulled on my gloves, rolled the corpse onto the plastic sheet and, gathering up the corners, lifted the *zonbi* into the cello case and tucked the sheet around it. Shutting the case and snapping the lock, I grabbed my tools, and stuffed them into the rucksack. Hoisting the sack onto my back, I took the handle of the cello case in my other hand, and gingerly stepped around the disarray of books and mortar toward the side door.

Keeping my head down, I squeezed through the door and shut it behind me. The case felt weighty in my hand as the remains shifted inside. I turned down Broadwick, away from the ruined bookshop, and approaching my Volvo from the rear, unlocked the boot. I slid the cello case inside, shrugged off my rucksack and tucked it beside the case.

I sped out of the parking space, trembling as I drove, the adrenaline from the heist draining away to leave me feeling unutterably exhausted. I felt light-headed, and as I traced my way back home, a feeling of horrible nausea came over me.

Tearing into my driveway, I leapt from the car, heaving the contents of my stomach onto the driveway. Wiping my mouth on the back of my coat sleeve, I slowly righted myself and retrieved the rucksack and cello case and brought them into my study.

Situating the case on my dining room table, I brought in additional desk lamps from my study and floor lamps from the lounge. Retrieving some disinfectant and a cloth, I wiped down my large dining room table, then covered it with a sheet from the linen cupboard. I then proceeded to dress myself in an unused painter's suit from the garage, as well as gloves and a knit hat to keep any skin and hair from contaminating the sample. The wooden hands on the pendulum clock clicked towards two a.m.

At last, the crucial moment had arrived! I had Edward's horrible little secret before me. The mummified corpse had survived into the twentieth century, and now it was up to me to prove to the world what it signified—the remains of a young Haitian boy, poisoned by a *Vodou* witchdoctor, or something even more nefarious…

With adequate illumination, the corpse of the young boy was something to behold; the constant air temperature within the vault had preserved the body well. The ebony skin was in almost perfect condition and the body, although bony, had retained a good amount of flesh. The boy was dressed in a cotton shirt—the blue stripes now faded—and trousers, both of which were darkly soiled and quite deteriorated. The spine curved forward at the shoulders, neck extended, with knees tucked up underneath. I deduced from the way the body had dried that Henri had been kneeling at the door, trying to paw his way out when he slumped forward and expired. Each of his fingernails had been broken off; he must have tried to scratch and pry at the vault door.

Turning my attention to his face, I noted that his mouth had deteriorated around the cheeks to form a gruesome smile with teeth showing along the curve of the jaw. Facial decay had exposed part of the skull; the cartilage of the nose was gone, and the left upper cheek sported a hole.

Despite myself, I suppressed a faint shudder when my gaze turned to the eyes of the corpse. Typically, when one dies, the eyes are the first features to dry out and deflate, comprised as they are predominately of fluid; Henri's eyes, in spite of a slight shrinking back into the head, remained open and staring. The gaze, similar to the one described in Edward's journals, seemed suspended between death and life, the last part of his soul caught within. Retrieving my camera, I returned to take photograph after photograph of the remains, from every perspective. Then, using plyers, I removed a tooth from Henri's skull, dropping it into a labelled bag. With a scalpel, I scraped out a piece of the tissue from the exposed area around the jaw and deposited the samples in a fresh bag. Next, I retrieved hair and fingernail fragments, and scraped a measure of bone from the jaw. This done, I collected up the samples and dropped them in my rucksack, to analyze at the university lab upon my return.

Now, the time had come for me to put Edward's claims to the ultimate test. Within the wall behind the couch, was a live trap, and within it a large grey mouse. Grabbing the mouse by the base of his tail, I dangled him over the desiccated black hole that had been the boy's mouth.

The dead unfocused eyes stared upward at the dangling mouse. The corpse did not stir. The mouse twisted and swung in my fingers, trying desperately to right itself and escape my grasp. *The boy is dead, isn't he? Of course he is. Look at him.* I passed my hand over the head of the corpse, felt its brittle hair, and taut, dried-out skin. I looked into its eyes and shivered at the hideously inert expression.

The mouse jerked in my hand, almost causing me to drop it. "All right, I was a fool. I must now kill you proper, little pest." I swung the mouse away from the corpse and turned toward the counter in search of my kill jar, when I felt the mouse torn from my fingers.

Turning back to the table, my eyes widened in horror at the scene—where, a second before, a rigid, half-deteriorated mummified corpse had lain on my dining room table, now a reanimated corpse sat upright, its bony fingers gripped around the mouse, sucking the lifeblood from its suddenly severed body—feeding a hunger that had waited 125 years to be satisfied. The *zonbi* raised its head and, in growing terror, I studied its face. Those dead eyes, my God…they were…glinting—the centers like the well of black candles, where hot liquid pooled. Those eyes stared at me with hatred, with an evil that penetrated me to the core. The head cocked to one side and the corner of the left side of the mouth pulled back to reveal yellow, aged molars. Did the *zonbi* think that I was Edward? I started to back away, but those eyes held me and whispered, I imagined: *You're next!*

Henri moaned in a tone low and long, and my mind raced to recall all of Edward's conclusions; I knew I could not kill this beast. Inexplicably, it existed still.

My only chance was to sedate the creature. Edward had proved—*No! I had proved*—that neither time nor circumstance could kill it. I had only one chance to get this right and I had to act now. Backing into the dark hallway, I heard its dried skin crack as the child-beast turned its partly decomposed head toward me: my retreat had caught its interest. In mere seconds, I assumed, it would toss aside the mouse and come after me. It had just woken so its strength would be weak and its speed slow; could I reach the bathroom before it did?

Passing out of its line of vision, I kept my eyes glued to the dining room entrance, waiting for the thing to come after me. Moving backward along the wall, my hand outstretched behind me, I groped for the door to the bathroom.

From the dining room, came the telltale thump of the *zonbi* dropping from the table to the floor. Then it crawled out of the light, emerging in the dining room doorway, to join me in the shadows, tracking me like the prey I was. A cry of panic and fear escaped my lips as I watched the thing slowly drag itself after me. My hand hit up against the door trim and I ducked into the bathroom, slamming the door on the aberration that stalked me.

Hands trembling, I turned the lock and exhaled in relief—the door, a flimsy barrier between me and this bloody thing from hell. Legs trembling beneath me, I steadied myself on the towel rail, feeling that it would be a quick slide into a pit of debilitating fear and anxiety. I did not recall a single instance from the journal in which Henri had broken through a barrier, so I hoped I would have sufficient time to ready the sedation. Pawing frantically through the contents of the medicine cabinet, I tossed pill bottles and tubes of ointment aside, desperately seeking the small brown bottle I had been keeping there. It had been used to exterminate small vermin, now it would save me from the most dangerous one of all by rendering the *zonbi* corpse motionless, à *la Edward Walker*.

Outside that door lurked Edward's curse, the scourge that I had tracked and pursued through time, a curse that was now my own. This was my inheritance, the one I had insisted upon. Had I chosen to become Edward's heir or had Edward chosen me? I, the newly converted, wished with all my soul that I had not found the journal, had not become curious, and above all, had heeded the warning to burn the bones and send this creature's soul to hell. But perhaps it wasn't too late. I had my samples, mined from the body of the boy—I could burn him, destroy him, and still provide compelling evidence of his anomaly, of his *zonbi* aberration. I could win my accolades with or without the body.

Pulling the stopper from the bottle, I tipped it upside down onto a face cloth. One tiny drop teetered on the rim before soaking into the cloth. Oh God, I was out of chloroform! Without the ability to sedate the fiend, I was done for. It would rip me apart and feast on my heart. I prayed that this remnant would be sufficient to subdue the creature in its currently weakened state. It had to be.

CHAPTER THIRTY-FOUR

I snapped my head around to see the creature making his way down the hall, blood dribbling down its chin as its jaws worked to crush a mouthful of mouse, another in its hand. This was not the weak, clumsy, newly awakened *zonbi* I had left in the dining room moments before. It was now agile, spry, and calculating, its gaze sharp and threatening as it fixated on me.

Heart racing, I braced myself for combat. The thing advanced toward me with double the speed, and as it drew close, I recoiled against the smell of its rotten flesh, now yellowed, oozing, and hanging in jagged ribbons from its body. What had moments before been mummified flesh, was now, inexplicably, putrefied tissue. I was trembling with fear and repulsion, gulping air to keep from collapsing as I steeled myself. I took a step toward the thing, and it leapt at me with teeth bared. Spinning away, I clipped it with my elbow and caught it in a tight headlock, weeping flesh smearing my arms as I held it against me, clamping the cloth over its face. Head twisted back, the *zonbi's* eyes locked onto mine, and with swift, targeted swipes, it clawed at my arm, but its strength was not enough to resist my efforts. Not yet. Blood pounding in my ears and the taste of bile at the back of my throat, I prayed that the last drop of chloroform was enough to subdue the newly awoken creature, enough to buy me the time I needed to prepare the fire. The *zonbi* thrashed its head, trying desperately to escape the cloth, no doubt reliving in its 125-year memory the implications of a cloth to the face. With all the strength I could muster, nerves alive with adrenaline, I held that oozing *zonbi*, mouse blood and putrefaction dripping down my arm, until it slumped to the floor, body limp, as the chloroform did its job.

Releasing the horrid thing, I sprinted to the garage and then returned to where the creature lay, throwing a fistful of rags on it and dousing it in gasoline. The fumes filled the room, making my head swim and my gut turn. Arming myself with the fire extinguisher from the kitchen, I struck a match and lit the now-twitching corpse.

In a blinding flash, the rags ignited, hissing and curling against the rotten flesh as a cascade of blue and orange flame spread across the length of the body, encapsulating it in a burning blaze. The *zonbi* came to life with a shriek, twisting as it clawed at the floor, trying to escape its fate.

The smell of burning flesh hit my nose, acrid and cruel, and I choked as smoke filled the room. With blasts from my fire extinguisher, I beat back the flames that threatened to jump to the curtains, as the *zonbi's* skin boiled and crisped before me. From within the blaze, those eyes stared up at me, narrowing in anguish, but never breaking from mine. The creature bared his gnashing teeth and uttered the most prolonged ungodly shriek I'd ever heard in my life. It undid me, and I braced myself against the doorframe, my gut turning inside out. All around me, fire leapt across the carpet and I aimed the extinguisher in an arc around the flaming *zonbi*, trying to quell the runaway blaze.

As if in answer to the creature's shrill intonations, my smoke alarm suddenly came to life, in its own kind of deafening rage. The noise ripped at my eardrums and I longed to drop the extinguisher and cover my ears, but I didn't dare. The *zonbi* showed no signs of defeat, continuing to crawl towards me, writhing in pain, the flames still clinging to their fuel source.

It was impossible—the thing should have been dead in an instant, from the moment the fire erupted over its body. Mice scurried in all directions to escape the heat, the blaze, and the *zonbi* itself. I watched, horrified, unable to believe what I was seeing, as it reached out a burning hand in an attempt to grab at the fleeing mice on its way to me. *Holy shit!* Edward had been wrong. Not even fire could stop this insatiable creature, this immortal *zonbi*. It was fighting, crawling, and, yes, even eating, building the strength it needed to overpower and consume me.

I knew that soon I would run out of fire retardant and the blaze would spread out of control, burning my house down, and I'd be trapped inside.

Instinctively, I aimed the extinguisher at the thing and fired. In an instant, the blaze was out and the abomination began to rise unhindered, restored, to come after me—to rip my heart out. Abandoning the extinguisher in the ruin of my lounge, I sprinted for my study and locked the door. Seized by panic and desperation, I paced the room, running my trembling hands through my hair.

Had I thought of everything? Had I explored everything in that journal, every clue? The sweat rolled off my forehead and I felt I would collapse from fright. I couldn't breathe; my heart filled my throat. Then it hit me. There *was* something I had neglected!

Falling upon my bookcases, I began to tear every book from the shelves—a flurry of color and paper raining down to the floor. With a sob of relief, I pulled from the pile a brown book with a worn cover—*Encyclopedia of Folklore Around the World*. Tearing through the pages to the section on the Caribbean, I examined each picture carefully until at last I found it: the woodcarving of a heavy breasted Haitian *Vodou* statue, eyes closed as if in rapture. *Erzulie Manser*, the caption read. *Represents motherly love and protects children from harm.* The idol wasn't intended to protect Edward, it was to protect Henri! *The idol must be the key to Henri's immortality!* Edward had needed only to destroy the idol and not the *zonbi*. And now, that's all I needed to do. But I didn't have the carving. I had forgotten to retrieve it from the safe!

Outside the door to my study, the animated corpse of the boy who had once been Henri shrieked and my door vibrated with a terrible bang as the thing threw itself against it. Trembling with an all-consuming fear, I pushed my desk against the door, and then my chair, barricading myself in. Climbing onto the desk, I peered through the small window at the top of the door and my jaw dropped at what I saw. The charred corpse of the hideous creature scurried around the room in a frenzy, shoving mice into its gnashing mouth, blood squirting out between its teeth, and soaking its tattered shirt.

Catching sight of my face in the window, the *zonbi* launched itself off an adjacent bookcase and hurled itself at the window. Leaping back in shock, I fell to the floor, coming down hard on my ankle, and rolling it. I writhed in pain, and the horror and hopelessness of it all consumed me. The ankle was most assuredly sprained, if not broken. Were I to attempt to escape this room and make a break for it, the *zonbi* would absolutely catch me and I would die a painful, horrific death, with that thing on top of me, ripping me to pieces, pulling my heart out of my chest.

My mind flashed back to the ruined bookstore, the vault, and the carving inside. It was a crime scene now. Soon the police would be crawling all over it. They would find the idol, confiscate it and it lock it in the police station for years, labeled as evidence. They would never destroy it and end the *zonbi's* rein of mayhem and terror. Were I to try to get it back, I would be implicated in the crime, locked away. I was due at the meeting with HR at nine a.m. When I didn't show, they'd be concerned. They'd phone someone trying to find out what had become of me. They'd phone Clara! And she'd try to come here again, to find me! Put the key in the lock and then... *Oh God! What if she brings Tommy with her? Christ, no!*

I crawled across my study floor, amid the rubble of books, the shards of glass, the debris of drywall and mouse crap, to where the broken phone lay on the floor. *Please, God, please!* I prayed as I attempted to press the faceplate back into place. It seemed to hold and I plugged the phone cord back into the wall and brought the receiver to my ear. And miracle of miracles, the happy hum of a dial tone jetted to my brain.

With fingers impossibly shaky, I managed to dial Clara's number. The phone rang. And rang. And rang. *Clara! Answer!* My mind screamed. But she didn't. Then the machine clicked on.

"Clara! It's Dad. Please answer!" Nothing. She wasn't home, or not answering on purpose. I shouted into the receiver, above the scream of the fire alarm. "Look, I know I've been cruel to you. And... and I'm sorry I hurt your feelings, darling. But please. You must understand—you must trust me. I need you to promise me you will *not* come to my house. Even if you never hear from me again. You mustn't come here, do you hear? In fact, get as far away from here as you can. Pretend you don't know me. I...I know this is painful to hear. I love you, Clara. I love you, and Tommy, more than life itself, and that's why you must stay away. Please, just promise me. I'm sorry my darling, I'm so—" The answering machine cut off and I smashed the receiver down and quickly picked it up again. I dialed her number again and this time when the answering machine clicked on, it told me the mailbox was full and to please call back later.

Tears welled in my eyes and I dropped my head in my hands, as with sudden horrifying realization, I understood what I'd done. I had again released this curse into the world and now it had come for me, for my family, and like Edward, I was powerless to stop it. Instead of the *zonbi*, it was me who had become trapped. I had no sedation, no weapon, nothing by which to subdue the terrible creature on the other side of the door that threatened to slaughter me. All I could do was as Edward had done: wait for the monster's supply to run dry and hopefully he would return to a state of lethargy where I could escape from here, if I didn't starve first.

252

Curling into a ball, my stomach a painful knot, I cried out in terror, my hands gripping the phone until my knuckles turned white. I couldn't catch my breath, and my heart raced out of control. Sounds of crashing furniture punctuated the blare of the alarm, as on the other side of the door, the *zonbi* rampaged through my house.

Make it stop, make it stop, make it stop, I whispered so only I could hear this mantra designed to keep me anchored to life, to keep me from slipping into unconsciousness. If only no one opened the door to my house. I'd be safe here. When the *zonbi* ran out of food, and returned to its comatose state, I could crawl from here and subdue it, keep him under sedation until I could figure out how to get the carving back and destroy it.

The world would be safe, if only Clara didn't open that door. I must keep trying to ring her. I must—another panic attack gripped me, and I curved forward, shoving my head between my knees. The anxiety was bearing down on me like a freight train and my stomach began to go into deep convulsions. I rolled onto hands and knees and vomited. The room swirled around me, every sound was loud in my ears, caving in on me, the high-pitched insistent alarm from the lounge, and then another siren, growing closer, louder, as flashing lights filled the tiny windows of my study and bounced off the walls.

Dear God, No! They're going to open the door! I must... I tried to pull myself up on to the desk, to get to the window, to shout at them, to warn them somehow to chop at the thing with their axes, when I put weight on my shattered ankle, I collapsed again to the floor. The final line of "A Tell-Tale Heart" flashed in my mind: "I admit the deed!—tear up the planks! Here, here—it is the beating of his hideous heart!" The last thing I heard was the *zonbi's* horrific shriek as the whole of my world imploded into darkness.

EPILOGUE

Dyscrasy. The word pushed through the haze of my mind, past the confusion of cool white sheets against my damp skin, and the sharp smell of antiseptic. My throat was a Sahara of pain. I struggled to swallow, in a failed attempt to lubricate it. *An imbalance of humors. Of course!* I closed my eyes against the brightness of the room and its stark white walls. Whispered voices drifted in from somewhere beyond, feather soft, anchoring me to the present.

"We have him under a mild sedative. He was quite distressed when we brought him in."

"What happened to him?"

Distressed? I clambered through a litany of images, leaping mice, a combination safe, a cello case, and then—*oh God, no!*—Henri. The wild, twisting corpse, engulfed with flame crawling after me, mouth dripping with the blood of half-eaten mice. Then, my last moments in the study—the thing hurling itself against the door, my fall, and the shriek of emergency vehicles. I struggled to rise but an explosion of pain sent me falling back to the white-sheeted hospital mattress.

"He's had a bad fall, shattered his ankle, but he'll be okay, I should think."

"Oh, dear. What was he *doing?* I heard there was a fire…"

Clara! It's you. You're okay! I tried to call to her, but my scratchy voice was little more than a froggy croak. Again, I tried to rise, but my shaking arms wouldn't support my weight, and I collapsed again, my head swimming.

"Yes, you'll have to talk with the fire chief, but I'm afraid when they broke down the door. Your dad's poor dog was so frightened it escaped."

"Dog? You must be mistaken; my dad doesn't own a dog."

"How odd. I was certain they said the fire chief was bitten by a dog before it ran off."

Dear God! I have to… I must. Summoning a burst of strength from deep inside, I rolled to the edge of the bed, one hand on the bedrail and the other behind me and hoisted myself up.

"Nurse!" I rasped, finding my voice at last before the contents of the bedside table went skittering to the floor.

"Dad," Clara cried as she rushed to my side, followed by a blur of white uniform and cream stockings.

"Clara…help me. I have to…get out of …" I panted. My mind was a soupy mess, struggling to piece together a thought, to string a sentence. I fought to kick free of the sheets that tangled around my feet, my ruined ankle shrieking. "…here. Must… get out… of—"

"Professor Clarke, I'm going to need you to calm down. You're under sedation, do you understand? You'll only hurt yourself if you continue. Please lie back in the bed."

"You don't…you don't…know what…"

"Dad, please. Lie back. Do what the nurse says."

"…what he…can…*do!*"

"What *who* can do? The dog? Dad, when did you get a dog?"

The nurse's hands, surprisingly strong, clenched my shoulders and forced me down. I resisted with everything in me and the nurse lost her balance, falling against me as she yelled, "Code yellow!" over her shoulder. In an instant, I was surrounded by two men, who held me, kicking and thrashing, while the nurse plunged a needle into my thigh. Then Clara's face, a mélange of concern, pity, and the faint glow of love, disappeared in a swirl of black.

ACKNOWLEDGEMENTS

Thanks to my editor, Jaynie Royal, who showed me that my characters had more to reveal about their wants and needs. This book is better because of her hard work.

Thank you, Robert Beckwith, for your prompt answers about Britain and its history. Thanks Greg Cossey, for your knowledge of genealogy, and shipboard protocol.

My gratitude to James Patrick Kerry for your expansive scientific knowledge, plot suggestions, and coffee getaways that kept me sane.

Thank you, Kim Martins, for always providing an ear to natter to. Your friendship and support mean the world to me.

Thanks to my beta readers, Kim Martins, Andrea Cotman, Delphine Kelly, Mark Gilmore, Ray Andrews, Robert Beckwith, Leslie Wibberley, and Spencer Cossey. Your mistake-finding skills are beyond compare.

My appreciation for the late William Kelly, for giving me an appreciation for the power of horror, to exhilarate, tantalize, and explore fear, an important part of the human psyche.

Thanks to my parents Steve and Annie, who instilled in me a love of history and literature; my siblings Lisa and Trevor, who always have my back; and my kids, Spencer and Eden Rose, who understand and support my need to create.

My love and thanks to my husband Greg, who works hard on all fronts so I may pursue my dreams.

To those I've failed to mention, your support has not gone unnoticed or unappreciated.

Special thanks to Eden Rose. If they had not brought home 100 stick bugs when they were fourteen years old, A Peculiar Curiosity would have never been born.

Lightning Source UK Ltd.
Milton Keynes UK
UKHW041831131118
332286UK00003B/33/P